HOLIDAY FOR SIX

KELLY FINLEY

The Queen
Of Spice
©KELLY FINLEY BOOKS

DEAR READER,

This is a story celebrating all consensual adult love. It's a sweet and spicy tale about finding your happiness and family.

Along the way, polyamory and consensual non-monogamy are celebrated, and real-world challenges are explored such as discovering bisexuality and polyphobia. The use of terms varies as do the people and communities who use them.

If the idea of a lot of love for all excites you, this story may be quite the holiday for you.

All of these characters have their standalone, interconnected romances available for free on KindleUnlimited.

For details and a suggested reading order review
Also by Kelly Finley

For bonus content on their sweet and spicy life together,
visit my website at
KellyFinley.com

For every smutty reader who deserves a hot holiday ...
every day.

HOLIDAY FOR SIX PLAYLIST

AVAILABLE ON SPOTIFY

Sinners by Ari Abdul, Thomas LaRosa
BAIT by Kim Petras, BANKS
more than friends by Isabel LaRosa
Lost in the Fire by Gesaffelstein, The Weeknd
Sex Calls by Harrison Brome
Talk Dirty by Daniel Di Angelo
Taste by Ari Abdul
Coffee (F***ing) by Miguel, Wale
I Want It by Two Feet
Body High by Harrison Brome
love me by Ex Habit
Make Me Feel by Janelle Monáe
Apartment by BOBI ANDONOV
Best Friend by ASHWARYA
Count On Me by Bruno Mars
Listen Here

HOLIDAY FOR SIX

Charlie

"I'M A HAPPILY MARRIED WOMAN WITH A PISSED-OFF PUSSY."

What kind of liquor do you buy for a holiday for sex? I mean... for *six*?

There are so many choices.

Any glistening white bottle on the glass shelves with the word "cream" on the label makes me smirk. This holiday we're about to begin has my mind swimming in salacious thoughts. Who knew I could be so risqué?

Me.

The tequila bottle with the red smiling cat makes me sigh. I *wish* my cat was happy. She's been a little lonely lately.

The bottles next to it, standing erect with the word "Amigos" taunting back on numerous labels, find me chewing my lip. I'm a storm of emotions: curious, excited, wondering—*will I fuck my hot friends this week?*

Or is the crystal vodka bottle on the opposite shelf shaped like a skull a giant warning?

Whore alert! Whore alert! You're a wife and mom. No swinging allowed.

I could play it safe and just get that simple malt whiskey with the word "Reserve" on the label. *Humph.* Yeah, my mouth craves that as much as a teeth-cleaning.

Or I could go for it and buy those "Just The Tipsy" frosted bottles of bubbly rosé shaped like giant penises, the corks on the tips straining to burst.

I stare at the hard... tall... thick... full glass, licking my lips, wanton wishes teasing my mind.

Me? Thirsty?

Yeah, I could swallow that thing in one gulp.

"Bloody hell," a deep English accent booms over my shoulder, making me jump, "is that a bottle shaped like a giant cock?"

I grab it by its base, pulling it off the shelf in this high-end liquor store.

"Yes, it is." I turn to my husband. The father of our three kids. The towering hulk of muscles. The sexy, famous A-list face that people in this store instantly recognized.

I'm so used to it that I'll give you zero fucks.

I'm not a mom this week. I'm not a bodyguard or a boss of a security firm. I'm not a former Marine or a woman publicly stalked to news-worthy levels; people recognize me, too. I'm not even the wife of Daniel Pierce, the global celebrity, a superhero turned James Bond turned serious actor.

No, this week, I'm a woman who better get fucked.

A lot.

Preferably by my sexy-as-hell husband. Yes, I love him. The man makes our bed every morning. He even stacks the mountain of throw pillows right and never bitches about it.

But it's been so long since we've fucked... my pussy ain't picky right now.

Daniel shakes his head.

"If you buy a wine bottle shaped like a cock in a Miami liquor store, it will go viral."

I lift my chin, giving a one-shoulder shrug.

"Yeah, well, I'm so infected with horniness, let it. At least on Instagram and TikTok, we have a sex life."

"Babe," Daniel towers over me, that sexy, dark tendril falling over his furrowed brow, "we've been busy. We have kids and jobs, and we're bloody knackered by the time we're home."

"No, *you're* tired. You fall asleep while I'm horny. I'm not breastfeeding anymore. We're not having any more babies. You've been fixed, and I want to fuck."

"I do what I can."

"It's been two months, and I'm having an affair with a vibrating rabbit."

He rolls his blue eyes, his thick lashes framing his frustration. "This pressure really gives me a stiffy."

"Daniel," I whisper low while customers mill around us. They're filming us and snapping pics, too. *Whatever.* "We used to fuck all the time. We used to have kinky sex all over the house. You couldn't get enough of me. And now... if we ever get a chance, it's two quick minutes every few weeks, maybe five minutes if we're feeling kinky."

His full lips purse, straining with the frustration I feel.

"That's bloody normal, Charlie. We're married. We're busy. We work long days and come home to change nappies, feed mushy peas to our children, give them baths, then read about bloody 'good night moons' until we fall asleep, too. When the fuck do we have time to fuck?"

As a reminder of our smutty days gone by, I stare into

his eyes, lifting the frosted rosé bottle to my lips. Slowly, I drag the tip of my tongue over the cold tip, laving over the glass while I softly moan. Like I'm on my knees for him again. Like I'm his shameless POV porn again.

TikTok, there's your "Caught in 4k". Imagine the viral meme.

It barely lifts Daniel's grin.

"Cheeky," he rumbles.

"Cocky," I correct him, putting the lucky penis bottle in the black plastic basket hanging from my arm. Then... I put two more penis bottles in my basket.

Subtle hint?

Maybe.

"We'll have time this week." It's instinct; I touch his concrete chest, rousing him. "We have six nights on a yacht with our friends, and I don't care how jet-lagged we are... we're fucking as soon as we get there."

Our holiday plans change the light in his piercing eyes. It goes from tired dad and stressed-out husband to horny man remembering how we used to fuck like rabbits. Toys optional.

He lowers his lush lips to my ear.

"I want to know what naughty little gift my wife bought."

His sexy accent. His baritone voice. His warm lips skimming the shell of my ear and me thinking about the kinky-as-hell present I bought for this trip zing my pussy with a bolt of electricity.

She's alive! She's alive!

Here's the plan—three couples, six people, each bought a naughty adult gift. All had to wrap it in black. Cade even sent us matching large boxes with wrapping paper and gold bows so no one will know the other's gift.

She's such a detective. I love how she thought it through, how we could deceive one another.

We've shipped the gifts to her ahead of time. They're waiting for us on Silas's yacht, and the plan is we roll the dice when we arrive, and that's our number. One through six. Whoever rolls number one picks a box from the mystery pile first, and so on. One gift per night.

Culminating on New Year's Eve.

No one can tell each other, even our spouses, what we bought. And no one can confess it afterward. Sworn secrecy 'til death.

What happens each night after we open the gift?

Well... it ain't Vegas.

It's a luxurious superyacht sailing from Miami to the Bahamas with three couples on it. But the real gamble is... who is fucking who? And with what?

I don't answer my husband. If he knew what I bought, what I'm suggesting...

But he sees my horns, knowing I'm secretly a horny little devil, taunting me.

"Tell me, Charlie. What's your naughty gift?"

"Nope. That's a secret threesome between me and Adam and Eve." I tease right back. "But I'll know *your* gift. It'll have ass play written all over it."

We've been married for over four years. I know Daniel too well. He has a fetish for bodystockings. He likes recording us, turning our sex into amateur porn. Well, when we were fucking. Now, it'd be like a six-second GIF of a dog humping a stuffed animal. I swear, we rarely get a moment alone. And he has an ass fetish. Then again, what man doesn't? Hell, I do, too.

"You think you know me so well, Mrs. Pierce?" He rests

his massive hand on my lower back, guiding us to the register. "I bet I surprise you, too."

After we check out and he takes selfies with fans, we finally make it to the limo waiting for us outside, and I'm not used to such extravagance. Low-key is safer.

Not that we don't have money either, but Silas is spoiling us with his billions.

He's still the boy I used to babysit when I was a teenager—my cute partner in crime. We ruled Daufuskie Island together like we owned it. And now, Silas could. He's inherited his family's energy fortune and insists on sparing no expense for our holiday.

And his yacht? It's a *superyacht*. A ship, actually, with seven luxury staterooms, a movie theatre, a spa, a gym, multiple lounges, a sun deck, and a pool on the fifth deck, with a helipad too.

It's an opulent vessel built for a Russian oligarch.

But that's not Silas.

No, he still walks around in flip-flops, cargo shorts with marine grease on them half the time, and he won't waste ten of his twenty billion dollars on a shirt. No matter the high society he can run in, he won't cut his long brown hair, licked blond by the sun, either.

His only splurge is his superyacht. He owns that and a humble Grady White center console boat for fishing.

That's life. Some things change. Some people don't.

But me? I need some changes.

Like when you've bought your dream home but have lived in it for years and want to remodel. I love my husband. I love our kids. I love my job, and I love our life.

But for seven years before I met Daniel, I didn't have sex. Long story. So imagine, when we finally fucked, it was a

July fourth fireworks show. Every time. I got used to the stars he'd make me see all night.

Now? Our sex is a bang snap—the smallest, fastest firecracker, made for noise only.

And I... need a bicentennial show.

I feel like somewhere along the way, from college to job to marriage and kids—yeah, there was drama, but you get the drift. I feel like I missed out. It seems like everyone had their fun but me.

Every steamy book I read or show I stream, who lives these sexy lives? Not me. I have Goldfish crackers for my kids, crunched in the bottom of my purse, not hot red lipstick. I have children's toys strewn over our floors, not sexy lingerie ripped off in the heat of passion.

I even fully waxed my kitty for this trip, and when that shit was ripped off, she screamed back, "Bitch! This ain't the kinda special attention I crave!"

I don't know what'll happen this week, but like hell, I'm not prepared. I'm like a horny Girl Scout wanting to share her cookies. Tagalong for this erotic ride.

As the limo whisks us down Miami's streets lined with palms, Daniel pours us a second glass of champagne. He must sense my excitement laced with frustration, so he gets playful.

"So, what shall we wager?"

For the first time in forever, he seems relaxed.

"Bet on what?"

"If I guess which naughty gift is the one you bought," he asks, "what do I win?"

He hands me a full flute, bubbles dancing through golden champagne to the surface for my lips.

"We're not supposed to confess whose gift is whose."

"Who made these rules?"

"Cade and Eily. They came up with the idea—a holiday getaway the week before New Year's Day, and I think it's brilliant. After the Christmas Olympics we perform with our families, we're exhausted. It's nice to take a break before we go back to work. Adults only."

"With the gift I bought," Daniel grins, and nuns everywhere cream their granny panties, "it's going to be *very* adult."

I smirk back. I know I am. It's written all over my guilty face because I've been waiting for this chance. Hoping for it. Okay, fantasizing about it. It's why I said yes to this steamy vacation. The champagne in my bloodstream is the liquid courage I need...

"Question is, dear husband, how adult are *we* going to be?"

He waggles his brows. "I shall perform my husbandly duties."

Bye-bye, Cliff. Here I go.

"With who?"

I have my answer, my secret desires, because I'm a happily married woman with a pissed-off pussy.

But Daniel scoffs, "With my wife, of course."

And shit.

Shot down before I even took off.

Daniel can see my disappointment smack the smile off my face.

"Charlie," he lowers his gaze and voice, "are you suggesting something *else* this week?"

It's rare that I can't read my husband like an open book. We're soulmates. We've survived so much together; I never doubt Daniel's love. I swear he's a chamber in my heart, beating only for him. But...

"What if I *am* suggesting something else? Just for the week?"

He stares at me.

I stare back.

One of us needs to breathe, but it's not me. I'm holding my breath.

I'm not a woman, easily scared, but this? Asking my husband to open our marriage? And with our closest friends? Fine, I might be crazy. But if you saw our sexy friends, you'd give up your sanity, too.

The exhale that heaves from his broad chest is long, heavy with doubt. His gorgeous eyes narrow. He clenches his square jaw. Shit, is he jealous? Afraid? Pissed off? This is new territory for us. It's always been just me with Daniel. He's the second man I've been with, and I love no other.

Daniel, on the other hand? He fucked half of Hollywood before he met me.

"Tell me exactly," he says, "how you think that would work."

"Cocks and pussies fucking, that's how it usually works."

"Don't be daft. It's more than that, Charlie." He sets his flute down. "Let's start with Redix and Cade. They're married, too. They have a child. You went to high school with them, you have a history, and now I work with Redix. We're mates and co-stars on the same show. Fuck's sake, he and I start shooting season two next week, and now, you work with Cade, too. Well, *she* actually works for *you* at HGR Security, so you're her *boss*."

I twist my lips.

I want to argue every point, but those are facts, and he keeps laying 'em down.

"We all know Redix and Cade are with Silas, too," he

says. "They were public about their throuple. Then, Silas found Eily Dove, and she joined them. She married Silas, and now the four of them have... what do they call it... kitchen table polyamory love... something like that."

It makes me grin.

"Since when did my husband get so enlightened on his terms?"

"Since everyone on set knows about Redix's lifestyle. It's all they whisper about in the hair and makeup trailer."

"Redix and Cade, and Silas and Eily have nothing to be ashamed of. Why are people whispering about them behind their backs?"

It pisses me off.

I go way back with Silas; I'll always protect him. And I adore Cade. Yeah, we have a history. I beat up some assholes on our school bus who were bullying her when we were in high school. I've also worked with Redix on set. His fans are a security nightmare, but he's a sweet, sexy devil. And I'm getting to know Eily. We haven't spent much time together yet, but whenever we do, I've never seen Silas so in love, so happy.

"They're not ashamed of their love," Daniel answers me. "That's my point. They're public about it. And it is *love*. The four of them love each other, and us coming 'round, wanting a shag, we could bugger it up."

He leans my way. "And I love you, Charlie. I'm not insecure. I'm not some wanker who judges or gets jealous."

I cock my eyebrow. *Puhlease, Mr. Alpha of the bet.*

"Fine then," he answers. "I'm not jealous of *them*."

Is that a glimmer of hope? Sparkling like a stripper pole on the horizon? Like the promised land of real-life porn?

"Why not?"

"Because every man fantasizes about watching his wife

with other women. Go for it. It's the porn we were raised on."

Is it scary that we think so much alike?

"That's so damn sexist." I shake my head. "Like other women aren't a threat, but other men are?"

He studies me, wrapping his seductive gaze around my soul. "No one threatens us," he vows. "We'll always love each other."

"Exactly," I reach for his hand, "so why aren't these men in particular, why aren't Silas and Redix a threat?"

"Because I trust Silas. I trust our history with him—our secret. And Redix and I have gotten close. We're mates. We're... " He pauses. "We're... Bloody hell, I don't know... "

He falls back in his seat, watching the harbor as we cross a bridge, our limo heading toward One Island Park, where Silas's ship is docked. It's the only place large enough for his vessel.

Yeah, that metaphor is perfect for Silas.

Not that I've seen his large vessel. I've just watched it tent his board shorts around me for years.

Talk about a big circus in your pants.

"Daniel," I set my flute down before turning to crawl on top of him, straddling him on the bench seat beside me, "I love you. You know that."

I caress his granite jaw, and it clenches in my grasp, straining under stress, but I trust our love, so I keep pushing.

"We've tested our marriage; we know nothing can tear us apart. But our sex used to be so kinky. It used to connect us, too, and I miss that part. We need to spark it again. *I* need to spark it... because the truth is... you got to explore a lot more than me before we were married."

I'm right. He knows it.

"How many threesomes were you in before me?"

He huffs, his shoulders dropping, "Three."

"And you've been with sixty-one women because you count everything, and you've also been with a man."

"That man hardly counts." He grabs my hips like it's instinct. "It was hand jobs."

"But you got hard." I grin, feeling his cock stiffen with me sitting on his lap. "You got off on it. Being with a man. Being with more than one partner. You came. You can be *very* kinky, and you got to explore it, and that's my point—I haven't."

My logic is strong, but he keeps questioning my lady-boner.

"All this because we're too busy to fuck lately?"

"Maybe." I shrug. "Or maybe it's more. I don't need to justify it."

"I'm. Your. Husband."

He's my husband whose linen pants can't hide his cock surging at my suggestion.

"Exactly. And I love you, and we'll always be together, but what if I want to be with someone else sexually? Just for a few days? What if I need it?" I pause before broaching a subject I've been waiting to mention. "And *you* do, too?"

Something flashes across his eyes.

Is it thrill or terror? I'm not sure yet.

"Even if I were curious," he says. "Even if I say yes to your crazy idea, you can't be sure they're interested. We've spent time with Redix and Cade. Nothing happened. We're friends and colleagues.

"And you grew up with Silas. For ages, he was in love with you, but you always said he's like a little brother. You two are best mates. You're so close, I used to be jealous, but now I bloody love him, too. And I haven't met his wife yet, but I'm sure he loves *her* now because that's the kind of man he is; Silas has a heart of gold."

I chew my lip, questions swirling deep inside me. Urges I didn't know I had.

Yes, Redix and Cade have become our friends. But I can't deny that Redix Dean is one of the sexiest men alive. He always looks five seconds away from taking you hard against a wall.

And you want to be slammed by him.

And his wife, Cade Bryant? She's a former model with a body I gotta admit is hot. She tries to hide it, but I can't. I can't help that she makes me very curious.

Because I know Cade and Redix are with Silas and Eily. I'm one of the first people Silas came out to as bi. That was years ago, and I supported him. I just hated how he kept getting his heart broken.

Then he met Cade, then Redix. How those three came together? Damn, I bet it's a story that would warm my heart and wet my pussy; I can't lie.

And Eily, Silas's wife? She's the kind of beauty that seduces grown men into very bad deeds. She's a talented artist and a grown woman, but she has that look of innocence that tempts you into sin.

I don't know who I want or what I want.

But you just know, right?

When you want... *something*.

Daniel can read it in my silence. His eyes lower, doing that wolf-gaze thing he gets paid millions to do.

"*Who* else do you want, Charlie?"

I can't answer him.

Or maybe I shouldn't.

The minute Cade suggested this vacation and shared their naughty gift idea, my wheels started turning. It put my frustrated pussy into fifth gear, speeding down the Autobahn of sex at Mach One, headed toward an orgy.

So I turn the tables on him.

"Who do *you* want me to be with, Daniel?"

"Don't be coy."

"My coy has got your cock rock hard."

Daniel's my equal, my true match, so I start grinding on him, confident I can make his growl slide into a grin.

I taunt him. "So you won't get jealous watching me with someone else?"

You'd think that'd be our deal-breaker, but I know my husband and all we've been through. The man is unbreakable.

"No," he answers, clutching my hips, "that's not the problem."

"Then what is?"

"How will we work afterward?"

He's not worried about us. We're strong. I know who he's curious about, who he works with.

"It'll work if we want it to." I grind harder, his thick firmness turning me on, passion slicing through my veins as I lean forward, brushing my lips over his. "And I know you secretly *want* it to."

He taunts back, nipping my lips. "Do you now?"

Daniel can be so bad when he finally lets go. I know he wants this, too. The heat is scorching between us as his hands caress my thighs, pushing my sundress to my waist until all that's between us are my white lace panties, his drawstring linen pants, and a very big question.

I pull the drawstring, snapping it free to reach in; my hand could find his hard cock in a blinding snowstorm. But it's not cold. It's getting very hot in this limo on a mild December afternoon in Miami.

I taunt him, staring into his eyes.

"It's turning you on, isn't it?"

"That my wife is naughtier than I thought?" His erection strains, swollen in my grasp. "That she wants a leg over with someone else?"

"Yes," I confess, stroking his hard shaft. "Who do you want to watch me fuck for you, Daniel? How naughty do you want me to be?"

I lift his thick cock, heavy with lust, as my other hand slides my panties aside. I swear my pussy has been wet for a month, anticipating this week. Missing my husband. And wanting to be free to fuck for days upon end.

It's going to be paradise.

A luxury superyacht with a crew of two dozen, serving our every need. Our every desire will be met as we sail across turquoise waters, seeking even warmer temperatures. Pampered by a spa staff. Fed by a gourmet chef. Everything you can wish for, and that's just the crew.

Then there are our friends—two other couples. And I don't know who's the hottest because they all are. The thought of them together? All four of them? I'm not jealous. I'm so curious.

I want to join their fun.

Just for the week.

Daniel slides the spaghetti strap of my black dress down, exposing my braless breast. His fingertip circles my thrilled nipple, tightening even more as he taunts.

"Do you want to be with Cade?" he asks as I wedge his fat tip into my excited pussy. "Does my naughty wife want to lick nipples and eat pussy too? Is that what you're trying to tell me?"

I don't answer him. I can't. I moan instead, sinking down his rigid length. Leaning forward, I start riding him, bracing my hands against his broad shoulders as I rub my hard clit up and down his shaft. My orgasm is so close; it's only a block away. All the desires I have storming inside my body held at bay for so long, I want to unleash it all.

Like he knows, Daniel reaches down, thumbing my clit, pressing in firm circles over it, making pleasure burn up my thighs until it's a luscious attack of my senses. My husband has trained my body to always receive his dirty demands. We used to be so kinky.

And now we're back.

"Or do you want two pussies, Charlie? Cade and Eily?" He nips my bottom lip again. "Do you want me to watch you with two women?"

"Oh fuck," I gasp at the idea, at his other fingers; they're pinching my pearled nipple.

"Do you want to be with Cade and Eily while I fuck you?" He doesn't let up. "I can fuck your naughty little ass and fill it with my cum while they lick your sweet pussy clean."

I knew it. I knew this was in him, too.

I press my forehead to his, grinding down on his cock; he has me. I've missed him so much, and I want to greet this too, a new experience, a new lust like I've never had before. If Daniel shares it with me, then I trust it. It'll work.

We can do this.

"Redix," I sigh, and his eyes change. "You can fuck his ass too." His lips part. His breath thins. My pussy soaks his cock as I crack him so fast, revealing his secret. "I see how you look at him. You fucked him in a scene, and you weren't acting, Daniel. You want him, too, and it's okay. We can both fuck Redix."

"Oh fuck," Daniel grunts, grabbing my hips harder, his

desire exposed, and he loves it. "Fuck yes, babe, you're making me come."

I clasp his face, our eyes locked.

"Come in this pussy you're going to share."

Daniel's my anchor no matter how far I explore. My clit, his thumb is teasing it, pressing down, binding my core so tight; *I'm gonna come.*

I can barely huff. "Come knowing that I'll watch you fuck Redix, too."

The veins in his neck strain; he stares at me, his helpless grunts filling the limo as he comes so hard. I don't care if the driver can hear us; I cry out, too. The orgasm I've been craving, the one with my husband deep inside, seizes my sex, and I convulse. I see fireworks against the bright afternoon sunshine outside our limo as it parks beside a yacht so big it eclipses the sky.

My hands still clasp his face. We're still panting, our bodies connected, recovering from the sex we needed so badly.

"Is that a yes?" I ask him. "Will you share me if I share you too?"

His answer is his deep kiss. He yanks my long blonde hair, pulling me into one, his tongue taking mine, and we haven't kissed like this in so long, either. But when we do, I know his answer.

Yes. I love you.

There's only one question. One name we didn't confess in our passion. The man who's wanted me since we were teenagers.

Silas.

Will I do it? Will I finally fuck my hot best friend?

Cade

TWO

"I GUESS AMAZON WON'T PUT A 'CUM BLANKET' IN
YOUR CART, BUT YOU GET THE PRIME IDEA."

"This is crazy," I marvel. "*This* gift weighs a ton, but
this one weighs nothing at all."

This dirty game may get a little crazy, too, and, hey,
that's exactly my plan.

I arrange the sleek black gift boxes in a neat row on a
matching black credenza in the "owner's lounge." That's
what the captain calls this room, but Silas never would.

This ship isn't his style. It's Art Deco meets Manhattan.
All the sleek furniture either gleams in shades of black or
wraps you in luxe whites and ivory. Every shared room is
designed in circles with crescent sofas and plush chairs,
while the staterooms have massive beds with black silk
sheets and ivory pillows. Chrome accents are everywhere,
from the railings around the five upper decks to the fixtures
in every spa-like bathroom off each stateroom.

But Silas says this yacht was a steal at one hundred and

sixty-seven million dollars, and I don't know his world sometimes.

My sweet friend went from being a boat mechanic to a billionaire, and it hasn't changed him because I know why he bought this ship. The hull is dark indigo, so dark it's almost black, and he bought it for his wife, Eily, changing the vessel's name from *Phoenix* to *Indigo Dream*.

Eily said we should play our nightly naughty game in this upper lounge, and I agree.

It's breathtaking, with wrap-around views of the water. It has a massive ebony velvet sofa and a matching ivory one, both big enough for multiple people and shaped like half circles that don't touch. They're separated by a stately round onyx coffee table with crystal chandeliers in deco designs gleaming above.

Yep, someone designed this room for group sex.

I grin, knowing that's another reason why Silas bought it.

"No matter your tricks," Redix, my playful husband, wearing only black board shorts, taunts me from across the lounge, "I'm gonna know which treat is yours."

"What makes you think you can guess my gift?"

"I know my wife's kinks. Hell, I taught 'em to you," he says. "I'll know which gift is yours the second it's opened. Watch: it'll be black leather."

No, I watch *him* set out our supplies on the coffee table.

It looks like Adam & Eve opened an adult store on this yacht. My favorite strap-on. An array of cock rings. An assortment of vibrators. Nipple clamps. A prostate massager. Personal wipes. Toy cleaner. Eily's magic wand, charged and ready to go.

It's all here.

I swear—it looks like an epic porno series—like Lords of the Ass and Pussy Rings is about to be filmed here.

Yes, my precious, all week long.

"And look what I got you, Candy Cade."

Redix uses my nickname. We met as kids, sharing our candy, and now we share everything, even the partners we love, too.

Reaching into his black carry-on for orgy flights, apparently, he sets out his next surprise.

Three boxes of candy nipple tassels in pastel colors.

Will he ever stop?

Hell, no. He's paid to perform, but his daily occupation is making me laugh. Opening a box, he peels off the adhesive and sticks a tassel to his nipple, smirking at me. "Wanna lick my candy, Cade?"

We're on a yacht, no shirts or shoes required, as he starts rolling his naked, sculpted chest like a burlesque dancer, making the rainbow nipple candies twirl.

Laughter bursts from my lungs.

"Where the hell did you learn that?"

He jumps up. "You don't play a male stripper in two movies and not walk away with some sweet skills."

Redix pops his hips, swinging his package and candy around the salon while he sings, "Welcome to my candy shop." He winks, giving a half-hearted attempt at a twerk, and I grab my splitting sides. "I'll let you lick my lollipop."

He starts untying his shorts.

"Oh, my god! Stop it!"

I hope he never does.

"Fine," he gives the tassels two more silly twirls, "I'll let you lick *ALL* my candy later."

Leaning down, tassels dangling from his nipple, he pulls more boxes from his carry-on.

Candied cock rings. Candied G-strings. Candied bras. Even three candied penis pouches.

"Sweet Jesus," I gasp, "I came for orgasms this week, not cavities."

"That's why I packed toothpaste, too," he replies, pulling out a big box of condoms next.

"Holy prophylactics, how many condoms did you buy?"

"They're just in case."

He pours dozens of Magnums in gold foil into a glass vase on the table, and yes, Silas and Redix fill Magnums and then some.

Honestly, they need Magnum Cum Laude condoms because *praise their girth.*

"Just in case?" I huff. "I have an IUD, and so does Eily."

"You got asses, too," he grins, "and *we* are in the mood for poke parties."

WE are Redix and Silas.

And *WE*, me and Redix, and Silas and Eily, haven't had a sin fest in months.

Redix has been too busy filming, and Eily's been traveling to Europe a lot, visiting the Mercier hotels in Paris and Madrid, where her next two paintings will hang.

We have our own homes with busy lives, but when we have the time, we don't usually do anything unless it's all four of us. But occasionally, I'll walk in on Silas and Redix in the shower and just watch. Or one of them will catch me and Eily in the kitchen and watch, too.

Yeah, I've caught Redix's food fetish.

What can I say?

Kink is contagious.

Redix pulls more surprises out of his bag.

"What are those?" I ask.

"They're called 'Liberator Fascinator Throws,' or some

shit like that." He drapes three plush white blankets over the ivory sofa. "Silas told me to buy a dozen. They're supposed to help with... *moisture.*"

Redix tosses me a cute grin, and I don't care if we've been in love since we were kids and fucking since we were eighteen; he still makes my kitty purr like a fucking lioness.

His guilty grin grows, teasing me.

"Guess Amazon won't put a 'Cum Blanket' in your cart, but you get the prime idea."

He's such a bad boy. Cocking that half-smirk at me, making me laugh with his long, golden brown hair covering one of his sky eyes and those lush lips. He's sweet, too.

Redix earns millions seducing the camera when all he wants is to seduce me every day.

And we do. We try to fuck daily, even if it's a quickie; I don't care. We stay connected. My husband gets me off every damn time. He was my first, and I was his. It's like our bodies were built for each other. Dynamite and a fuse. BOOM!

We're so close; our love is so great, it's big enough for others.

But having enough time to share it?

That's the issue.

That's why Eily and I came up with this week. We're going to make it a tradition for our nontraditional family.

The idea to invite Charlie and Daniel too? That was mine. I know they're not part of our group, but they're close friends.

Redix has gotten close to Daniel. They've shot one season of their new show, *Breaking Laws*, a dark detective show, and I like Daniel Pierce, too. He's so fucking alpha, like Redix. No wonder their show is number one, making panties and boxers spontaneously combust when you stream them together.

But when I see Daniel around Charlie, it's even hotter because she's his match.

I love working with her. Well, *for her,* technically. She works hard, though she doesn't need to; Daniel makes millions. Charlie works for the same reason I do; we love it.

The detective in me can read people, and I could tell the last time me and Charlie met for lunch... *this woman needs a fucking break.* Literally. She needs time off *and* fucks.

Every woman does.

It's like, women can save the world six days a week, but on the seventh day? Save us with sex. Dirty sex. That's why I invited Daniel and Charlie to join us.

Am I trying to seduce my hot boss? *Maybe.*

Don't hate.

There are some people you'd lose your job for. Your mind for. Because I've worshiped Charlie Ravenel since we were teens.

You know that person who changes you in two, maybe three minutes? You didn't know someone like that existed and want more of them?

That's Charlie.

At the least, she'll have fun with her hot husband. At the most, we'll fuck too. It's a win-win situation, and Eily agreed. She liked the idea of inviting them. She said Silas's yacht is too massive, too incredible not to share.

I grin... *kinda like his dick.*

Eily and Silas are down below, on the main deck, waiting for Charlie and Daniel to arrive any minute while Redix and I are tasked with getting the festivities ready.

It's a task I love because I need this week away, too.

Don't get me wrong. I loved Christmas with our daughter and our families. But if I have to hear sleigh bells, Mariah Carey, or Santa "Ho, Ho, Ho" one more time, this ho is gonna unload her 9 into the flatscreen—Elvis style.

I'm a good mom. A good wife. I'm so damn good all the time; I need to be bad.

Real fucking bad.

I got no shame. Just a suitcase full of sexy bikinis and fancy lingerie, but who are we kidding? They won't stay on long because Eily and I decided to spice things up. We devised the adult gift idea. Like Secret Slutty Santas sliding orgasms down your chimney and wrapped in a golden bow.

That's the kinda ho, ho, ho we want.

"I got lube." Redix lines bottles up on the coffee table like a bartender serving kinky cocktails. "Silicone. Water. Anal. This organic shit that Eily likes. Some oil-based—" He pauses, cutting a serious look at me. "Do *not* lick this off my dick again. You said your tongue burned for days." He pulls more bottles out while I lean on the ebony sofa. "And, of course, flavored. Watermelon for Silas. Apple for Eily. And our favorite—Salted Caramel—for your sweet pussy."

"My pussy tastes great without flavored lube, thank you very much."

"You're always welcome and so right." Redix admires his work. "But our lube pairs perfectly with the banana pudding I've asked the chef to prepare for your pussy too."

I laugh, covering the distance between us; I can't resist him. Reaching my arms around his neck while he wraps around me, too, I'm tall, but Redix is taller. I love that about him. How no matter how much ass I kick on my job, working as a protection officer for Charlie now, Redix loves me. He's even stronger. He kicks my ass, metaphorically.

Well, actually... he likes licking my ass after he's drizzled it in mango juice and served it with a banana.

Y'all, Jamba Juice ain't got nothin' on our sex.

"You're something else," I tell him, gazing into his sky eyes.

"And you're all mine," he says, gazing back at me, and yes, Redix is my home.

I lost him for so many years to drinking, drugs, and almost death; it took him a while to recover from our past. But he's sober and home for good. Because now he won't stop being the most amazing dad and husband, loving me so damn much it hurts my smiling cheeks.

He kisses the tip of my nose before warning me.

"You keep wearing itty bitty bikinis like this, and you're getting fucked six ways from this Sunday, Candy Cade. For seven days straight, but don't worry; I packed ice packs for your pussy, too."

"And *your* ass."

It's true, and it makes him kiss me. *God, Redix's kiss.* It still makes me tingle, from my scalp to my toes. His lush, possessive lips. His talented tongue dancing across mine. He claims my mouth while his hand tugs at my bikini bottoms, his candied nipple pressing against mine, his cock firming against my belly.

I murmur over our lips.

"What are you doing?"

"I'm about to make my wife grab her ankles."

I grab his long hair, pulling it gently instead.

"Mr. Dean, I told you last night—no fucking until you tell me what *you* want."

He half growls, half rolling his eyes.

"I told you; I don't know what I want. I have to talk with Silas first."

"Redix," I sigh, "I love that you love him. That you honor Silas. You know that. But you're allowed to have an opinion, too. You've done it your whole life, sacrificing your-self for others, but not anymore. *You* can decide what you want and *then* talk to Silas about it."

I know Redix has feelings for Daniel, Charlie's husband. He told me. We have no secrets.

Redix started getting anxious months ago when he read the script for the final episode of their first season—the one everyone is talking about. The episode where Daniel Pierce fucks Redix Dean.

Well, their characters did.

And though the men are seasoned actors who've had to shoot sex scenes with dozens of gorgeous women, this was different.

The scene was one of the hottest ever filmed, allowed to stream on STARZ without going straight to gay porn because it wasn't porn. It was drama. It was intense. It was two men coming out to each other, and it was raw and passionate and beautiful.

Both men brought so much to that scene. They shot it on a closed set over three days. Intimacy coordinators and the crew did their jobs. They were professionals.

But Redix came home drained after the third day of shooting and worried.

"Cade, I'm scared," he admitted to me. Sobriety has Redix stone-cold honest about everything, and I love that about him. "Three days of kissing Daniel, even on a crowded set with bullshit lights and mics everywhere, and I... I felt something."

"But aren't you supposed to feel something?" We were in bed, him holding me with my head on his chest while he bared his soul. "Isn't that doing your job? Won't those feelings go away after a while?"

"Maybe," he mumbled into my hair. "But I've never felt that shooting a scene with a woman. I'm so focused on the blocking and my lines. But with Daniel? Man, I forgot where I was. I got so hard with him on top of me, and he did, too. I could feel his big cock under his modesty pouch thrusting against mine, and I almost lost it. I almost came on set."

"Okay, so it was intense. Y'all are good actors." I rubbed his chest. "It's okay. Maybe you should talk with him about it."

"Hell no. That'd be harassment."

I glanced up at him, surprised. "Are you serious?"

"Yeah. Think about it. If I got turned on and started to catch feelings for a woman actor, and I forced her to talk with me about it? It could make her feel awkward as hell. It's borderline harassment."

We laid quiet for a while until he finally shared, "I feel like I cheated on Silas."

"You didn't cheat on him. You were doing your job."

Our relationship is closed. It's just been me and Redix, and then Silas joined us until finally, Silas found Eily, too.

Silas had been searching for her, saying he wanted a love like what me and Redix share, and I was happy for him. He and Eily's story is like a tragic fairytale with the happiest-ever-after ending.

And I'd been with other men and women before. But Eily had been with no one. Silas was her true first, and then she wanted to join us, and I adore her. Eily always makes me laugh after a shitty day. A filter has never met her mouth. And now? Hell. She's the most sexually ambitious of us all, and I love that about her, too.

Still, Redix hasn't told Silas about that scene with Daniel and what it made him feel. That's why I insisted that Redix and I decide now what our vote is on including Daniel and Charlie in our love. Maybe just for the week?

If they're interested.

Maybe they aren't.

I can't read either, but Charlie has always attracted me. With that scar on her gorgeous face? She's breathtaking. And search "pussy magnet" on Google, and Daniel's face appears.

Think I'm kidding?

Start typing.

"Redix." I stare into his eyes now. They're searching mine for an answer that's not mine to give. Outside on the dock, a car door slams. *They're here.* "What do you want? You know I want to be with Charlie. Eily and I aren't closed like you and Silas are. We're with other women at the club, so you have a choice. Do you want to be with Daniel, too?"

"Hey, Asshole."

A deep Southern voice booms from the main deck below. We left the lounge doors open, and the sound carries across the water, making Redix smile.

Silas *always* makes Redix smile. The bond they have is special. Between the two of them, I don't know who saved who.

"We got company," Silas shouts again, sending his taunt four decks up to us.

"Shit," Redix mutters to me, fear and lust swimming in his eyes, "do we ever have fucking company now."

Eily

THREE

"I'm married to clit bliss."

"Do I have stalactites?"

Silas glances down at me, laughing at my question. "Do you have *what*?"

"Boogers. Do I have a booger hanging from my nose like one of those crusty things hanging from a cave?"

I put my nose in the air, requiring a full inspection from my husband, but he just wraps his big arms around me.

"No. But you have a heap of damn cute filling my heart."

"Silas, I'm serious." I pull back from his grasp, staring up at him and the sun. "Do I have something in my nose, spinach in my teeth, or is my mascara smudged like bukkake porn, or does my breath smell like ass?"

His knuckle lifts my chin even higher.

"Baby girl, are you nervous?"

"Hell, yes. Daniel Pierce is about to arrive, and no offense, but I've had a crush on him since I was a girl, and he was wearing capes and codpieces. And now he's bringing his wife, Charlie Ravenel, the love of your life."

His face falls.

"Eily, *YOU* are the love of my life."

"Yeah, but you were in love with Charlie long before me. You wanted to marry her until Daniel stole her from you."

I'm not mad about it.

I'm standing on the deck of my husband's yacht. The one he named *Indigo Dream* for me and my art, and it's more like a cruise ship. And if you think this fancy ass yacht is jaw-dropping, which it is, you should see my husband.

Silas Van de May is digit disco.

Your fingers immediately wanna dance with your sex in his presence.

Tan shredded muscles wrap over even tanner ones on his tall frame; you can plant seeds in the crevice of his washboard abs and sprout orgasms daily.

He usually wears his long hair in a knot, and all that does is show off his hazel eyes that sparkle with mischief. But it's his lips. They're full and soft and sweet but say the dirtiest shit when we fuck.

I'm married to clit bliss.

I know Silas loves me, and I've been in love with him since he saved me at fifteen when he fought for me. Then, I tried hiding from him for years. I didn't want to be remembered as *that girl* who survived, who left her clunky shoe behind, but he found me again, and now he's never letting me go.

Silas spoils me rotten in little and big ways, and I don't know my heart without him.

But I know he had a life before we were reunited, and it involved a lot of sex and exploration. So now? Hell, yes, my

HOLIDAY FOR SIX

husband can Marco Polo my kitty all day long with his
skills.

I'm secure in our love.

He's the prince, and I'm his Cinderella.

We're a fairytale meant to be.

"Daniel didn't steal Charlie from me." Silas wraps his
arms around me tighter, smushing my face against his naked
pecs. "That woman does shit of her own free will."

"Yeah, but," my husband is allergic to shirts, "you
crushed on Charlie hard since you were ten. You said she
didn't marry Daniel until you were like, what, twenty-five?
That's fifteen years of pining for the same pussy."

He huffs, "That's fifteen years I also fell in love with a
man who broke my heart, and I fucked other women trying
to get over it. We all have a past."

"So you're telling me you don't find Charlie attractive
anymore?"

"She's hot. Daniel's hot. That doesn't mean I want to
fuck them."

"Well, *I* do." Craning my neck, I look my husband in
the eye. "And I bought a kinky-as-hell gift to make it
happen."

Silas may be much bigger than me, but I stand up for
myself. Yeah, I was an awkward, artsy girl, all quiet, lop-
sided, and limping while I grew up, but I've blossomed
under Silas's love. After everything we've been through,
now, I'm not shy; I'm shameless. I owe no one a justification
for the love we share. Silas and I have earned this. We've
fought for this.

He grins down at me.

"Whatcha get?"

"We're not supposed to tell."

"If my wife bought it, it'll be the kinkiest gift of all."

"One woman's kink can be another man's *hell no*."

He scoffs, "I ain't ever heard you say no to a damn thing when we fuck. You're usually the one wearing *us* out."

I slap his chest.

"You flatter me."

"No, we fuck you, all three of us at the same time," Silas plays with me, rutting against my belly, "because you tell us to. You love being our dirty little cum princess, don't you?"

It's official. Call me anything taboo, and my pussy licks her lips. Silas relishes it, too, because he's the filthiest of all with that talented mouth.

My devoted husband is half-saint, half-sinner. The proof? He's smiling sweetly at me, proudly wearing his golden wedding band, gently lacing his hand through my long brown strands, his eyes full of love before... he tugs my hair, grinding his firming cock into my body.

Y'all, I married a Centaur: half romantic man, half wild horse.

Don't be jealous.

I'll tell you all about it.

"Are you getting a chub for me, Mr. Van de May?"

"My wife gets me fat and happy at least twice a day."

"So, you're gonna fuck me right here? For all of Miami to watch?"

Put down the binoculars, folks. You won't need them. He's that hung.

"Yo, ho, ho, hell yeah, and a bottle of rum,"—he tugs my hair harder, seeking my lips—"because my wife wants to set sail on the Sea of Sex this week, and I fucking love her for it."

His kiss suddenly takes me like it always does. Like he owns me. Like he adores me. Like Silas won't live without me, he won't breathe, and it's mutual. That's why I'm not afraid. That's why we'll last forever.

I lift from his lips, gently gasping.

"So if they're interested? You're okay with me being with Charlie? Or Daniel?"

I'm open with Silas, Cade, and Redix. Those three have sexual pasts that would make a porn star retire. So now, it's just them, dedicated to each other.

But I'm just getting started.

Yeah, I love Cade and Redix, but in a different way.

Because Silas is my first and only love. The kind of love when you belong to someone. Yes, like in a sexy, fist-your-hair-while-I-fuck-you hard way, but it's more.

It's how whenever he's inside me, Silas grabs me so tight, either growling or sighing in my ear, "I'm your first and last, Eily."

I belong with him like the stars align in the sky. Shining on each other. Always by your side. You need their gravity. They're your light. They're your world.

But Silas lets me explore. He said he got to, and so should I. Not that he could stop me. I'm small but stubborn as fuck. I admit it; I make a mule look like a Xanax poster child.

I'm with other women at Ms. Faye's sex club. Cade is, too, sometimes. I don't fuck other men but Silas and, sometimes, Redix. But I love it when they watch.

I love being the bad one.

That's what happens to a strict preacher's daughter. You'd think by now, preachers would get the joke about their kids and quit having them. We're loads of delicious trouble.

Because I don't believe in shame or sin.

So when Daniel Pierce arrives, why do I have the

sneaky feeling that I'll be tempted to *whoops* break something just so he can punish me? So he can spank my naked ass and call me a "very naughty girl" in that English accent.

All three men can take me over their knees and...

Shit, that slaps my clit.

It makes me twist my thighs, trying to hide my dirty imagination from my even dirtier husband, but he grins down at me, all sweet and cupping my cheek.

"You have my permission, Mrs. Van de May."

Permission? No, I have his sexy smile and stirring cock aimed my way.

He likes sharing me.

"What about you, Mr. Van de May? If Daniel and Charlie are interested, will you join us?"

"I need to talk to Cade and Redix first."

"I've already talked to Cade. We're in."

He rolls his eyes, the mood shifting.

"Dayum, woman. We don't stand a chance with you two."

WE are Silas and Redix. And the two of us, Eily and Cade, their wives, pull their strings like puppets.

As if we could make our husbands, two Eiffel towers of matching looks and muscles, do a damn thing they don't want to. They go along because they love it, they love us, and they love each other. Yes, we're one big happy fucking loving family.

But I like growing families.

I'm not ready to have babies with Silas yet. Give us a few more years. We've only been married for two. But I need to explore before we settle down.

"What did you two decide?"

"Cade's always been attracted to Charlie," I answer. "I

think she's hot, too. And who doesn't want a three-ring circus with Daniel Pierce?"

The sparkle dims in Silas's eyes, his usual smile fading. *That's not like him.*

"What?" I ask him. "Didn't you tell me you already shared a kinky moment with them? Why are you acting like it bothers you now?"

"Yeah, I busted them in the dunes once."

I bounce my brows.

"What were they doing?"

"Charlie was sucking Daniel's cock. He likes her playing with his ass, too, while he comes on her tits. And then he finger fucked her so hard; that woman can squirt like a fountain. It's hot. And they knew I watched them. I couldn't help it, but they weren't mad about it. I think they got off on it."

"Damn, Silas." *I'm getting off on it.* "Then what's the problem?"

He shrugs.

"There's more than sex between us, Eily. Me and Charlie go way back. We've been through some shit. And then she brought Daniel Pierce home, and they were perfect together until they got into a big fight. They almost divorced, and Charlie came to me. Not to be with me. Just to, you know, be with a friend, but Daniel didn't see it that way. It's like I was a threat to him."

This is news.

And oh fuck, we invited this story to join us this week?

Cade thought Charlie needed a break, and I loved the idea of friends hanging out. But I'm not inviting drama into my life. I've survived enough for three lifetimes.

"So, is Daniel still mad at you?"

"Nah," Silas sighs. "We went through some scary shit

together after that when Charlie was stalked. It's a long story, but let's just say me and Daniel are... *very* close now."

"What about you and Charlie? How do you feel about her now?"

"Me and Charlie Girl?"

His eyebrows jump, his eyes lifting from mine to the horizon.

I hear it, too.

Turning around, I watch a black limo weave toward our yacht. It takes them a few minutes to exit the car, even with the chauffeur waiting patiently by their door before they signal him to open it.

And when *THE* Daniel Pierce steps out first... my lungs seize.

Yeah, Redix is as famous as Daniel and equally clit tingling.

Redix's beauty used to make me nervous. So did Cade's. She was a teenage model with iconic short brown hair, long bangs skimming her pillow lips, and captivating violet eyes. She still looks the same—jaw-dropping.

And me?

I was a geeky virgin who got more than a makeover when I married Silas. He makes me feel so beautiful. I've changed because my husband is hotter than a fresh-fucked fox in a forest fire.

I always want to play now.

But I've only seen Daniel Pierce on a big screen. In person? Holy shit, his muscles are bigger than a movie. His white linen shirt and pants can't contain him.

And with Redix and Silas here, too?

This week will be an adult trilogy, greater than my favorite books and movies. Like, yeah, okay; Bella had Edward and Jacob. They were like hot young ponies, all frolicking in a teenage, misty, dark mountainy sorta way. Plus, the whole vampire-werewolf thing was sexy.

But now? With these real grown men?

Redix and Silas threaten in an all-powerful, all tan and buff, *please, trap me between you and make me your slut* way. And with Daniel Pierce here, too? Like, *yes, Daddy, I've been so bad.*

This week ain't gonna be no ponyland in *Twilight*.

No, this is the dawn of three raging stallions charging my way. Plus, with our kinky adult game? With the naughty gift I bought?

Holy fuck, and crack some spines; don't ever let this book series end.

Reaching behind him, Daniel holds his hand out for Charlie. As she gracefully slips her palm into his and exits the limo, Silas reaches for my hand, too.

It makes me glance up, and he's smiling down at me. Like he did at our wedding. Like we're forever. Like he wants me to be sure—*I love YOU.*

"Hey, Dude."

When Silas greets Daniel with a back-slapping hug, it's genuine.

"Hey, y'all."

When Charlie hugs me, it's warm.

But when the two stand together, Daniel beside Charlie —beefcake married cheesecake—and...

Close your mouth, Eily. You're drooling.

"Bleeding hell, Silas." Daniel takes in the main deck of the yacht. "You've come a long way from your old Jet Ski."

"Go big or go home."

"I'm so proud of you," Charlie says, gently hugging him again.

And did my husband just blush at her touch?

"Before I forget, I, uh, found something of yours." Charlie reaches into her bucket bag, telling Silas, "I was cleaning out a closet at home and finally found this again. I kept it for you."

She pulls out a baseball mitt, and with wide eyes, Silas accepts it.

"I threw this away," he mutters. "My dad gave it to me, but after he kicked me out, I threw all my childhood shit away and—"

"I know," Charlie answers. "But I knew y'all would make up. Your parents love you. So, I did a dumpster dive in your trash and saved some stuff for you. There's more. I'll send it to you and—"

"Shit, Charlie Girl." Silas yanks her into another hug, whispering against her scarred cheek, "Thank you."

"You're welcome, you little shit." She smiles, shrugging in his grasp. "I'm still babysitting your stupid ass."

They gently laugh before he lets her go, but I sense it.

Electricity sparks the air around them, the pressure getting heavy, like the weather's suddenly changing. Like it's getting very hot. Flowers are opening, bees are buzzing, and nature awaits them. Their attraction is palpable, and I... I... I can't find a jealous bone in my body about it.

No, I feel something else.

Something blooms inside me, too.

Silas turns and starts showing Daniel around, but when Charlie turns to follow, "Hey uh," I tap her shoulder, noting the bullet scar through it. "Your dress," I tell her.

"Oh shit." She giggles, realizing that it's tucked into her panties. "Oh god, how embarrassing. Thank you." She fixes it, smoothing it down. "Daniel and I, uh... started our holiday in the limo."

"I get it. I ride Silas every time we're in one."

She laughs, wrapping her arm around my shoulder, making goosebumps blossom across my flesh.

"Thank you," she says, "we really need this week away. I just hope we aren't crashing your party."

"Girl, I love bumping cars. The more, the merrier."

It blurts from my lips and...

SHIT!

My mouth hits SEND on every damn message in my brain.

What if she doesn't love like we do? What if she's not interested? What if I freaked her out, and she uses her lethal skills to kill me?

Charlie's like a ninja with a sexy scarred Barbie face.

But she softly grins, gently reading my half-embarrassed, half-eager eyes before pausing to offer me the gold gift bag in her hand.

Hopefully, she's giving me the verbal filters I wasn't born with.

"Well, then here," she says. "I bought these for you, our hostess. This is *your* ship. We're at *your* command this week. Whatever you wish."

I peer into the heavy bag, relief and delight dancing through my veins when I see three frosted rosé bottles shaped like cocks, wrapped in black and gold bows.

Message received.

I didn't fuck up.

It's fucking ON.

"Actually," I grab her hand, sharing a knowing grin before we follow our husbands, "I like sharing with my ladies. Have whatever you desire this week."

And everything that intimidated me about Charlie Ravenel drops overboard.

Yes, with that scar on her stunning face, she could

threaten the sun not to rise, and it'd listen. It's a bullet graze, and she's that badass.

But not now.

It's like Charlie's relaxed. She's vulnerable around us. It's like she's home around Silas, and I like her—a lot.

I can feel why Silas fell in love with her so long ago. She's protective. She's the warm sun on your cool skin, making you open to her, and a plan forms deep in my loving heart, firing schemes in my thrilled little head.

Light bulb

Silas deserves closure with Charlie.

You think you love your husband, wife, boyfriend, significant other, partner... whatever... okay, you probably do.

But me?

I love Silas so much. His only dream is to make mine come true, and my daily goal is the same for him. He's given me everything, so I want to give him this...

I want him to finally fuck the woman who gave him his first wet dream. The person who introduced him to desire. The one that got away.

Because she's back.

And she's gorgeous.

And if that's what Charlie wants too? If she's always known how Silas has crushed on her, how he desired her, and if she feels the same way now? If they finally fuck? And if Daniel Pierce won't kill Silas if they do?

That's love, bitches.

Charlie

FOUR

"You're soaking wet for us."

This superyacht is a five-star Manhattan hotel on the water. I can't believe my eyes. Every room you enter is a "holy shit."

The dining room, with its view of the dark ocean outside, has walls of open glass doors, a long, shining black dining table with twelve white upholstered chairs, and crystal sparkling on the table *and* the ceiling.

Who puts crystals on the ceiling?

A ship designer who had a fifty million dollar budget, that's who.

This is *not* Silas's style or Eily's, I can tell. But neither gives a shit. He sits at the head of the dining table, relaxed with Eily on his lap.

"What's for dessert?" she asks him.

We've finished our gourmet meal of lobster thermidor, creamed leeks, and the best salad. The dressing on it would make me eat greens 24/7. We've enjoyed either wine or whiskey while Redix sips ginger ale.

"Our creamy game will be our sweet dessert tonight."

Silas answers Eily, kissing her neck and making her giggle. He's actually wearing a linen shirt, though it's hanging open and teasing her, too.

Daniel and Redix wear the same.

The dress code is yacht-casual.

But I seriously keep glancing at Redix's tan, shredded abs, then at Cade's amazing breasts under her silky purple slip-dress. She's not wearing a bra; her nipples are hard, and...

I'm in trouble.

Twice, Redix has cut me a sexy look, busting me admiring his body and wife's tits. It made him grin while Daniel holds my hand tight.

Is Daniel's palm sweating?

He has the same view of Redix and Cade, looking sexy as hell, and I wonder if they have the same effect on him.

They have to.

We're all hot and bothered.

We know what's next.

The game begins tonight.

All have prepared. Each couple retired to our state-rooms for a couple of hours, where Daniel fucked me again in the shower. We're both so turned on by what we've agreed to. It had us kissing more than we have in months as we laughed, cleaned up, dried off, and got ready for dinner.

I can only imagine what the other couples did, as Silas suggests we refresh our drinks before we begin.

He gets up, not expecting his staff to serve him, while Redix says, "Dude," and Silas can read his mind.

Reaching into a small refrigerator hidden in a buffet cabinet, Silas grabs another ginger ale for Redix before refreshing our drinks at the bar in the room.

He serves us first, but when he offers the cold, wet can to Redix last, he mashes it against his neck.

"Fuck!"

Redix jumps, laughing and grabbing Silas's hand, yanking him down into a retaliatory kiss. We watch them, Redix moaning against Silas's generous lips. The love between them is obvious, all four of them, as Silas turns and gently kisses Cade's neck, making desire flame up her cheeks. Then he stands behind their chairs, gently pulling Eily into his arms again. Like he owns her, his lips claim hers last, his hands sinking into her dark hair, tumbling to her waist, his body dominating hers.

It's like, I've always known Silas has a big heart, but now I see him in a new light. A very passionate, commanding, and seductive adult light, and I'm not used to it.

It's flipping my world.

It's storming my flesh with heat, tingling my sex, pearling my nipples, and pounding my heart.

What is happening to me?

I told Daniel I wanted my pussy to run free, not be on the prowl like a hungry cougar.

Okay, Silas is thirty, and I'm thirty-five. That's not cougar territory, but he's my best friend.

I've never looked at Silas this way, in a lusty lady way. There's no denying he's hot as hell. But to me, he's always been... just... *Silas.*

The boy I protected.

And he did the same for me.

Nothing separated us but age.

But now? Silas seems invincible. Like so powerful and sexy, I don't know how I feel about it as I hold Daniel's hand, our group ascending the spiral staircase to the upper deck lounge.

"Alright," Cade holds one crystal die for this special occasion, "let's roll for our number, starting with the youngest, Eily, and if you roll a number already claimed, roll again until we have one through six covered."

Eily goes first, tossing the sparkling die on the round coffee table with trays of sex toys, lube, and condoms.

Is my mouth watering?

Yes. I'm already so horny I'm dripping everywhere.

Eily rolls a six, making her clap with glee as Silas rolls a one. "Of course I am," he jokes. Cade rolls a four, Redix gets the three, then I roll twice to get the unclaimed two. So by default, Daniel, the oldest and looking so Daddy tonight, is number five.

"Before we open anything," Cade reclines beside Redix on the ebony sofa, "we should discuss boundaries and limitations and—"

"I'm okay with fucking *everyone!*"

Eily blurts, and Silas falls back, laughing on the sofa protected by blankets.

I blush, knowing why they're there.

"Of course, you wanna swing, baby girl." He pulls Eily, giggling, into a kiss. "You always wanna play."

"So do I."

Cade backs Eily up, and Daniel adjusts his pants. I catch it. So does Redix.

"I do, too."

I hear the words escape my lips as I jump off the cliff.

First, I look at Cade while I fall.

"You sure, Boss?" she asks with the sexiest grin.

This has always simmered between us. No shame. No need to be afraid. We're fearless women; we know what we want.

"If we take turns playing boss, then sure," I answer,

biting my lip but not backing down from the allure of her violet eyes.

"Fuck, y'all are hot," Redix softly proclaims. "All three of you women, give us a sapphic show."

"Hell no!" Eily blurts again. "I like cock too much, too. And lots of it *ALL* the time."

She keeps Silas laughing so hard, holding onto her tiny waist. I can't believe this little woman who's so cute. She's got a pixie face, big green eyes, and long brown hair. Her lips look like a doll, and her curves are demure. Eily's so small next to Silas, but her lust is big and shameless.

I see why she's perfect for him, why he loves her so much. I think she's adorable... and hot.

Daniel suddenly pronounces, "Yes, you may have my wife, too."

And in his old-world accent, it sounds like, "Hear, ye! Hear, ye! All townspeople may now bury their wick in my woman!"

I elbow him, amused.

"I don't need your permission."

"The bloody hell you don't." Daniel warns with a grin, "If someone wants to roger my wife, they'd better get my permission, or I'll bloody well murder them, then spit in their dead, open eyes."

I kiss his cheek.

"You're so sexy when you're aggro."

We make Redix laugh.

"You should see him on set if someone takes the last donut," he says. "He gets so pissed and possessive. Like he's gonna flip the craft services table if someone touches his Krispy Kreme."

Redix has Daniel laughing, challenging him, "So what? You saying I can roger your wife too?"

"Please do," Cade coos.

"Me too," Eily piles on. "I want all five of y'all to roger me." She pauses. "Wait. Is that fucking my ass or pussy?" She shrugs. "Whatever. I'm down for it. I got lots of holes. I'll make you fit."

She won't stop making us laugh; our sides are splitting. But then Eily blurts again, which I'm learning is her cutest trait.

"What about you men? We women are down to daisy-chain, but what about y'all in a butt chain?"

It's the obvious question, but it dims the laughter. My glance bounces from Daniel to Redix. Cade's doing the same, like she knows something too, but it's Silas who speaks up, clearing his throat.

"Let's uh... Let's not make the dude uncomfortable."

The dude is Daniel, and everyone looks at him.

"Look," Silas says to him, "you know I love Redix, and he loves me, so we'll keep it just between us."

I glance at Redix. Yes, love fills his eyes, looking at Silas, hearing him proclaim it.

"I'm not uncomfortable with you loving Redix," Daniel answers. "You know, I feel totally fine with it. Actually, I feel, uh... "

Daniel's sweating hand twitches in mine. I catch his nervous glance at Redix. Their pause is heavy; it's too long and awkward, so I jump in.

"I tell you what—all of us. Let's go slow and have fun. You four are together, obviously. Daniel and I are, too, so we talk it out. We ask, and if we have a boundary, it's okay. We say 'pass,' and that's it."

Daniel squeezes my hand. I'm sure we'll talk more about this when we're back in our stateroom. Because I don't think he can hide his secret attraction to Redix. Not all week.

"And tonight," Redix adds, "no fucking. Just foreplay, if anything. We can fuck in our cabins."

"You're no fun," Eily protests.

"Lookey here, Ms. Hot In The Biscuit," Redix teases her. "Four of us gotta work together next week, so let's slow this moresome down until we know what we want."

"Agreed," Daniel adds, relieved, while Silas jumps up from the sofa, heading toward the gifts.

"No shaking the boxes," Cade orders. "Once you put your hand on one, it's yours."

"Do we have to play with our gift?" Eily asks.

"Your box," Redix declares, "your choice."

"That's what *she* said," Cade adds, and we chuckle as Silas grabs the black box in the middle.

Sitting back on the sofa, he opens it, and it's a board game. An adult board game. While he sets it up on the coffee table, we refill drinks and settle back down.

"Okay," Silas says, "looks like we got CONFESSION, ACTION, and TRIVIA cards. And it came with a blindfold and feather tickler." Eily plays with it, tickling Silas's neck while he grins, explaining, "It's simple. Each player rolls, and you land on a different card."

Redix studies the circular board.

"A hundred says we don't make it around the board."

Daniel adds, "A thousand says we don't get through one *round*."

"Silas," Cade chimes in, "it's your night; you go first."

He rolls, lands on a CONFESSION card, and picks one up. "Who do I ask?"

"The person on your right," I suggest, and it's Daniel.

Silas grins, reading the card aloud. "Would you rather have sex with the lights on or off? And why?"

"Easy," Daniel answers, "on, so I can record it."

"Hell, yeah." Redix elbows Cade. "How come I can't record us?"

She scoffs, "Because you're too damn famous. If you ever get hacked, we're screwed."

"Darlin'," Redix wraps his arm around Cade's shoulder, squeezing it tight, "TMZ has busted my dumb ass so many times screwing when I was drunk; at least I'd be sober and fucking my wife."

"I mean," Eily shrugs, "we've already circle fucked in shows in a sex club."

"You *have?*" Apparently, blurting is contagious because I'm intrigued. "Where? How?"

Silas chuckles. "Charlie Girl, you know what *fucking* is, so imagine us doing it for an audience in a private sex club in Charleston. No phones. Everything is secure. And we all get off on it."

Us? We? Who?

The foursome I already know he's in?

Or is Silas suggesting something new? With me? And in front of others?

When Silas was thirteen and I was eighteen, yeah, he was hella cute, but I wasn't attracted to him. That's eons apart in teen years, but now we're equals.

Now I'm noticing details about his body, like his tan sculpted pecs, his perfect erect nipples, his carved abs, the sexy dark thin trail of hair below his belly button, disappearing under his pants, his big bulge obvious. My visual has always stopped there.

But now? I know Silas desired me. Does he still? And what do I want?

I don't know. My tingling pussy has an opinion, but my mind is still processing the kink as Eily rolls next and lands on an ACTION card.

"For two minutes," she reads aloud, "kiss the lips of the person on your left or your partner if playing with two."

Redix sits to Eily's left.

"Pass," he says. "Y'all know the only women we kiss are our wives."

"Why did you make that rule?" Daniel asks.

"It was mine," Redix answers. "After all my bullshit, when I came back for Cade, her kiss was all I lived for. But our wives wanted to kiss and wanted me and Silas to be free to kiss—"

"Because it's so hot," Eily swoons, "and beautiful."

Redix grins. "That too."

"I like that rule," I offer as Eily draws another card.

"Okay," she shares, her grin growing, "this one says, 'Put on the blindfold, then let two players kiss your nipples.'"

Eily grabs the silky strip while Silas leans over, reading her card.

"It says, 'Let two players kiss your *neck.*'"

She giggles, blindfolding herself.

"My card, my action."

Leaning back on the sofa, she drops one spaghetti strap, then the other. Her gauzy indigo dress flutters to her waist, revealing her small, pert breasts, and my nipples harden too.

"Who do you want?" Cade asks her.

"Surprise me," she purrs.

Silently, we look at Silas. Eily's his wife. Clearly, he likes this, too, because he points to Daniel and me. Like he knows exactly who she wants, and he's not denying her.

I glance at Daniel.

He glances at me.

Are we really doing this?

He tugs my hand, and quietly, we stand. Carefully, Silas moves aside while we try not to make a noise.

Calypso music lulls softly through the sound system on the boat while I swear everyone can hear my heart pounding. I think I can hear Daniel's, too.

Carefully, we sit on either side of Eily. She has to feel the weight of the sofa cushions shift, suspecting it's a man on her right and a lighter person, a woman, on her left.

We're making her narrow ribs lift with anticipation as Daniel glances at Silas, and Silas nods, giving his blessing. Then Daniel looks at me, and I do the same.

Watching my husband lower his parted, full lips, his face neatly shaven this morning, he still gets a dark shadow by the evening. It's so sexy, making my body flame as his tongue slowly laves over Eily's hard, apricot nipple. He makes her gasp at his touch, arching her back but sitting on her hands so she won't grab; she won't know who it is by their hair.

Then Daniel looks at me and grins. Lust swims in his eyes, and it pools in my lace panties. I can't believe I'm doing this... *and I want to.*

Lowering my head, my long hair tickles Eily's flesh before my tongue rings her pearled nipple. I lick her how I like to be licked, and she groans as Daniel joins me. He caresses my bare thigh, exposed by my short dress, as we suck and lick Eily's nipples, making her writhe and moan; it makes me so wet, too. Two minutes pass fast before Silas rumbles, "Time."

I'm dizzy with desire, rising from the sofa. Daniel takes my hand and leads me back to our spot, and I lick my wet lips at the hard cock in his pants.

We're definitely fucking again tonight.

Eily removes her blindfold and sighs. "Ten thousand if I can have the next turn too."

"No, it's mine."

Cade leans forward, rolls the dice, and lands on a TRIVIA card. She turns to Redix and asks, "What's the average length of a penis?"

"In this room," Redix chuckles, "or the general public?"

That makes Eily innocently blurt, "Wait. How do you know *Daniel's* dick size, too?"

"Because we shot a sex scene together." Redix laughs harder. "For three fucking days, we rubbed cocks under modesty socks."

We're all amused, but Silas catches on quickly.

"So, it got your dick... *hard?*" He slowly asks Daniel, his voice almost a growl, "Frotting with *my man?*"

Oh shit! Is Silas angry or aroused? Or both? My eyes dart from him to Redix.

"We were *acting,*" Redix assures Silas. "I can rub my dick against a wall and get hard."

"Same," Daniel answers. "If the wind blows right, I get a stiffy."

"Well, then answer the question." Cade asks Redix again, "What's the average length?"

"If I'm right?"

"A blow job of your way above average."

Redix shrugs. "Google says five point one inches."

Eily snorts, "Not in this room."

"You've Googled it?" Cade asks him, and Redix shrugs again, answering, "Every man has."

Daniel and Silas nod, backing him up, and suddenly, I'm curious. How big can Redix and Silas be? Because I know how hung Daniel is.

Oh, my dear Slut Goddess.

Please tell me I'm trapped for a week on a luxury vessel with three huge man mountains.

Though... I'm not sure if I should climb Mt. Silas.

He's the guy who used to bring me fresh strawberries, and together, we'd make strawberry shortcakes with whipped cream to devour while we watched the sun go down over the river. Then we'd get in a whipped cream fight.

With sweet memories like that, should I fuck him, too?

Redix rolls next, gets another ACTION card, and reads it aloud.

"It says, 'Tickle the bare ass of the second person on your left.'"

I'm shaken from my tender memory, now my current pussy puzzle, realizing... *shit, that's me.*

Redix grins my way. I snap my eyes to Cade, and she's smiling too. Then I glance at Daniel, and he's smirking like a cat who ate a canary.

"Well, go on then, Charlie," Daniel challenges me. "Will you let Redix have a go at your ass? In front of everyone?"

Daniel thinks I'm backing down? That all that stuff in the limo was just dirty talk? *Hell no.* I need a kinky week like this just once in my life.

Jumping past go, racing right through awkward, I arrive in Slut Land. It's a magical place.

I stand and unbutton my black linen shirtdress, watching Redix the whole time as he takes the feather tickler from Eily.

Dusting it over his lips, his eyes comb my flesh, his smirk growing and...

Fuck, Redix is hot.

And fuck, we've worked together. And fuck, this is gonna make my ankles so weak; they'll break.

"Come here, my wife,"—Daniel pulls my gaze his way—"and look me in the eye while you bend over, and I'll *LET* you give your ass to Redix."

Holy fuck, my husband sounds turned on.

And *holy hell*, I am, too.

Standing in black lace panties and a bra, I catch Silas eyeing my body, too. He's seen me in bikinis. And my bullet scars don't bother me anymore. They're not on my mind as I step between my husband's strapping legs and lean forward, bracing my hands on his granite shoulders, smiling with my breasts in his face.

Then I feel body heat behind me. I smell a new cologne —vanilla and leather—before, *yes*, I gasp as another man's hands softly grab my bare hips.

"Say what you want, Charlie."

Redix's deep Southern voice is like bourbon, and I look my husband in the eye as I drink.

"I want you to play with my ass... *Redix*."

Suddenly, Daniel's eyes ignite with lust. Hearing another man's name over my lips. Watching him touch me. Allowing another man's hands to caress my flesh, Daniel's so aroused.

I am, too, as I stare at my husband, feeling Redix's warm fingertips slowly tug my lace panties down, leaving them an inch below my cheeks, barely exposing my soaked sex.

"Oh fuck," I sigh at the cool air dancing over my excited clit. It swells with lust while Redix slowly tickles feathers across my ass, one cheek, then the other.

"She's getting goosebumps," Redix shares, feathers lingering down my crack. "I can smell her lust too."

I close my eyes, trying to stay sane at the maddening tease but hearing my husband's question.

"You like it, don't you, Charlie? Letting Redix play with my wife's incredible ass. The one you love for me to fuck. For me to record it too. Tell him how you like my cock fucking your tight ass so much it makes your pussy drip on the floor, doesn't it?"

"Oh god," I gasp. "Yes."

I can't open my eyes to the truth. I can't believe feathers are about to kill me. I can feel the heat of two men trapping my wet sex between them, and I can't help it. The ache is sudden and strong. Deep and demanding. I need something, anything to pound my throbbing pussy. I'm dying for it.

"More," I pant. "Please."

"Give her more."

Daniel's deep accent makes you obey, so Redix gently tugs my shoulder, pulling my body until I stand with my back against his hard, bare chest, his muscles pressing like smooth, warm stones into my flesh.

"You want more, Charlie?"

Redix's voice in my ear is new and exciting.

"Yes," I sigh.

"Cade," he calls, "come help me give her more."

Oh my god, he can read my mind.

As she walks over, I hear her heels clicking, approaching from my left while Daniel sits before me, watching the show.

Glancing, I look to my right at Silas and Eily on the sofa, and I gasp, shocked by what I see. How Eily's head bobs over Silas's lap, sucking his massive exposed dick. How he's opened his pants, how he's so hard, watching us, and my eyes widen at his size. *Oh my god, Silas is huge, too.* Eily can barely get his cock in her mouth, but she's sure trying while his hand reaches under her, finger fucking her pussy, her mouth drooling over his fat tip.

Still, Eily keeps her eyes open. Licking Silas's crown, she watches; Silas does, too, as Redix slides his hand between my thighs, thrilling my flesh, wedging it between my wet pussy and panties.

"Suck her beautiful tits," he commands Cade, and I moan, loving that Redix is a Dom, too, just like Daniel, and Cade complies.

She pulls down the lace cup of my bra, exposing one breast, then the other.

"God, you're beautiful," she sighs.

"You are too," I tell her right before I feel the slow penetration, the firm stroke of two of Redix's thick fingers sliding into my clenching cunt.

"Oh fuck," I cry out.

My eyes seek Daniel. He's all I've known when I feel pleasure like this, and he's right here with me. He's pulled his cock out, too, stroking it for us, watching us. Watching another husband and wife play with me as Redix glides his soaked fingers out of my pussy, reaching to find my hard clit while he grabs my throat with his other hand.

"Fuck, you are soaking *wet for us*," he growls, rubbing my clit as Cade's warm mouth sucks my nipple, and I buck in his grasp, pleasure spilling through my sex.

This feels greater than I thought it would, and I want more. So much more, and *don't stop*.

"You like this, Charlie?" Redix steams over my ear. "You like being a whore, just like my beautiful wife?"

Cade moans over my dripping nipple, sucking harder before flicking her tongue over it while her fingertips tug at my other one.

"Yes," I rasp at the taboo, at the delight. If Redix's big hands weren't rubbing my clit and choking my neck, I'd collapse, falling into lust and never coming back.

Fuck, this is so goddamn dirty and hot.

Redix steams over my ear again.

"Look at your husband's cock. He's so hard watching us."

From his vantage point. From the growl in his voice, Redix is looming over my shoulder, watching Daniel stroke his dick for us. It makes Redix sink two fingers inside me again, pumping them, matching his rhythm to Daniel's fist.

"Fuck," Redix grunts with his lips to my ear. "Fuck, his cock is huge. I bet you *do* love it fucking your ass."

Oh my god, Redix wants Daniel. I can hear it. Feel it. Redix's hard cock grinds into my ass, and I glance right again.

Silas is riveted, his gaze dragging from Daniel's pumping fist to my body getting mauled, and I'm about to come, I swear.

"Cade," Redix licks her name down my neck, "be my good little whore and eat her pussy for us."

"Oh fuck, yes," Daniel groans.

But I'm stunned silent. My knees wobble, weak. My eyes can't believe it as I watch Cade kneel before me, between me and Daniel. I wanted to kiss her first, but this? How she slowly drags my drenched panties down until I step out of them. Then, Redix gently kicks my trembling legs apart, and I obey.

I want them to use me.

"Lick her clit," Redix orders Cade while his thick, long fingers pump in and out of my pulsing walls.

"Now, spread your legs, our little whore," he whispers

in my ear. "That's it. Let my dirty wife taste your sweet cum."

"Oh fuck," I gasp, feeling Cade's tongue swipe my clit, but I can't look down anymore because Redix's grip on my neck gets tighter. I swear it's matching the intensity of Daniel jerking off at the sight of us.

I can't stop moaning because it feels like forever and not long enough as Cade's tongue circles and licks, worshiping my little throbbing nub like a goddess while Redix fucks my aching cunt with his fingers. Then he pulls them out, and I hear Cade sucking them before he thrusts them back inside me, making me groan, my eyes rolling back, my legs quivering.

"She's coming." Daniel knows my body. He demands my pleasure. "Go ahead. Make my naughty wife squirt on another woman's face."

"Daniel," I gasp, thrilled by his kinky demand as Redix takes his slick fingers out. Reaching them around my front, he uses them to spread my lips for Cade's tongue.

It exposes me. Raw air and lust thrilling my clit. It becomes a luscious assault on my senses, feeling Cade's fingers, three of them, start to fuck me where Redix's were while he stretches me open for her to devour, for her tongue fluttering over my roused nub.

"You're a squirter, Charlie?" Redix's lips graze my ear. "Come on then, and show us what a wet little whore you are."

My knees shake, my thighs quiver, and when I feel Cade suck my clit with a vengeance, I cry out. Coming over her mouth, feeling Redix's grasp of my neck, watching Daniel's lustful face, but I don't do it this time. I don't completely let go; sometimes, I'm afraid to. It's so intense I go insane.

"We're gonna make you come again." But Redix won't relent. He insists, "Come on, show us how you squirt, Charlie. It's what you want, and my wife is thirsty for it. Your husband is too, and I wanna watch his big cock spurt his sweet cream for us while we make you come."

The desire in Redix's voice—he can't disguise it while Cade keeps going. Her fingers don't stop, and as a woman, I guess she knows how to lighten her touch and take me from one wave to the next so fast while I hear soft gasps and glance again to my right.

Eily's shaking over Silas's hand. She's stripped her dress off, and I can tell she's coming on his fingers, her lips gasping over his swollen tip. And Silas doesn't stop either, his eyes taking us in; he's about to come, too. He grabs the back of Eily's head like that's her warning.

"Keep coming while you suck my cock, my little slut," Silas growls. "That's it. I'm gonna fill your dirty mouth so you can let me see my cum on your tongue before you swallow every fucking drop of me."

Oh my god, their dirty talk is next level.

It alone could make me come because I am. I'm right here again as Redix presses his hard dick into my back.

"You're gonna make us all come, being our new whore to play with this week." Redix's grip tightens on my neck. "Do you like it, Charlie? Being our whore?" It doesn't hurt. He moves my neck so I'm staring at Daniel. "Tell your husband."

"Yes, I like it."

I pant for air. It's turning me on even more. It's taking me there along with Cade's tongue that won't stop flicking my clit, her fingers pounding faster into clenching my pussy. My thighs shake so hard.

I didn't know it'd be this dark and dirty, and I'm not

afraid. I can do this. I'm staring at my husband; he's watching me; he wants this. He's about to come, witnessing my renewal.

"Is that what you want, Charlie?" Redix's voice is so haunting; it's hot. "You wanna be our new slut? You want three cocks to fuck you while our whores eat your pussy too?"

Yes, I dangle in his grasp, my whole body shaking, trembling against his. I can't speak. My massive orgasm is my answer, and I can't stop it. It's overwhelming. It's cracking my bones, tensing my muscles. I'm coming. The seizure of my spasming sex is too hard; it's too strong...

"Cade!" I wail, warning her. But she loves it, moaning into my gushing, pulsing pussy as I come, light slashing across my vision, making me scream as I pour over her chin.

"Fuck, babe," Daniel grunts.

I barely open my eyes. Watching me squirt over Cade's gorgeous face makes Daniel come so hard; ropes of his creamy lust paint his abs where he's parted his shirt.

"*Fuuucckk.*"

I hear Silas. I glance over in my haze, watching him shake, coming in Eily's mouth with his eyes glued to me.

"Shit," Redix huffs over my ear. "Shit, y'all are so fucking hot." His grip on my neck lets go; his voice softens as his hand soothes over where my neck burns from his grasp. "You okay?"

"Yes."

"I didn't hurt you? Did I, darlin'?"

"No."

I'm more than fine. I'm reborn, though I can barely stand, so Cade helps Redix lift and lower me into Daniel's lap. I crawl into his welcoming arms and hardly notice how

Redix grabs Cade, throwing her over his shoulder; he makes her giggle while he slaps her ass.

"Woman," he grunts, taking her out of the room, "get ready to get the hell fucked out of you."

But Eily and Silas stay in the room. They catch their breath, too. I'm sweaty and satiated, my muscles liquid after the release, my focus returning to see Eily in Silas's lap. Her face nuzzles his neck, her eyes closed against his flesh while Daniel kisses my hair, adoring me, too.

But I catch the look Silas is giving us, *giving me.*

And for the first time, I don't know the emotion in Silas's eyes.

Eily

FIVE

"You alright, Charlie Girl?"

Concern lulls through Silas's voice, so I open my eyes and check on her, too.

"Yeah," she sighs over Daniel's chest. "That was just intense. I've never done that before."

"You've never been with a woman?" I ask her, surprised. "I would've thought in the Marines and all."

"That's just a stereotype." She grins. "I've never been opposed to it, but I didn't fuck on the job." She pauses. "Clearly, that's changed."

Laughter shakes Silas's body under mine.

"What the hell's gotten into you, Charlie Girl?" he asks.

Daniel jokes with him.

"Redix and Cade's fingers."

But Charlie gets quiet; we all do before she adds, "I guess we all change." She exchanges a long look with Silas, a question churning between them before she kisses Daniel's scruffy cheek. "And I love my amazing husband who changes with me."

They belong together. You can see it in how Charlie wraps around Daniel and how he holds her back, full of love with no doubt. I know the feeling.

"Silas didn't want to share me either. And now... " I gaze up at him, and he glances down at me, "he loves me just the way I am."

"Yeah," he grins, "cuz' I married Dora the Explorer of sex."

He wrestles me back onto the sofa, nuzzling my neck, making me giggle. I want him now and always, but this time, just us.

"Take me to our room," I demand, "and we'll explore more uses for a champagne bottle."

His smile grows.

"See what I mean."

Then he's just like Redix, yanking me up and throwing me over his shoulder. He even slaps my ass while I tell Charlie and Daniel.

"Night, y'all. Breakfast is at nine... and nude."

I WAS SORTA KIDDING ABOUT THE NUDE PART LAST night.

Standing in our bathroom, as big as a marbled bowling alley, I throw on a coral crochet mini-dress for breakfast. It's meant to be worn over a bikini...

But that's no fun.

Bikinis belong in the dresser drawer this week.

"Baby girl," Silas steps out of the shower, noting my

naughty outfit, "you look so cute; you're gonna make cocks cream before our first cup of coffee."

"And?" I ask, "Isn't that the point this week?"

He wraps a white towel around his dripping Adonis belt, and I can tell *you* the point this morning. At the sight of me, it's waking up between his thighs.

But, "No," he answers before spraying some stuff in his hair that keeps it from tangling. "We're also good friends, so let's just hang out today. Lay by the pool. Go snorkeling. Play some volleyball—"

"Those *aren't* the balls I wanna play with."

I joke before looking down to load my toothbrush with minty paste, but then I feel heat standing behind me. I glance up and see Silas in my mirror's reflection.

And... *he's pissed?*

"What's going on with you?" he asks.

"What are you talking about?"

"I love you being so free and frisky, Eily, you know that. But it's like you're on a mission this week."

"Don't shame me for my sex drive."

"I ain't shaming you. Just don't assume we all share it."

Okay, that hurt.

He knows my past, how my family is, and I drop my chin, setting my toothbrush down.

"Hey." Gently, he tugs my arms, turning me around. "Hey, I'm sorry. I didn't mean to make you feel bad; it's just that—"

It's just that I tried talking with him about this last night after we had the most passionate sex in bed. It was like Silas was searching for something inside me, staring into my eyes, and it was powerful. As I lay in his arms afterward, I tried asking him about his feelings, but he said, "The usual—I love you so much, Eily." Then he got quiet again and fell asleep.

But this morning, we're talking about this.

"You don't know *what* you feel, do you?"

He doesn't answer me.

He's clamming up again.

"Silas, it's okay. You have my blessing, my permission, my whatever. You don't have to feel guilty about what you feel. I *want* you to be with Charlie."

"We're too close," he answers, shaking his head. "Me and Charlie Girl. It'll fuck up our friendship."

"How? You and Redix are best friends. You're close with Cade, too."

"That's different, and you know it."

"How? Because I don't see it. Cade and Charlie are so much alike. So are Redix and Daniel. It's like the six of us were made for each other; don't you feel it, too?"

"Yes, I feel something." His grip on my arms tightens. "But I don't know what to call it, so I got no business fucking anyone until I do."

"What if there's no name for it?"

"No name for what? Lust?"

"No," I beg his eyes. "*Love*. It's the one word we have to describe a million ways we can feel for different people, and it's not enough. We don't have the words to describe the difference between how I love you versus how I love Cade or Redix. Or how I could start to love Charlie or Daniel. I know it would be different with them, but I'd feel something, too."

His eyes widen.

"But you've just met Daniel."

"Yeah, but *you* haven't. You feel something for him, too,

more than just friends, and you definitely do for Charlie, and that makes me love them because I love *you*."

He keeps shaking his head, so I crane my neck for his lips to stop him.

"You know I love you because I'm breaking my rule." I mutter over our mouths, "I'm kissing you with morning breath."

"You're confusing me."

"It's not confusing. *I'm* very sure. *I* like them. *I* want to be with them. *I* want to fuck them. I want to hang out with them, and yes, I'll play volleyball with them too. You want it too; you just have to stop feeling guilty about it."

"What about Redix?"

"What about him? He finger-banged Charlie last night and got off on it. So did Cade. She was drinking Charlie like a fuzzy cup. I thought you could make *me* squirt, but she's a gusher. It's so hot."

Silas rolls his eyes.

"What?" I ask him. "Like it didn't turn you on?"

"Of course it did. It turns anyone on knowing a woman is feeling pleasure. That anyone's feeling pleasure."

"Yeah, but... " I linger my fingertip through the center canyon of his abs, "Daniel coming turned you on, too. That's when *you* came."

He gently grabs my hand.

"We're late for breakfast, Mrs. Van de May."

And this conversation will be continued later.

And I do keep my end of the bargain.

Silas needs more time, so I don't tease anyone at breakfast. I put on a bikini. Later, I lay by the pool with everyone. Then we play volleyball together, and no one gets naked, and everyone has fun.

And none of us can get over the view.

Overnight, we sailed to Little Exuma, an island just south of Grand Bahama Island. The ocean surrounding us is electric blue, so shallow and pristine in some spots that we have to use the tender, the smaller ski boat hoisted by a crane from the top of this one, to go snorkeling.

TWO HOURS LATER, THE SIX OF US STAND IN CRYSTAL clear, waist-deep water with white powder sand beneath our feet. Tranquil beaches of little, green, uninhabited islands dot the horizon. We're standing in paradise, taking a break from snorkeling with our masks resting on our foreheads.

It's paradise.

It's peaceful.

I'm so happy and relaxed until I see the scheme in my husband's sexy eyes.

"You better not!" I warn Silas, watching him drop pieces of wet bread in the water beside me.

"What?" He grins, guilty. "I'm just feeding the fish."

No, the Jaws theme music begins to play.

Duunnn dunn. Duuunnnn duun. Duuunnnn duun. Duunnnnnnnnn dun dun dun dun dun dun dun.

"Silas Henry," I fuss, "if you bring those fish around me, I'll never fuck you again."

He's laughing. He's not listening. He knows I'm afraid of fish and is determined to cure me.

"They're just little angelfish," he says.

Like his vast knowledge of marine life comforts me. I'm standing in the warm middle of hell.

"No," I gaze down, "they're little orange devils, and I swear if one of them bites me—"

"At least they're not sharks," Daniel says, chuckling beside me, admiring the school of dwarf fish in neon oranges and dark blues swarming our way.

"Eily, look," Silas points, "some are all indigo."

"Don't butter me up because that's where these things belong. On my plate, with butter and tartar sauce." My pulse skyrockets, watching the swimming devils surround me. Twisting toward Daniel, I try to escape, my voice rising, too. "I swear to god, if one of them bites me!"

And one does.

It nibbles my calf, and *fuck this*.

I squeal, jumping on my only option—Daniel Pierce.

I squeal again, *I'm an idiot*, but I don't care.

I turn Daniel into a human ladder, climbing up his colossal body and wrapping my arms around his neck. He grabs my waist, securing me here, laughing with Silas while instinct has me wrapping my legs around him, too.

Shit, he's enormous.

I'm hugging Mt. EverFuck.

"Make them go away," I mumble into Daniel's chest.

"I got bugger all," he answers, holding me tight. "We're standing in the middle of their home. *We'll* have to leave."

"Then act like a superhero again and carry me to the boat because my husband is a wicked villain, and he's never getting laid again."

"Baby girl, come back," Silas calls out for me. "They're just little fish."

I stick my tongue out at him as Daniel sloshes us over, wading through the water while I watch Charlie splash Silas.

"Quit torturing your wife, you little shit," she says through her chuckles.

"I ain't torturing her," Silas replies, splashing her back. "She loves it when we play."

Daniel lifts me, setting my uneven feet on the teak deck of the ski boat.

"There we go," he says. "All sorted."

"Sorta pissed," I mutter while we throw our masks in the boat before he jumps up beside me, his body dripping with salt water and sex appeal.

"I'm bloody starving." He calls out, asking Silas, "What's for lunch?"

"You gotta catch it," Silas answers.

"No, I'll catch *you*," Charlie warns, leaping from the water like a flying fish before hooking her arm around Silas's neck. He's big, but she's skilled, twisting her body and taking him under while they drown laughing.

Daniel watches them, telling me, "They do this all the time. They always scrap a bit."

Charlie and Silas keep wrestling in the water, play-hitting, choking, and grappling while Redix and Cade wade toward the boat, too.

"They scrap *a bit*," I answer Daniel while I climb over the back bench, grabbing some towels. He follows me as I hand him one. "Because they want to fuck *a lot*."

He takes the towel, studying me.

"Are you alright with that?"

"Yeah." I ask him, "Are you?"

"I think so."

He dries his dark waves, and I can't help but watch every hulking muscle on his body react to simple efforts. He's a brick, no, a *British* shithouse. Wherever that phrase comes from, I don't know. I just know my eyes are superglue.

"You *think* so?" I ask him. "You better be damn sure before they fuck."

He plops down in one of the white bucket seats.

"I'm fine with it," he says. "Part of me, for the longest time, felt like it should've been Silas with her. He loved her. He'd never hurt Charlie while I bloody well did, and if you knew how, I sort of owe her now. I love her so much, and by some bloody miracle, she still loves *me*. She always will, and now, I can see how Silas loves *you* even more than he ever fancied Charlie. I've never seen him this happy."

When Daniel Pierce smiles at me, comets fly across the clear sky. He does have supernatural powers. That shit ain't Hollywood. His blue eyes alone can fuck you powerless.

"And I love *him*." I plop down opposite Daniel. "I'm fine with it too. I want Silas to be more than happy. It's like he has a burning question about Charlie inside him, and I want him to answer it. I want to make *them* finally answer it together."

He tosses his stubbled, cleft chin up, laughing. "You can't make my wife do a bloody thing."

I nudge his dripping-wet foot with mine. "Wanna bet?"

His eyebrow cocks. "Maybe."

"I bet I can make it happen."

"How?"

"Don't know yet. But I'm sure one night, the opportunity will... *arise*."

He rubs his chest dry. "Careful what you scheme. You may regret it."

"Look, Supersexy,"—I cock my head—"I'm not scared of Silas fucking Charlie. I'm confident in his love for me. I know his heart is so big I can share it. And I love him so much; I want this for him."

Daniel gets quiet, drying his tree-trunk legs next.

"What does Charlie want?" I ask him.

He chuckles. "I think there are so many options for her this week; she wants a lot."

"What about you? What do you want?"

Thud.

Redix tossed his mask and snorkel into the boat. I glance up to see how he's climbed onto the teak deck, eavesdropping on our chat with his eyes searching Daniel's.

The water sloshing against the boat slaps the air and sudden tension. There's no other sound. There's nothing but the question I asked as Redix silently waits for Daniel's answer, too.

Both men drip with attraction. Yes, everyone felt it last night, but no one's saying a word, even me. I may blurt shit, but I swear I'm holding back on this one. You should feel this between them. It's dangerous floating on the water because lightning cracks between them.

Daniel stares at Redix, slowly combing his hungry gaze down Redix's wet, buff body in black boardshorts. His intense stare makes Redix flare his nostrils, his lungs huffing for Daniel's answer before he turns back to me.

"I don't know," Daniel mutters before everyone climbs aboard.

And when they do, Silas aims for me, scooping me up in his wet arms.

"You still mad?" he asks.

"You're never getting this pussy again."

"That's fine." He kisses my nose, dripping salt water on my face. "I married you for your cute little farts anyway."

I slap his chest.

"Uh, I don't fart."

"No, you don't." He softly glides his wet lips over mine. "And you don't have my heart either, Eily, every damn piece of it."

Over a late lunch on the *Indigo Dream*, we exchange childhood stories over steaming plates of paella and glasses of sparkling sangria while Redix swigs ginger ale, propping his bare feet on the outdoor dining table by the pool. Grinning from behind his black Wayfarers, he declares, "Shit, I just can't believe it."

"Can't believe what?"

Cade pops a shrimp in her mouth.

"I can't believe I finally hooked up with the hottest girl in our high school."

Redix toasts Charlie, who laughs while Cade throws a shrimp at him.

"Way to insult your wife," she huffs. "*We* went to high school together, too, you sexy dickhead."

"Yes, my darlin'," Redix answers her, eating the shrimp. "But Charlie Ravenel was a senior, and we were sophomores. That gave her more hot points back then." He shrugs. "*Gossip Girl* made the rules, not me. Right?"

He turns to Silas to get his back, who sucks down an oyster before answering him, "I didn't go to y'all's high school. I went to private school hell, but yeah, Charlie Girl had everyone hard for her."

Charlie punches Silas's arm while I sit across from them, wanting to know more.

"Why do you call her 'Charlie Girl' and not just 'Charlie'?"

She answers, "Little Shit,"—that's what she calls Silas a lot—"gave me that nickname because people teased me and said I was a boy with my name. That I acted like one, so

Silas started calling me 'Charlie *Girl*' like he was defending me. He'd get in fights over me, too, and I'd feel bad. But it was also kinda cute."

"You didn't do me any favors." Silas sucks down another oyster, slime dripping from his chin as he grins, talking with his mouth full. "You kept winning spitting contests and wouldn't shave your legs for years, and you'd beat up all the boys, especially the ones I couldn't. The whole island thought you were a man. Then you became a fucking Marine, so—"

"She sure shaves now, and she ain't no man," Redix insists. "That's for *damn* sure after last night."

"We all enjoyed last night." I grin at my husband. "The show *sure* popped Silas's cork."

Shit, did Silas just blush again?

Even under his tan skin, I know my husband. He's not usually shy. He goes after what he wants. And it's obvious he still wants Charlie, but it's like he's thirteen again and doesn't know what to do.

This would make such a cute rom-com.

Well, a XXX-rated one where the boy gets the girl... and two more girls... and two boys. At the same time. And the happily ever after is when the boy, I mean, *the man*, doesn't wonder anymore. He gets all the love and orgasms he deserves.

Yep, I'm pitching this to Netflix.

"Last night sure popped Charlie Girl's cork, too," Daniel adds with a wink. "Like a bursting bottle of champagne."

Did Charlie just blush as well?

Okay, she's like the senior—the pretty prom queen who'll kick your ass, too. But a cute freshman wants her, and she secretly wants him... but will she risk it all to be with him?

Charlie's clearly a risk-taker. Of course, she's attracted to Silas. His sex appeal could rouse the dead. But Charlie's no fool either.

Will she risk their friendship for something more? Even for just one night?

I don't know, and I don't worry. It'll work. Memories of last night make us all laugh and tingle. The six of us are getting quite comfortable together, and it's only the second day.

I may be the youngest. I may joke a lot, but deep down, I know pain, and I learned the only way out of it is love. I know all about being the quiet geek who finally gets the hot guy, the best friend who becomes your forever. I'm married to him because we all deserve a happy ending.

And I catch it—Daniel smiling back at me from across the table like, *"Game on."* Like he trusts in love, too. Like he wants to watch their happy ending.

Cade

"START FLICKING YOUR BEANS."

The glass doors are open to the warm night, and I swear I can smell coconuts and suntan lotion in the gentle breeze. Cuddled beside Redix on the ebony sofa, anticipation for tonight shimmers through my veins as we watch Charlie pick the next gift.

Eily suggested the ladies wear lingerie tonight, and hell yeah, we agreed. She's like a Tinkerbell, sprinkling happy, smutty fairy dust over everyone because the guys are wearing the black silk bottoms she left in gift boxes at the foot of our beds, too.

And all those black silk pants do is drape over what we crave. Like a curtain we want to drop to reveal the big show —the triple cocky feature.

Of course, the black leather lingerie I prefer is too hot for the Caribbean. So I compromised on a black lace body-suit with a halter top plunging past my belly button.

Score: Redix keeps ogling my ample cleavage spilling out of it.

Eily, of course, tempts in a white lace babydoll. *Such a naughty bride.* She makes me remember her bachelorette party at the sex club.

But Charlie shines in a nude bodystocking, covered in sparkles. It's a fancy one that captures Daniel's stare while I study him.

Do I desire Daniel Pierce?

Yes. Me and millions do.

And that includes Redix.

I don't think Silas would be jealous if Redix tells him how he feels. They're too close, and Silas isn't the insecure type. But again today, when we all took breaks in our state-rooms, I urged Redix to talk to him.

"What am I supposed to say?" Redix played with my toes while we shared a bath. "Hey, uh, Silas, you know I love you," he mocked himself, dropping his voice way too deep, "but I wanna fuck Daniel too. I get all squishy inside when I'm around him."

I flicked water at him.

"Quit joking."

He splashed me back.

"Darlin', I ain't jokin'. That scene did something to me."

"What do you mean?"

"It's like when I was with Silas, our first time together. Remember it? And we called you from my phone, and you watched us."

"Yeah, it was beautiful because I knew you loved Silas."

"Exactly," he massaged my foot, "I was more than hard for him. I had deep feelings for Silas, like butterflies and shit, and I got them again in that scene with Daniel, too. And I don't know if they're legit or acting."

"Oh. My. *Goddd.*" I threw my chin up, rolling my eyes. "Quit piddlin' and just say something to him."

"To who?" Redix raked his hand through his wet hair. That's his tell. He was stressed. "Who do I talk to first because either could go sideways so fuckin' fast? I could hurt Silas. I could freak Daniel out."

"Silas loves you. Y'all are so close. He only wants you to be happy, and Daniel won't freak out. Yeah, he's all alpha and shit, but so are you. Deep down, y'all are good men. You got open hearts and open minds. Clearly, because Silas got off on me slurping Daniel's wife right in front of him."

Redix grinned, the mood shifting like rapid fire.

"Shit, baby, that *was* hot." He grinned. "You gonna do it again for me tonight?"

I watch Charlie pick the last gift in the row, and I don't know what's happening tonight.

Part of me doesn't want to push Redix; I promised him I wouldn't, and he promised to talk to Silas tomorrow.

That's how the four of us work; we talk. We share what we feel and say what we want. We don't argue. We don't judge. We respect each other. Adding two more people to the mix should be no different. Right?

That's my big heart talking.

The other part of me? That's my kitty purring to play, excited to see the next gift. We all are. We're half-naked with bodies primed with lust. The sexual tension in the room is palpable, and three women dressed in scanty lingerie only make it worse... in the best way.

"What in the... ?"

Charlie opens the black box on the credenza, peeling back gold tissue paper.

"This is yours." She whips around with a massive tube in her hand, accusing Daniel, "Who else would buy three Clone-A-Willy Vibrator Kits?"

"Don't look at me," Daniel snorts, half laughing. "There are *three* willies in this room."

"Lemme see."

Eily jumps up from the sofa and joins Charlie. "Hell yeah," she grabs another tube, "they'll be our vibrating vacation keepsakes!"

"You know... "—I can't help it—"... most people bring home magnets, mugs, or T-shirts from their vacations. But *noooo*. Not us. We're bringing home clones of our men's cocks to give us big O's, not memories, for years."

"Wait, y'all," Eily shouts again, digging through the tissue paper. "There's three dildos in here too!"

She lifts one in the air like the Statue of Liberty—liberating orgasms for everyone.

"Oh," Charlie calls out, reaching into the box, "they're not just dildos. They're *ejaculating* dildos with... " she reads the red bottle in her hand, "... 'Splooge Juice' to go in them?"

Redix bursts out laughing, rolling and slapping the sofa. Tears form at the crease of his eyes, and if he had stitches, he'd be popping them.

That makes him guilty, right?

But then, Silas also looks too damn amused.

And I'm suspicious.

"They sell those at Delta's, Stacey's adult store, so I suspect this was a local crime."

Stacey Evans is my close friend; lucky for me, she also owns the best adult store in the South. She and her men even give demonstrations for her customers, and as her close friend, I'm willing to sacrifice; I buy everything she sells.

"Quit being a detective." Silas throws an ice cube from his rum and coke at me. "You can buy that shit online at Adam and Eve too."

"How do *you* know?" I interrogate him.

"Cuz' I got a wife who's ready for Freddy every waking hour, that's how. Toys keep my dick from falling off."

Eily nods, "We've earned Frequent Fucker cards from Delta's," like a proud, horny customer, "*and* Adam and Eve."

"I'm no engineer," Daniel says, "but I assume our willies have to stay bloody hard if we're going to clone them."

"Yeah, well," Silas adds, "if one of y'all fuck a dildo in front of my face, with that fake cum dripping outta your pussy, my willy will cut diamonds for you."

Redix is still laughing so hard; I admit it; I'm amused and stumped. Still, "Seems you figured this out already, Silas."

He throws another ice cube at me, taunting, "My Caprihorny wife lives near Charleston, too, you know. She loves going to Delta's for her toys. *She* could've bought them."

True. Obviously, it's not my gift, but no one else is fessing up.

It's like we're playing Clue with Colonel Mustard jerking off in the library.

"Alright, y'all. Listen up." Charlie takes charge. *She's so sexy when she's boss.* "This gift is self-explanatory. You guys gotta get hard so you can stick your dick in this tube full of molding powder mix, and then you gotta stay hard for two minutes."

"How long until their willy molds are ready?"

Eily wonders, bouncing like a kid on Christmas morning, and I don't even notice her limp anymore. She doesn't hide it from us because I swear Eily's always jumping up and down, excited for cock. Or pussy.

Charlie reads the instructions. "They'll be ready tomorrow."

Daniel surmises, "So, we play with dildos and dripping fannies tonight?"

"Oh," Eily perks up even more, "you want us to put the squirting dildo in our ass for you?"

"No," Daniel joins Redix and Silas, laughing so hard, "fannies are *cunts*, pussies where I'm from."

Eily cocks her head, raising her eyebrow at Daniel.

"Nuh-uh. Y'all got that English shit backasswards, cuz' fannies are *asses*."

Charlie pecks Eily's cheek.

"It confused me too at first," she says. "But both are great, so stick it in whichever fanny you desire."

"Hey," Redix finally has his composure... sorta, "is that Splooge Juice edible, or can we put whipped cream in the dildos instead?"

I backhand him.

"Of course, you'd ask. And no, we're not shooting whipped cream way up our pussies. Talk about yeast infections ruining a vacation."

"Oh darlin'," Redix bats his thick lashes at me, "I get so hard when you say *yeast*."

"Quit it."

The sexy asshole makes me laugh.

"How do we decide," Daniel asks, "who keeps who hard for this?"

Charlie shrugs. "The women roll the dice, and we entertain the man with the corresponding number."

"I'm three," Redix points to Silas, "and you're one, and you," he points to Daniel, "are five, right?"

Daniel nods, and we're all caught up as Eily rolls first and gets a three—Redix. I roll twice before I get the five—Daniel. That leaves Charlie entertaining Silas by default, and her teeth grab her bottom lip.

Oh shit.

She's nervous.

"You can always pass," I tell her. "This is supposed to be fun. Or hot. Never uncomfortable."

But Charlie studies Silas. He's sunk into the sofa and searching her eyes, too, as Eily touches Charlie's arm.

"It's totally fine with me," she tells her. "I'll think it's so hot."

No, it's so sweet. Eily doesn't have a jealous bone in her body, either.

I take it for granted; not everyone is wired like us. Then again, there are some women I'd snatch bald if they lay a hand on Redix. Hell, I almost shot two one time. Anyway. That's not the vibe, the love between us. And Eily's no pushover, either. She doesn't just share Silas with anyone. And for the women who try, she's better with a gun than me —don't piss Eily Dove off.

But something settles down Charlie's spine. She relaxes, grinning at Silas like she's staring at a monster roller coaster she's about to ride. Half terrified. Half thrilled. But not backing down.

"Silas," I ask, "do you pass?"

He grins back at Charlie. He's known her too long. He's rising to her challenge.

"Nah, I'm good. Let's play, Charlie Girl."

Daniel jumps up. Redix joins him. They assemble the mixes after Silas goes down below to the kitchen for some mixing bowls.

I can only imagine what the crew thinks about our nightly games. Surely, they know we're up to something kinky. We don't need the ocean. There's enough lube on the coffee table to glide this ship home.

Once the molds are assembled, ready for hard cocks,

KELLY FINLEY

and Eily's done giggling, filling the dildo's up with faux cum while she informs us, "It's non-toxic, safe for pussies, and kinda tastes like vanilla," I take charge.

I help Charlie because she's not used to orchestrating a theatre in the round. But I am.

"I think you guys should sit on the same sofa," I say. "It's big enough to leave room for us to stand over you."

"Hell yeah," Redix crows, jumping in the middle between Daniel and Silas.

We line up—me in front of Daniel, Eily beside me with Redix, and Charlie beside her, looming over Silas.

The guys each have their tubes filled with molding mix. Like giant test tubes for cocks, and Redix studies his.

"You sure our dicks won't get stuck? These look small."

"If your dick gets stuck, I got you, dude." Silas grabs his shoulder. "I got pliers in the Engine Room or a helicopter on deck to take you to an Emergency Room."

Redix huffs, "Imagine what that'll do for my career."

"It'd be a cockbuster," Daniel snorts. "I mean a *blockbuster*."

Redix laughs with him while Eily hands them lube.

"Use this," she says.

Then... it becomes a standoff.

We're all quiet.

Staring at each other.

"Well, go on," Eily waves her hand like a cocky conductor, "start beating your meat."

"It don't work like that." Silas grins at her, flitting his hand back. "Y'all go first. Go on. Start buttering your muffins."

Redix copies him. "Start flicking your beans."

Daniel does it, too. "While you toss your pink salads."

I look at Eily, then Charlie. *These fuckers wanna joke?*

Charlie winks back at me, Eily nods, and we step up for the win together.

As we straddle their legs on the super-long ivory sofa, Redix bunches the blanket under him into a little pillow under Eily's left foot to steady her uneven stance. That's the only sweet moment because once we start...

It gets real dirty.

I go first, spreading my thighs so Daniel can see that my bodysuit is crotchless, and his eyes darken at the sight of my bare pussy, glistening a foot from his face.

Eily knows how to tease Redix. She starts licking and sucking her dildo first.

Then I glance over at Charlie, and Silas's jaw drops as she tears her fishnet bodystocking at the crotch, barely ripping it open, before taunting him.

"Go on," she says, "and rip it open, big boy, if you really wanna watch this wet pussy fuck for you."

Holy shit, she's going for it.

Don't challenge that woman. She'll win.

Silently, Silas grins up at her. Grabbing the mesh, he rips a gaping hole between her thighs, the snaps of threads filling the air. It exposes her pussy as she smiles down at him before gliding the big dildo between her waiting lips.

Daniel's watching them, too. I gaze down, and he's soaring hard under his silk pants.

"I'm gonna get so wet, playing with my pussy for you."

I get his attention back. He turns to stare up at me as I pull my halter open, revealing one breast, then my other, to him.

"You're gonna get so hard watching me play with my wet pussy." I tickle my nipple with the dildo. "Do you like my tits, too? Do you want me to play with myself for you, Daniel? Can I drool over your hard cock while I do?"

"Fuck yes," he murmurs, pushing his pants down, exposing himself, lubing his hard cock up with the bottle beside him and...

Holy shit, grab saddles. He's as hung as Redix and Silas.

I lick my lips at the size of him, gliding the dildo into my eager pussy like it's his massive cock. Daniel Pierce is so goddamn sexy with those eyes; I moan for him as Eily teases Redix.

"You're gonna stay so hard, sucking up all my pussy cum while I drip more sweet cream all over your face."

Since she's been married to Silas, Eily rarely wears panties. He only rips them right off of her, and now she's giving Redix one helluva show with her dildo, teasing it into her entrance.

"I like to imagine all the ways you jerked off, thinking about me." Charlie's voice fills the room. "Didn't you, Silas? You wanted to fuck my pussy," she sighs, "just like this."

I glance over, and Charlie's sliding the slick dildo in and out of her sex, rolling her hips for Silas, too. So we match our cadence, making our men watch our filthy show with their jaws dropped.

Who's joking now, horny fuckers?

"Take out your cocks," Eily tells Redix and Silas, "and lube them up; get so hard for these wet pussies."

She takes her glistening dildo out and offers it to Redix's lips. He sucks it while he frees his hard cock, fisting it and moaning with a big dildo in his mouth.

"Oh fuck," Daniel huffs, watching Redix suck cock before looking up at me.

"Yes," I tell him, "look at all these fists pumping hard cocks. Look at all these wet pussies fucking for you, too. You love it, don't you, Daniel? Being naughty with us?"

I slap the dildo against my clit while he groans, not able to resist our kink.

"Fuck, yes," he growls. "Play with that wet pussy, Cade. Go on. Show me. Be a naughty little girl for me."

Eily moans at Daniel's taunt and accent. I cream to it, too, while Charlie baits Silas.

"Is that what you want," she asks him. "You wanna watch me be a dirty little girl for you, Silas? Like this?" She steps closer to his face. "Like this is your *big... thick... cock..* fucking my *tight... wet... pussy?*"

"Fuck," Silas huffs, "fuck, I'm hard as fuck."

I scan the men, and they are.

"Use your molds." I keep teasing them, "Stick your huge cocks in them and keep them hard for our pussies so we can have your dicks to fuck forever."

"So we can share them," Eily adds. "Right, Redix? You like it when I share a dildo with your wife? When I'm your nasty little princess for you to share? For you all to use my holes and fuck me at the same time?"

"Goddamn," Daniel mutters with his cock in the mold. I have no doubt he's hard as steel hearing how we play and talk.

"Daniel, you like it, don't you? Joining our little group? Letting us be whores for you too?" I pull out my shiny dildo, slowly offering it to his parted lips. "Wanna join us?"

I tempt him, and he answers by licking my cum off of the big tip of it.

"Shit," Redix grunts, watching him. "Fuck, man."

I know my husband. I know his dick is so swollen in that mold at the sight of Daniel licking a cock, and I'm so wet. This is so erotic. So taboo. How sexy Daniel looks. How hot my husband is. How hungry Silas appears. How we all have bodies screaming for more, but this filthy tease is so damn good.

I glance farther down the sofa because Silas is quiet. So is Charlie, and for a second, I worry.

This won't work for them.

Then I see Silas's face.

He's gazing up at Charlie as she thrusts the dildo into her pussy, making her thighs shake because she's stunned silent too. He doesn't touch her, he keeps his hands on the rigid mold over his cock, and she doesn't touch him either, but their eyes are connected, and it's intense.

"That's enough time," Eily says. "Take them out," and carefully they do.

Their cocks are still hard, swollen, and throbbing as Daniel picks up the personal wipes we put on the sofa, taking one before passing them down for the men to clean themselves. Then Redix finds the lube beside him, and once he's clean, he lubes up again. All three of them do.

Good god, this is kinky and hot because now we get to finish them.

"Show us," Redix says, stroking his shiny cock, his eyes gazing at Eily's pussy in his face. "Show us those pussies dripping with cum we can lick up."

Eily goes first. She and Redix love to play when they know we're watching, and she's so close; I know Eily. My husband is close, too. Thrilled by Daniel watching him jerk off, Redix pumps his fist fast over his tip, making Eily's lips shake as she starts crying out, pounding her pussy, inches from his sexy face.

"Yes, our dirty little princess," Redix knows how to taunt her, too, "fuck that tight little pussy with that big cock. Be our little slut and gimmie that cum." She's right there.

"Yes, that's it. Come on. Fuck that cock and come for Daddy," and she does.

"Silas!" Eily screams.

She always says his name when she comes, this time squeezing the bulb at the base of the dildo, her thighs shaking as Redix holds her leg steady with one hand while she jerks the toy out.

"Give it to him, baby girl."

Silas tells her, watching her too. We all are as Eily trembles, lowering her pussy, dripping with fake cum over Redix's mouth, and he growls into her sticky folds. Cream starts dripping down his chin and neck. He's slurping it up like he's starving, jerking his cock to it as he moans, coming so fast.

"*Yeessss*," Daniel groans because he's not watching me. "Fuck." He's watching Redix's cock, his cum spurting from his swollen crown, splattering his shredded abs. Then Daniel looks at me like he's busted again but can't stop. He can't help himself. His fist furiously pumping his cock, he's going to come too.

"Yes, we're whores for you," I tell him. Because so am I; I'm gonna come so hard on this dildo, holding Daniel's desire by a thread; it's so hot that he wants me and my husband. "Yes, you want all this pussy and cock. Don't you, Daniel? Don't you want us?"

His eyes are helpless, answering *please* and *yes* and *fuck me, both of you* and *take me however you want,* which is so damn sexy, making me grunt, "Fuck."

It hits me so hard. My orgasm heaves my ribs, my hands trembling while I fight to stay focused, squeezing the end of my dildo to give Daniel the creamy show I know he desires. I pull it out of my pulsing walls, and once he sees fake cum dripping from my swollen pussy, over his thighs and cock, he comes with such intensity he can't even speak, his grunts filling the air.

"Oh fuck," Silas huffs. "Oh fuck."

In my haze, I glance over; we all watch him and Charlie now.

She can't talk, either. She's just moaning, her body writhing and standing over Silas with the dildo buried deep inside her. She holds it there, jerking it hard.

"Fuck," Silas huffs again. "Fuck, yes, do it." His fist strokes so fast it's a blur. It's like he's losing his mind watching her. "Yes, Charlie. Squirt all over me."

Charlie screams, yanking the dildo out like it almost hurts her, the letting go, the rush of lust, the desire jetting out of her. It showers Silas's cock and lap, and he's going to come, but his neck strains, holding it back, grabbing Eily beside him.

"Do it, Silas," Eily coaxes. "Come for Charlie."

With Eily's permission, with her voice, with that name in the air, he lets go.

"*Fuccckkkk*," he howls, his back arching, his eyes slamming shut as he convulses. "*Fucckkk!*" he shouts again before grunting repeatedly, painting Charlie's legs and his fist with his milky cum.

Damn, that was intense.

We're all panting and quiet, catching our breath, searching each other's eyes, and... *what do we do now?*

Sex and tension and need perfume the air like a fog, and we can only see each other.

"Damn, y'all," Redix marvels, looking at our spent bodies and the furniture. "Who spilled all the milk? Seems making cock art is *messsssyyyyy*."

He breaks the tension, making us laugh as we flop on the sofa, too.

"I told y'all we'd need these blankets," Silas adds, starting to clean up like he wants to change the subject.

But still... I can't wait for gift number three.

Charlie

SEVEN

> **"I GOT A BLACK BELT AND THREE WILLIES, AND I AIN'T AFRAID TO USE THEM."**

I double-knot my sneakers while Daniel sits beside me on the bench at the foot of our bed, doing the same.

Watching his big hands with our matching platinum wedding bands... I wish they were tying me in knots. Teasing me with nipple clamps. Dousing me in lube and making me do more dirty things in a fuckathon with our friends and...

Okay, Wanda Wannabanger.

Pace your pussy.

Last night was another intense fuck in our stateroom inspired by our games with everyone else. It was just the two of us, and our sex was as if it was our first time together, but now, it's so much more. It's passionate and deep. It brought tears to my eyes before we fell asleep, wrapped in each other's arms.

All three couples disappeared into our cabins after we cleaned up our big mess. I assume the others had a similar night, just them together. But maybe Silas and Eily spent the rest of the night with Cade and Redix?

It makes me wonder.

No, it makes me worry.

We need to confront the big pink horny elephant in the middle of the room.

"Daniel," I sigh, exasperated, "you have to talk to Redix. I've been patient like I promised I would, but come on. You know more will happen tonight, so you gotta talk to him first."

He stands up, knotting his gym shorts.

"No, I don't."

"Since when are you afraid of your feelings?"

"Since I bloody well have to work with Redix, and he loves Silas. It's clear, and I'm not coming between them."

I stand up, too, and it burns my nose. Holding back my pun.

Nope, I can't. Here it comes...

"Oh, you'll be coming between them, alright. With them. Inside them. Tasting them. I know you want it, and they do too."

"Quit pissing around, Charlie."

"Alright, I think they'll draw the line at piss, but... "

He glares at me—five seconds from yelling. Or laughing.

"Alright then," he says. "What about you and Silas?"

Shit, I should've smelled that cow patty. I'm stepping in it now.

"What about us?"

"Never thought I'd see you squirt all over the bloke you used to say was like your little brother."

"Ewww." I stomp my foot. "Don't say *that*."

"Why not?" He grins. "It's what you said. And *did*."

"Yeah, well... " I storm off to the bathroom, needing to

pull my hair back, then punch a wall or have a hissy fit; either would be so mature. "It's different now."

Daniel's on my heels.

"What's different? What's changed? Because clearly, something has."

"Fine," I snatch my hair tie off the vanity, "I've changed. He's changed. Silas is *not* the boy I used to babysit or the teenager who used to crush on me when it felt all innocent and sweet. Now, he's a grown as fuck man, and he's smokin' hot. It's like being with Eily; he's happy, he's found his power, and now he's clit bait."

"No, he's always been a pussy magnet, so what's changed with *you?*"

He swipes on his deodorant while I yank my hair into a ponytail.

"I told you. I want to experiment. I want to explore stuff I never got to. And there's something about loving you and feeling secure with you and sharing it with you that makes me feel powerful, too. Like I can do anything."

I catch my breath before I yank a knot in my hair.

"Why?" I ask him. "Are you getting jealous? If this is not okay with you anymore, please tell me now because I don't know what's next."

Tugging his blue T-shirt back down his carved body, he aims my way.

"I'm not jealous. I swear. I'm okay with it."

"Then why are you giving me such hell?"

"Because I want *you* to be sure. For *you* to be okay with it. If you fuck Silas, there's no going back."

"How is that any different than you fucking Cade or Eily tonight?"

"Because I don't love them. Not like you and Silas have cared for each other for so long in this odd way. I've never been able to name it, but we've all felt it. And yes, it used to make me jealous, but now, I love you so much; we've shared so much, and I want this for you. I want you to finally figure out what in the bloody hell is going on between you two because either way, I'm fine with it. Nothing can threaten our marriage."

I soften, my shoulders dropping, tears biting at my eyes as I reach for him because Daniel's right; nothing threatens our love.

"Then, why won't *you* explore too? Why won't you figure out what you feel for Redix?"

"Because it's different for men, Charlie." He clasps my face. "Talk about no going back."

"It's nothing to be afraid of. We celebrate love; we don't shame it. We never have. I like being with Cade and maybe Eily soon, and I'm proud of it. If you feel something for men, why can't you be proud too?"

"Because Redix is my mate."

I stifle a snicker.

It doesn't work. It escapes as a snort, and Daniel grins at his pun.

"You know what I mean. He's a good *friend*. I respect him, and we have to work together. We have to act like we're in love for the next five months in front of hundreds of people, but what if, in real life, it doesn't work out? Or what if it's so obvious to all, and then what? I fuck up his career and mine? And Silas? I'd never hurt him. Yes, I love him in some way, too, that I can't bloody describe, and what if I muck that up as well? All because I got a sudden twitch in my cock *for* cocks."

"You have more than a twitch in your cock for both of them, and it's okay. It's beautiful. It's new love, and I support you."

Sighing, he lowers his lips to mine. "Fuck, I just know I love you the most and always."

His kiss is deep, seeking, and passionate, sharing how much he needs me, and I caress his face. Taking his lips. His breath. His whole life. We can love each other through hell and to heaven and back, and we have. I belong with Daniel. I'll always be with him as his lips dust over mine with a husky whisper.

"Speaking of twitches in my cock."

"I feel you, big boy." He's rutting against my belly. "But pace yourself. We have a full day ahead of us."

"This is bull *TITS*."

Daniel and I follow Eily's loud curse. It summons us down the corridor into the ship's gym, where we're headed anyway. It's fully decked out, but we halt in the doorway at the intriguing spectacle.

"Don't you mean bull*shit*?"

Silas smiles down at Eily and Cade doing pushups on the vinyl plank floors.

"No," Eily huffs. "It's bull *tits* cuz' this makes as much sense as tits on a bull. How many more?"

"Y'all said you could beat us."

Silas teases her, spotting Redix while he bench presses. But he's doing a shitty job because Silas is too distracted, amused by Eily's bitching.

"We *said*"—Cade does her reps beside Eily—"that we could do as many as y'all. Not more." She grunts, "And that's twenty so far, fuckers."

Redix bangs the bar down. Good thing he didn't miss

the catches because Silas is useless, focused on the sexy women sweating at their feet.

"Come on, Amazons." Redix sits up, watching them struggle. "Make Wonder Woman proud."

"I can't." Eily eeks out another rep. "I'm gonna die in a pool of sweat... when I'd rather die in cum."

"Come on, sister." Cade reps out two more. "Team Beaver can't lose to One-Eyed Bob and his one-eyed brother."

"They can spit in my face for all I care."

Eily's arms are shaking. Her strength is wavering. She's about to give up.

Oh, hell no.

They can't lose to sticky spud guns.

"Oorah." I rush in and join them on the floor. Bootcamp style. "Come on, Team Fur Burgers, we got this."

I can do pushups til the cows come home, fall asleep standing, and wake back up, tipped over, and I'd still be doing them. Once a Marine, always a Marine.

"Fur burgers?" Eily grins my way as I join her, panting beside me, but she keeps going. "We got full brazilians for Senators Packwood and Johnson up there, and this is the thanks we get."

It ain't easy doing pushups while you laugh, but we soldier on.

"Baby girl," Silas taunts Eily, "you know I love your Fort Bushy. You ain't gotta burn it down for me."

Daniel's feet cross my line of sight.

"What's the wager when they lose?"

"*When?*" Cade huffs.

"Don't pile on with your bald Captain Picard." I don't huff. I got this, warning Daniel, "Or you'll never ride in my enterprise ship again."

"You want in?" Redix asks Daniel.

I hear hands slapping, men doing that whole "what's up, bruh" thing, and I can't help myself.

"Oh, *everyone* wants some big beef in them tonight."

Cade snorts, Eily giggles, and I wink their way.

"But tonight is *my* turn, darlin'." Redix leans down so we're in his sight if we dare to lift our eyes. "So when y'all lose, you three get to be little Oral Annie's tonight."

I've never wanted to lose so badly or win so much because nothing with these five would be a punishment. Still, I gotta take one for Team *V*.

"How many did they do?" I ask Cade. "Total?"

"A hundred," Silas answers for her. "Fifty each."

"Alright, bitches." I glance at Eily, then Cade. "Peel off when you need to. I got a hundred in me all day."

"That's what *she* wished," Cade jokes while Eily collapses.

"Oh, thank fuck." She rolls to her back, gazing up at me. "Charlie, I'll worship your high heels any day."

"Lucky for you," I wink at her, my shoulders ain't even burning yet, "I *like* wearing heels lately."

"Shit," Silas grumbles, "y'all got GI Jane all horny for tacos, too. She's fighting for *your* team now."

"Damn right." Cade glances my way. Her arms shake, but she still taunts the guys, "Nothing fires us up more than cream in our panties."

"Or taking the piss," Daniel adds.

"No golden showers for me."

I joke back, but after ten more, Cade collapses while I bang out the rest, then I add twenty more just to flick their sexy balls.

When I rest back on my knees, all three men are standing, arms crossed, faces half-defeated, half-aroused. I wink at them.

"Wanna bet on a hundred crunches instead?"

"NO!" they answer in unison.

"But you men are all *tough* and *strong* and got such *big balls*,"—it's like I'm in basic training again—"and we're just what? Little pussies, built to take more pain and live longer and be so much smarter doing it."

Silas smirks at me in the cutest *fuck-you* and *we-go-way-back* way.

"Charlie Girl, like you've ever heard me say 'pussy' as a slur," he says. "Any of us. We know better. Only little-dicked men and women who hate themselves say that."

"I fucking *love* pussy," Redix whoops.

"I love *fucking* pussy," Daniel adds, his eyes flirting with me, "especially strong pussy that can take this cock."

Redix elbows him. "*Our* cocks," he adds.

"You sure that's what the ladies want tonight? Cocks?"

I tease Redix, who's caught a case of Silas. He's not wearing a shirt either while Daniel's hugs his beefy body like pec pantyhose.

Redix lifts his sexy lips.

"It's still *my* turn tonight."

"Yeah," Cade adds, "but since we won, Team Clint Toris gets to decide how Team Connie Lingus will play with your mystery gift."

"I swear to god," Silas rolls his eyes, "if one of y'all put butt plugs in your gift, I'm—"

"But I love butt plugs!" Eily blurts. "And so do you."

"In *your* ass," Silas answers her. "But I ain't putting a bunny tail in my backend for no one."

Daniel quips, "He *is* called Peter Cotton Tail for a reason."

Redix howls back, slapping his arms around Daniel and Silas. They huddle like triple Tricky Dickies.

"They got us beat, y'all," he says. "There ain't no punishment we can give Horny Harriet and her hot sisters."

"We can cut them off," Daniel schemes. "Starve them of sausage the rest of the week."

"Yeah, while we tease them," Silas adds, "with a sausage party of our own."

"Nuh-uh," Eily scoffs, "we got copies of your cocks upstairs and—"

Eyes dart. Chins pivot. Schemes fire fast through the air, but I'm too quick. So is Cade. We jump to our feet.

"I got the cocks!" I shout, running out the gym door and down the narrow corridor, seeking the treasure three dicks... I mean... three *decks* above.

Cade's on my heels. Redix and Daniel chase right behind her while I glimpse Silas laughing and carrying Eily around his waist while we all race up the spiral staircases.

"Get the dicks, Charlie! Get the dicks!"

Eily screams so loudly the crew can hear us, and that's an order I've never obeyed until this week.

It has us laughing, scrambling to reach the lounge first. And there they are.

Like beige beacons glistening in the sunlight.

Three large silicone cock clones have been neatly stacked, base down on the credenza, by the cleaning crew, and that only makes me laugh more. Peeing my pants is an imminent threat.

"Got 'em."

I grab the big squishy willies, hugging them to my chest while Cade protects me.

"Back away from the cocks," she demands, putting her

back to me, spreading her arms wide to block the advance of Daniel and Redix, who slowly stalk our way.

"I got a black belt and three willies, and I ain't afraid to use them," she warns. "Stand down, or someone's getting beat."

Daniel snorts. "Precisely."

If they weren't laughing, they'd be menacing, all tall and muscular and shit as Redix puts his palm up like a cop.

"Put our cocks down and put your hands where we can see them."

"Don't do it, Charlie," Cade warns. "This is war, and these dicks will throw their cocks in the ocean to win it."

Eily and Silas march in behind Daniel and Redix, but they're too focused on kissing and laughing to give a shit about Dilbert the Dildos being held hostage in my arms.

"Y'all are *NOT* taking our cocks," I sneer. Hearing myself. Trying not to bust a gut.

Cade chokes on laughter, too.

"Leave the mother's little helpers alone, and no one gets hurt," she says.

"We will protect our plastic lovers at any cost!" I warn. "No one wants to hurt innocent marital aids. They're *educational*."

"Yeah," Cade adds, half-chuckling, "they're a woman's home companion."

"They make us happy, dammit!" I proclaim, lifting one in the air like the President, addressing the nation, "If everyone had big dildos, we'd have global peace!"

But Redix and Daniel don't back down. Shoulder to shoulder, they skulk our way until they loom over me and Cade, casting shadows over us, all sexy skyscraper-like.

"We know you want the cocks," I negotiate, teasing Daniel with a wink. "Right, Daniel? You want cocks?"

Daniel grins. His arm brushes Redix's, and Redix side-eyes him, smiling too.

"What do you say, guys?" I keep pushing. "How bad do you want cocks tonight?"

I swear I catch Redix's fingers brushing Daniel's, almost caressing them before Silas calls out.

"Dudes, just rush 'em. Your wives have lethal skills, but they won't *kill* you. They like your real *D* too much."

"If y'all don't hand us our cocks"—Redix struggles for a straight face, loving every second of this, too—"we're gonna use all six on you."

Don't threaten me with a good time.

"We surrender."

I offer the dildos to them before Cade slings her arm over my shoulder.

"Way to put up a fight, babe," Daniel says, taking two cocks while Redix takes one.

And a million jokes sit on the tip of my tongue at the sight, but Cade shrugs, summing it up.

"We all win with *six dicks* tonight."

OILED HANDS GLIDE UP MY BACK. THE PRESSURE squeezing my muscles is perfection. All tension releases as I sigh into the massage table's white sheet. It smells like lavender, and I've never been so relaxed until I wonder...

"What do you think the guys are doing?"

I ask Eily and Cade beside me on their massage tables. This afternoon is spa day "for the ladies" while the men go fishing.

"I can tell you what I *hope* they're doing," Eily mutters.

"They're being stubborn," Cade grumbles. I open my eyes to see her sexy pillow lips smushed against the table. "They need to talk instead of grunting like horny cavemen."

My masseuse focuses on my shoulders, and I gotta admit, after all those push-ups, I need some body work. I'm gonna be sore tomorrow in all the wrong places.

"I think they're more than horny; that's the problem," I share. "There's some feelings, too, and Daniel doesn't want to come between Silas and Redix." Eily snorts, and I chuckle. "Yeah, that pun keeps punching, but I don't know how else to say it."

"I don't know, y'all." Eily lifts to her elbows while her masseuse works on her feet. "Silas has a big heart. He's fine with sharing me because he knows I love him; I'm his. But I don't know if he can share Redix with another man. They have a special bond."

Cade props herself up, too.

"But Silas is so generous with everything. I've never seen him get jealous."

She genuinely sounds confused.

"Yeah, but," Eily answers, "the first man he loved hurt him so badly. Silas lost everything over him. Maybe he's afraid he'll lose Redix to Daniel."

"Daniel would never do that," I explain. "He'd never hurt Silas. They're close, too. And he'd never fuck things up with Redix."

Eily snorts again, and I giggle.

"Dammit. What are we? Soulmates in the gutter with the same dirty minds?"

"And men." Cade laughs.

"Well, if they won't talk about it," Eily's so cute when she's cunning, "let's do something tonight to see if they'll *act* on it."

"I don't wanna make them do something they'll regret."

"We won't *make* them," Eily answers me. "We'll put the opportunity in their face and see what they do. They can always blame it on passion later. Isn't it better that way? If they talk first, then there's no denying what they feel. But they can just say it wasn't their thing if they try it tonight and don't like it."

"Maybe. I've just never seen Daniel like this," I share. "Usually, he's so alpha and unafraid. But this is new territory for him, exploring his feelings for men."

"It's funny," Cade adds, "some men can be so brave, staring death down. But some act like living with emotions will kill them when emotions are what make life worth living."

"But our men aren't frat boys," I defend them too. "They're mature as fuck. This is just... new for them... for Daniel at least."

Cade flips to her back so her masseuse can knead her thighs before she wonders.

"How come we three happened so easily?"

"Because women aren't afraid of their feelings," Eily answers.

"And because," I add, "I never said I wasn't attracted to women. I just never met any before y'all. And y'all made it so—"

"*Easy*," Eily quips. "Yep, we sure did. We're easy sluts who like to feel, fuck, *and* share." Eily pauses. "Actually. Wait. I haven't felt *you* yet, Charlie."

I blush, lust flaming my cheeks, tingling my sex. "I'm not stopping you," I tell her.

"Tonight," Eily makes me wait, "let me direct the festivities, and we can show the guys just how good sharing feels."

Later, when we meet in the lounge after dinner, after the ladies returned to Eily's stateroom to get dressed for our game, the guys obviously did more than fish.

I hope they talked it out, but I scan their eyes, and they're on us. It seems the women are still the focus and not the men, which is kinda refreshing but kinda disappointing.

I really want this for Daniel tonight. I hate seeing him suffer, but at least they're getting closer. At least they're working together.

The men moved the sofas to the side of the room. The coffee table, too. Now, it's beside a large onyx sex chaise lounger in the middle, and I chew my lip, noting the ankle and wrist straps tucked under it.

"Someone's been busy," Eily coos.

"We're bringing a king bed up here tomorrow," Silas informs us, and I think the guys planned their outfits too.

Or lack thereof.

They're shirtless and only wearing gray cotton joggers over their dicks, arching long and thick. Like kryptonite for any pussy or cock in this room. But we also have a surprise for them, under our white silk robes—nothing.

We planned it.

That and our bodies are dusted in vanilla-flavored kissable powder with bright pink rouge on our nipples that tastes like strawberries. "The ladies" had way too much fun getting ready this evening. Because we also planned this—together, we open our robes, letting them drop to the floor, and the men's jaws follow.

"Go ahead," a nude Cade teases Redix, "and pick your box."

He eyes her pussy with a sly grin, declaring, "I pick the hot box that belongs to me," while Daniel and Silas comb our naked bodies, lust filling their eyes and dicks.

"Yes," Cade answers him, "but the winners decide how you'll play with the boxes tonight."

Redix quickly grabs one off the credenza, ripping it open.

"It's a bunch of stuff," he announces, lifting items out of the box. "Three Goodhead For Him kits. Silicone anal beads. A leather crop shaped like a heart, and—"

"Who went to the Walmart of Sex?" Eily blurts, but no one confesses.

"And some panties?" Redix pulls them out. "No. Wait. They're *pegging* panties."

I clock the crowd, and Daniel looks sly. So does Silas. Hell, it could be Cade. It's too hard to tell, but three things are getting hard, that's for sure. At least this brings us closer to desires fulfilled, particularly ones some are afraid to confess.

Whoever planned this gift is a genius.

Is Eily the guilty one as she sashays over to Redix?

"The ladies decided *I'm* in charge tonight."

She picks up the riding crop, playfully swatting Redix's butt. But he smacks her naked ass back, making her squeal with delight before she hooks her finger our way.

"Fellas," she says once we stand in a sorta circle, "time for Team Connie Lingus to warm your players up, please."

Eily reaches for Silas's shoulder, smiling as she pushes him to his knees. Daniel quickly falls to his. He loves eating pussy, and it seems Redix is the same. Once he's kneeling before Cade, he slings her leg over his shoulder.

Tapping Silas on the back with the riding crop, Eily demands, "Now, eat this pussy up like a real man."

Silas grins, his lips nearing her sex. "You're *soooo* getting spanked for this later."

At first, it's funny and playful, but then Daniel's too

good at this. Spreading my lips with his fingers while his others slide inside my cunt; he licks my clit with his warm tongue before blowing cool air over it.

"God, Daniel," I sigh, pleasure skittering over my flesh.

I gaze down into his hungry blue eyes while his tongue circles my clit like a lavish whirlpool before he does it again —gently blowing cool air over my nub before he pulls his fingers out and spanks it hard.

"Fuck!" I cry out, the rapture making me grab his granite shoulders to steady myself.

"I'm going to make you squirt on my face, naughty girl," he taunts in that deep English accent, and I hear two moans —Eily's and Silas's.

I lift my gaze to see how Silas has Eily lying on the credenza with her legs over his shoulders, her hands grabbing his long hair. He's devouring her sex, but they're moaning to Daniel, about to make mine explode.

Redix and Cade are beside us. They're so close to us that Redix's thigh touches Daniel's, kneeling beside him, and I wonder if it's an accident or if they keep seeking each other's touch.

Cade sinks her fingers into Redix's long strands while he slurps through her sex, and I start shaking at the luscious sight of three hot men worshipping pussy. The decadent sounds and smell of it, too.

I can't believe we're doing this, and who wouldn't? It's too incredible to be forbidden. It's too taboo to ever stop.

Then Cade moans, bracing herself against Redix's tall body, lowering my way, and I know what she craves. I turn my body so she can take my nipple in her mouth. And when she starts sucking it so hard while Daniel sucks my clit, I don't know who comes faster.

Her, as she groans, shaking and coming over Redix's

mouth, or me, grabbing her with one hand, my other fisting Daniel's dark, silky waves.

"Fuck," I warn them. "Fuck, I'm coming."

"Do it. Come for me, babe."

Daniel jerks his fingers so hard inside my clenching sex before his tongue expertly flutters over my clit. He knows how to do this so well, making me come so hard. He won't stop until the orgasm seizes my body; the only thing escaping is my scream, causing all eyes to turn my way as my body quakes, my lust pouring over Daniel's chin before dripping onto the rug.

"I wanna taste her cum, too."

Eily's voice is smokey with lust. It makes Silas groan, returning his tongue to Eily's clit, his fingers sinking deep inside her, and I swear I could come again at the sight of Silas eating pussy. It looks like he's so good at it, that he loves it, but Eily wriggles, gently tugging at his hair.

"Fuck me," she tells him. "Fuck me like your slut while I eat her out."

Oh my god. It's a whirlwind as Daniel fulfills Eily's request. He scoops me up and carries me to the chaise lounge while Silas does the same with Eily, but once we're here, she takes charge again, waving the riding crop around.

"Cade," she says, "put those pegging panties on, and Redix, get the anal beads and two Goodhead Kits."

It's like Eily's directing porn. Steven Spielberg would be so horny and proud.

"Charlie," she directs, "lie back on the chaise. That's it. Now, scoot down to where I can reach you."

I follow her instructions. This chaise was made for this while Eily drapes her petite body over the low, soft hump at the end of it. It puts her ass in the air for Silas and my pussy right in her face.

"Cade," Eily commands, "fuck Silas. Redix and Daniel," she waves her crop, "feed Charlie your cocks until she comes for us. Twice."

Smack!

It cracks the air as Silas gives Eily's ass a spank. He stands over her while she's kneeling before me.

"Someone's being a *dirty* little slut tonight." Silas gently pulls Eily's hair, making her smile. "You think I'm gonna get my ass fucked for you?"

"You'd do anything for me." She grins, looking over her shoulder at him. "And you love it when Redix fucks your ass while you fuck mine, but tonight is Cade's turn."

Silas doesn't say no. He doesn't resist as Cade steps behind him, her hands reaching around to untie his jogger pants.

Daniel does the same to my right, and Redix pushes his pants down to my left.

When all three men stand nude, their cocks surging veiny and thick, their swollen crowns jutting for more, I want to praise Eily.

I know what she's doing.

She's tempting Redix and Daniel as they share my mouth, knowing I can get their dicks to finally touch. And she's tempting Silas with everything he loves, fucking her pussy while his ass gets fucked and watching her eat mine.

Will she seduce him to eat me, too?

Wait? What?

What's happening to me?

I'm slipping into a new woman, and I like her skin. I love her lust. I'm changing and letting my body feel pleasure I denied myself for so long. All I knew was grief until I met Daniel. Until I felt his love.

And now? The thought of Silas's mouth on my pussy, too? It makes me moan.

I'm a new woman, touching myself for Silas's gaze while Cade steps behind him. She's wearing the red lace panties with the smaller black dildo designed for ass play secured to them. It's like she's about to take charge, but Silas turns the tables.

"If you wanna fuck my ass," he says, "I'm gonna play with my wife's first."

Picking up the toy, Silas grabs anal lube, glossing the clear blue beads while we watch. While I glance right, then left, at Daniel and Redix, slowly stroking off to watch this... and each other.

They've glossed their dicks in strawberry lube from the Goodhead kits, and Daniel put a tingling mint in my mouth for their pleasure too. But now? All we can witness is Eily's pleasure as she leans over the lounger with her eyes on my wet pussy before they start rolling back with her moan.

"You like that?" Silas teases her. "You like me shoving beads in your tight little ass, Eily?" He pushes them in, making her gasp. "Yes, baby, you do. You are *such* a beautiful, dirty little girl for me. I'm gonna play with your ass while I fuck your tight pussy so hard because it's *my* pussy to share. Right?"

He smacks her ass again, and Eily cries out, "Yes, Silas. Make me your slut."

"Then eat some pussy for me."

He grabs the back of her head, pressing Eily's face into my sex while his other hand guides his hard cock inside her, and I moan at the feral sight. How Silas looks like a sex god, controlling and powerful, but he fucks like a wild animal, my clit sparking at him holding Eily here, at the luscious feeling of her moaning, licking my pussy like a cat through milk, while Silas's shredded abs start flowing like water, fucking her like a pro.

"Oh my god," I sigh.

"Fuck yes," Silas groans, watching me, then watching Eily. "Fuck yes, eat Charlie's sweet pussy. Come on, my little slut," he spanks Eily's ass again, "make her squirt for us."

"Come here, Charlie."

It's a voice I know well. It's woven into my soul and pulling my eyes his way.

Daniel looms over me, his swollen cock hovering over my lips. It's instinct. I grab his base, guiding his fat tip toward my lips while he demands, "No. Two cocks. My naughty wife is sucking two cocks tonight, aren't you?"

"Yes," I huff, reaching left for Redix too.

Wrapping my hand around Redix's thick shaft, I'm fisting hard dicks, and losing my mind. I love it. With two cocks in my grasp, I let go of my sanity, my tongue laving over their sweet, swollen crowns. I start rubbing them together, licking and slurping fat tip over tip, all while feeling Eily's tongue circling my clit that's a firecracker about to explode.

"*Fuucckk.*"

We all sigh it, huff it, pant it.

Daniel and Redix can't rip their eyes away from the sight. There's no way they can fit in my mouth simultaneously, so I keep rubbing their cocks together before tightly grabbing their shafts, side by side, letting Daniel feel Redix glide against him as they thrust their cocks together. Then I lick them like strawberry lollipops stuck together, the mint in my mouth giving me the zeal to never stop.

"*Fuucckk.*" It makes Daniel lurch forward, grabbing Redix's shoulder for balance.

"*Fuucckk.*" It makes Redix grab him back, his other hand reaching, tugging at my rouged nipple until Daniel copies him, twirling my other one before gently slapping it like he knows how I love it.

And I do. I'm moaning and licking two huge cocks. Hands are toying with my tits, too, while I watch Silas. His eyes are savage, tugging at the toy in Eily's ass while his other hand holds her face, keeping it buried, her tongue licking through my slick pussy, as he sinks his cock over and over into hers.

It makes me writhe, rolling my hips, lifting higher for Eily's licking tongue, for Silas's riveted gaze. My empty sex is aching. I need more. *Please, fill my every fucking hole.* And like she can read my body, Cade, who's watching it all, quickly grabs one of the cloned cocks.

"This one is yours?" she asks Silas.

"Yes," Silas grunts, lust churning in his voice.

I don't say anything. I want this. It's so intense. It's so bad, it's right, and why have I waited so long? Why did I deny myself when this feels like nirvana in my sex?

Cade taps Eily's shoulder.

"Fuck her with Silas's cock," she tells her, making Eily grin with my cum glistening across her cute face.

Oh my god, this is hot.

Oh my god, I'm dripping.

Oh, my sex goddess, thank you. Someone put the vibrating mechanism inside the willy, too.

"Watch Silas," Eily taunts over her shoulder before pressing the large vibrating dildo into my entrance. "Watch while I fuck Charlie with your big cock."

"Fuck!" Silas growls, smacking Eily's ass again, but he can't look away, watching what I feel—a long, cool dildo shaped like his thick cock sliding deep inside my warm pussy, vibrating against my eager walls, stretching my sex wide to receive him.

"Yes!"

I don't know where it screams from inside me. I don't know what I feel. What to call this, but I do. I surrender. I let it happen. I *want* it to happen. The ache in my cunt goes away once Eily leaves the big toy thrumming deep inside me while her tongue flutters over my electric clit again.

"Oh my god," I gasp over Daniel and Redix's cocks. "Feed them to me." I've lost my mind, and sanity is overrated because this feels too goddamn amazing as I insist again, "Daniel, feed me Redix's cock."

Without a word, he does it. Wrapping his big hand around Redix's wide shaft, replacing mine with his, he taunts; he wants this too.

"Suck Redix's cock," Daniel commands me, and I do. Tasting Redix in my mouth, feeling my pussy drip over Silas's dildo, I moan at Daniel's praise. "That's it. Take it. My naughty wife wants so much cock tonight. We're going to cover you in our cum."

"Damn," Redix huffs at my moans that won't stop at Daniel's tease and touch. "Damn, that's it," Redix tells him. "Yeah, man. Yeah, stroke my dick. Fuck yeah, you feel so good. Fucking jerk me off over her mouth."

A loud grunt hits the air, and I focus on its source—Silas.

He's draped over Eily, humping her pussy while Cade's behind him. She must be pegging him because he looks blissed out, and so does Cade, playing with her nipples while she thrusts into his ass, watching our show; it's getting her off too.

"Yes," Silas pants. "Yes, eat that pussy. Look at my cock inside her."

His lips steam over Eily's ear, but who is he talking to? He's so close to my sex as she lifts away, fluttering her tongue over my clit so he can watch her do it.

"*Mmmmm,*" it makes me groan with Redix's hard cock in my mouth. With Daniel guiding him, making him gently thrust into my cheek while my right hand jerks my husband off as he jerks off another man.

Oh my god, I'm gonna come so hard.

Tasting Redix's early, creamy drops. My pussy stuffed full and clenching around Silas's vibrating dildo. Eily licking my clit. And my husband is watching it all, wanting it all. *Oh my god, I love him.* I'm safe with Daniel. I can let go and do this hearing Silas's voice, his dirty talk with Eily while he gets fucked too.

"My wife is so fucking dirty and all mine," Silas growls. "Your pussy's so fucking wet and tight for me, Eily. You love a good cock and cunt, don't you?" Eily moans, sucking my clit while he kisses her cheek. "Yes, lick that pussy up, Mrs. Van de May. Come on. Make Charlie come on my face."

I buck. I groan. This erotic reality is a dirty dream, my eyes rolling back, seeing a new heaven, desire ripping open seams in my body I didn't know I had. My thighs draped open over the velvet chaise shake violently at the pressure building as I squeeze Daniel's cock so hard, not sure and wanting this so much.

"She's coming," he warns. "Hurry. Take the cock out."

He knows what my body needs. How I can't stop this. How when a cock glides down my clenching walls, the lust, the pressure releases too. I want to scream at its power, seeing stars as my sex clamps down, pulsing so hard, coming and gushing, and I can't breathe. I groan, lurching with Redix's cock in my mouth, gasping over it as I search for air in the blinding light of ecstasy.

"*Dayum*," Redix moans at the sight. At the wet shower I must be giving, I don't know. I can't open my eyes. I can't stop it.

"That's it, babe," Daniel soothes, desire stirring deep in his voice. "Come again for them."

Them?

Suddenly, I feel two tongues, two mouths slurping up my dripping, spasming sex, and I barely open my eyes, moaning at the sight.

Oh my god...

Silas.

Silas.

He's licking my wet clit while Eily's tongue fucks me, and, *oh my god. Oh my god. It's Silas eating my pussy,* and I convulse, my legs shaking beside his face. Another wave hits me so hard I can't warn him. I can't stop it. He just does it to me. His tongue licking my pussy makes me cry out; it makes me gush into his mouth and Eily's.

"*God*," Cade moans. "Good god, that's so fucking hot."

She sounds so turned on, while all I hear next is gasping, high pitched, and about to come. It's Eily. Silas is fucking her so hard he's rocking the whole chaise.

"Fuck," he groans. "Fuck, Eily. I got Charlie's cum in my mouth and your cum on my dick. Come on, my dirty little wife," Silas growls, spanking her again. He fucks her like a beast. "Fucking squirt for me, too, while I fuck you so fucking hard."

"Silas!" Eily screams in pleasure. I can't focus, but she must be coming hard because Daniel's cock swells in my grasp.

I don't know time or anything, but wanting more. But grasping a cock, my husband's cock, feeling Daniel's hard velvet shaft get so rigid in my hand while I taste more of Redix's cream. I offer my tongue for it.

"You want this cock? You want my cum?" Redix palms my breast while Daniel keeps stroking Redix's shaft. "You wanna taste my dick explode in your mouth?"

Redix isn't just asking me. He's asking Daniel, too, and I love it.

"Yes," I beg. "Yes, Daniel. Make Redix come."

Those words hit him hard. Redix grunts to them... and grunts again... before he spurts across my tongue, drops dousing my cheeks. Most fills my mouth, but before I can swallow, Daniel's kissing me. His tongue searches, wanting to taste Redix's pleasure, too, and we moan, all three of us, before I gasp for air.

"Redix," I demand, "make Daniel come on my tits."

"Shit."

I glance at the voice. At Silas, who's taking a pounding from Cade. Somehow, in the haze of Redix coming, Eily's moved aside. She's standing up and stroking Silas's cock over my pussy while Cade fucks his ass.

"Both of you, come on her," Eily demands Daniel and Silas. And Daniel's so close.

Once Redix wraps his hand around Daniel's cock, making Daniel groan with his tip aimed at my breasts, he's going to come.

Daniel's hooded eyes slide from mine to Redix's and back, and his lips part. He's searching. He doesn't know where to look; he just gives in to his desire, to the touch of me grabbing his ass while Redix jerks his cock, aiming it at my nipple, and...

"Fuck, Charlie." Daniel lets go. "Fuck, man." He can't help it. He reaches for Redix with both hands, holding on to him while he groans, covering my tits and Redix's fist with his cum. And I shudder, my orgasms still singing through my flesh.

The sudden sound from Silas. It's pain and pleasure as I lift my eyes to see Cade shaking. She's holding his hips, kissing his back while she comes, and that takes Silas. In Eily's grasp, he growls, his neck straining to hold it back, but he can't. Not when Eily urges him, "Come on Charlie's pussy," and it makes him roar with release, watching his cock in her hand as it splatters my sex with his warm desire, and I still don't know, and neither does he.

What do we want?

What do we feel?

Maybe we'll find out soon. Or maybe some answers are never found; you just keep asking.

But Daniel's found his answer. He doesn't let go of Redix, grasping the back of his neck. They nuzzle their foreheads and can't deny it. They can't hide it.

The question in my worried heart. The question in my eyes, searching Silas's hazel gaze on them before he seeks mine—I've loved Silas in some beautiful way for so long—is... *what does he feel?*

Silas

> "You gave your best friend a tongue bath last night and drank her lady juice. Lines *have* been crossed."

What do I feel?

The fuck if I know.

Because I feel everything.

And that makes me a dick.

I love my wife, Eily. I don't want a single day if she's not by my side. It's ironic how she's the tiny one, but she loves me so much, and I love her even more. That makes our lives big, our love huge.

As long as I fall asleep with Eily and wake up like this, with her in my arms, her head resting over my heart, the sun has my permission to rise.

And I love Redix, too. It makes me feel selfish, but I ain't ashamed. Nah, I relish what we have because it's powerful; it's rare. It's so damn good, it's right, and we know it because we love Cade too. She belongs with Redix like Eily belongs with me, and the four of us work.

If it's true love, it doesn't need explaining.

Maybe that's why I can't explain whatever the fuck is happening between me and Charlie.

Yes, I love her. I always have.

Like a puppy dog at her heels, I've grown into a man by her side. She was there for me when the world outed me, abandoned me. She was my friend when no one else was.

Shit, she even saved the childhood stuff I threw away. She knew my parents would accept me one day. Charlie's always believed in me. We've never let each other down.

So now, I'm a big dick.

A dick who's so close to fucking his hot best friend.

My childhood crush on Charlie used to be innocent. Then, it ached in my teenage heart. But I matured, and it became a sexy joke we shared. Because before this week, Daniel Pierce would fucking kill me if I laid a hand on his wife.

And now I have *my* wife, who I'd kill for, stirring in my arms.

Burying my nose in Eily's long hair, I inhale lavender, lacing my fingers in the silky strands tumbling down her back and loving her so goddamn much but not believing... *she wants me to fuck Charlie?*

If that ain't enough of a mind fuck.

Daniel does, too?

Or is it a swap?

Is Daniel giving me Charlie while he takes Redix?

Don't think I didn't see that last night between them. Hell, since they got here, I've noticed. And I watched that love scene from their show. The whole world has. Daniel and Redix have been nominated for Golden Globes for it, and I saw why.

That shit was damn close to real.

But my globe? My world feels as clouded as my mind. As the sky outside. I don't know what I feel about it; I just feel Eily in my arms. I squeeze her tightly, loving how my body protects hers, how she's all mine. Ultimately, she's who I live for.

"If you don't stop tossin' and turnin'," she mumbles against my chest.

"That ain't me." I kiss her hair. "That's the storm."

Her little head pops up, her eyes scanning the large oval windows of our owner's suite.

"Shit," she gasps. "Is it a hurricane? Are we gonna die in a tsunami? Is a big wave gonna flip us over and—"

I laugh, flipping her on top of me.

"You think I'd risk your life and all my friends' lives in a fucking hurricane on a ship?"

"*Maybe.*" Her jade eyes twinkle. "You're not afraid of the water and storms. Or fish. But I am."

"I'm gonna keep bringing fish around until you ain't afraid. I'll even get you a fish tank for your birthday." I tuck her hair behind her ear to admire her gorgeous face. "A big saltwater one in our new house."

"You mean, you're getting me a big supply of fresh seafood?"

"Uh! You'd eat my pet fish?"

"Fish ain't pets. They're fried sticks that taste yummy with ketchup."

Thunder rolls in the distance, and her eyes grow wider.

"Silas Henry,"—she sits up, straddling me, trying to look tough, but she's too naked and cute—"you better not turn us into shark chum out here."

"We ain't *out here*. If you'd get your sexy little ass up and look out that window, you'd see we're docked in Bimini

Bay. The captain brought us in last night. It's just a little system. It'll blow off by the end of the day."

She whirls her fingertip over my nipple.

"So we're not sinking like Jack and Rose? Cuz' that's kinda romantic."

"No, we ain't on the Titanic. The water ain't freezing." I grab her hips. "And you'd *share* that wooden board with me because there was room for two. Just sayin'."

"He died for her."

"No, he froze his balls off for her, which made him stupid. They both could've lived."

She tilts her head.

"So you wouldn't die for me?"

I gaze up at her, and the answer is everywhere in my heart, in every breath I take, and every day I'm alive; I'd give everything for Eily.

"Nah," I answer, "I ain't dying for a fish hater."

She starts tickling me, going for my ribs, teasing, "Here, fishy, fishy," and I'm five years old, kicking the bed, begging her to stop until I can't take it.

Like my beautiful rag doll, I flop her onto her back, grabbing her wrists and pinning them above her head.

"I think," I spread her legs open with my knees, "all the fish in the sea need for me to give you a good morning fuck so you'll start loving them like you love me."

Because, *goddamn*, I can feel it. Love swells in my veins for Eily. It floods my mind, and even when she's not around, she's everywhere inside me. And she's so beautiful, her big green eyes gazing up at me as she lifts her hips. She knows exactly how to trap me inside her, too.

"I think," she teases, "that'll take more than *one* morning fuck, Mr. Van de May."

"Then open up, Mrs. Van de May, so I can fuck you forever."

When Eily lets me inside her, where I belong, it's like nowhere else and no one else. It's just us. It's her grabbing my back with her tiny hands and holding me so tight that I only need her, not oxygen.

"Deeper, Silas," she begs me, wrapping her legs around my waist, and that's where we go, as deep as we possibly can.

It's instinct. It's an urge. It's the animal in me every time I fuck her, *only her*.

"I'm gonna put a baby inside you."

"Not yet." She grabs my ass. "But keep trying. One day you will."

I do try. I give Eily everything I have this morning and always until we're a big, sweaty, satisfied mess in our black silk bed sheets.

We're kissing. We're smiling. We're quiet when we're done. I could die happy like this, with Eily back in my arms, but she's lifting the sheets, examining our naked bodies before she declares, "Black sheets and white cum don't mix."

I laugh. "That's what we have a cleaning crew for."

"No one gets paid enough to clean up cum."

"*I* like cleaning cum."

She grins up at me, dropping the sheet as it settles over our bodies.

"Are you gonna have a talk today?"

"With who?"

"Charlie. Who else?" She asks, kinda thrilled, "Why? You want Daniel, too, don't you?"

"Fuck." My brain is scrambled. My heart's so confused.

I drag my hand over my stubble. "This shit is getting complicated."

Eily sits up, twisting my way to give me the thirty-third degree.

"Silas, I swear. I don't know how you men wound up in charge of so much shit because when God was handing out common sense, y'all asked for sex instead."

"You're the one wearing hornied-rim glasses all the time."

"Yeah, I like sex, but I got enough sense to talk about it too."

"If folks wanna talk, they know where to find me."

"*That's* what's making this complicated—y'all avoiding the obvious."

I loop her silky hair around my finger.

"What's so obvious to you?" I ask.

"Uh-uh." She shakes her head. "I'm not doing the thinking for you. You tell me what *you* see."

Maybe if I say it, I'll know how I feel about it.

"I know that Redix and Daniel feel something."

"And that makes you feel... ?"

"Don't know." I search my heart. "Not mad, I guess. Just... worried."

"About what? Us?"

"No. Me and you are the one thing I'm sure of. I always will be."

She caresses my chest, and I hold her hand over my heart, needing her touch.

"Then, as long as we're good, what are you worried about?"

"Losing Redix to Daniel, or losing Charlie if we fuck up our friendship with sex."

"Breaking news:"—she grins—"you gave your best friend a tongue bath last night and drank her lady juice. Lines *have* been crossed."

Damn, all that does is make me remember how I lost my mind.

Fucking Eily's tight little pussy, I could feel the beads in her ass, making her even tighter, while Cade fucked mine. It gets me off that Cade likes fucking like she's got a cock, too, almost as much as she enjoys us railing her pussy so hard.

We've done that before, but last night, we added Charlie. And to watch Eily's pretty tongue lick Charlie's hard, pink clit? To smell Charlie's sweet, musky pussy so close to my mouth that it watered. To hear her moans as Eily's tongue slurped up her lust. To know that Charlie was writhing and moaning with a dildo shaped like *my* cock inside her, she was so fucking swollen and hungry for it.

I couldn't help it. It was a baptism when she came. I finally tasted her and went insane. I put my mouth on her pussy, needing more, and she came again, so wet and hard and fast; *what the fuck?*

I never thought we'd cross that line. Any line. But it's like time has erased them. And it's like my wife won't paint them back. Eily doesn't want us living in the lines. She has her reasons. Those lines hurt her for too long.

"So what are you telling me?" I ask her.

"That I wish your mind was as open as your heart."

"My heart belongs to *you*."

She traces over my chest like she believes it.

"Then open your mind because I love you. We're together forever, so answer your past. Don't live with questions in this heart." She pokes it, all cute and playful. "This heart that belongs to me."

"So, you'll just share my dick with anyone?"

I know the answer but watch this; Eily's so pretty when she's pissed.

"Hell, no." Her neck weaves. "I'm Mrs. Silas Van de May, and I'll fuck a bitch up if she messes with what's mine."

The fact that she ain't kidding makes me laugh. Jealousy is a waste of time for my wife. She goes straight to shooting your ass. She's done it before.

"Then what makes Charlie different?"

"Because I like her and could love her too, just like you do. And can't you just sense it?"

"Sense what?"

Eily can be so playful and free, but deep down, she has the wisest soul. I saw what she survived; we can't ever forget it. It's another thing that binds me to her forever.

"Can't you just sense when someone's walking around like they've got this hole in their heart, this spot to be filled?" she asks. "It doesn't hurt them, but life would be so much better if it's filled. That's you and Charlie."

"So you don't mind me fucking her?"

"How many times do I have to tell you that I *want* you to?"

"Until I believe it."

"No," Eily answers, "until you're not *afraid* of it."

EILY'S WORDS TUMBLE THROUGH MY HEAD WHILE SHE takes a shower, and I work my way up to the bridge to talk to the captain.

I'm afraid of fucking Charlie?

Like what? Her pussy's one of those vagina dentatas? You know, a pussy with teeth that'll maul your dick?

I ain't kidding. It's a horror movie.

But no, Charlie's pussy is perfect. Just like Eily's and Cade's and all pussies.

I ain't afraid it's a trap. That I'm gonna fall in love with Charlie. Not like I love my wife.

No one's like my incredible wife.

That's why I married Eily. That's why, when I almost lost her, I went crazy. I was willing to lose my life and my family's fortune for her because Eily's my family. She's where I belong and the one I love the most.

It's her above everyone else as I wind up the steps, not really liking all the mirrors and chrome everywhere, though the black and white marble is kinda sweet.

This ship ain't my style, but it is *mine*. I'm proud of it.

And shit... I guess that's it.

I'm proud of my friendship with Charlie. I count on it. I believe in it. If I fuck her, I'm afraid I'll lose it. And I already know what that feels like. To be abandoned. To have no one. No one but my grandma and my best friend, Charlie.

Losing people is the only thing that scares me, so I control the one thing I can.

My ship.

The captain tells me the worst of the storm is behind us. Mainly just clouds, swells, and wind the rest of the day, but no one wants to lose their lunch, rocking and rolling out to sea, so we'll stay docked today.

My ship's bosun is Bahamian. When I ask around for what we can do on a cloudy day, she suggests Radio Beach.

She says we can find sea glass there, and that's got Eily written all over it. She can use it for her art.

After breakfast, we rent two Jeeps and park near a beach bar. With the weather, there aren't many tourists crowding the sand, so half of us put on gloves and pick up trash while the rest look for sea glass.

That was Daniel's idea, and that man has changed.

As if he wasn't intimidating and perfect before, now, he's even more confident. Like he and Charlie have survived so much, he only cares about her and their kids. He ain't threatened by anyone.

Not even me.

And now he's got a little silver at his temples, making his dark waves even sexier—*such a fucking English Daddy*.

Yes, dammit, I've always thought Daniel was hot. The whole world does. I fantasized about him, too—me, him, *and* Charlie. I just didn't want to make the dude uncomfortable about it.

Did I ever see it coming?

That Daniel would be into dudes, too?

I don't know.

They say our sexuality or whatever is fluid. It can change over time, with who we meet, how we feel, what we're free to do, or what's safe. I get it.

You can't debate who someone is.

They just are.

Like me—I used to be so chill. I never got attached. But this shit, these feelings firing through my nerves?

What the hell do I want?

Back in the day, all I wanted was to fish all day and fuck all night. Alright, fuck while I'm fishing; I've done that too.

Now? The only part of me I'm sure of is loving Eily and our marriage.

The rest?

I don't know what to say to Charlie, which is weird because we used to talk about everything. We've shared everything, too, as if we could feel each other's emotions, and now we share desire. It used to be only me who felt it, but I saw it, tasted it; she feels it for me too now, and I sense it kinda scares her.

So will we do it?

Yeah, we're crossing lines already, and it's hot as fuck. But that final line? Me inside her? I've wanted Charlie for so long; maybe I *am* afraid to finally feel it.

What will it do to us? Me and Charlie?

Like Eily says, will it fill that space in our hearts that's always wondered?

Or, like I worry, if I scratch the itch and satisfy my lust, will it break us into pieces that can't be mended?

And Redix? Even if we never fuck again, he's mine, and I'm his. Trust is something he doesn't give easily, and I earned his, and he understands me. I used to feel so lonely, thinking I was the only man like this, but then I met Redix. He's my match, and I can't lose him too.

That's what makes this so fucking excruciating because I can't look him in the eye as I sense him walking beside me. He's picking up trash while I'm looking for treasure.

"You mad?"

He grumbles, grabbing a plastic water bottle from the sand before tossing it into his trash bag.

"I ain't mad."

But my damn pulse starts racing near him.

"You sure seem fucking mad. You ain't talking to me. You won't look at me... "

My feet stop.

They start sinking in the sand, like my heart, forcing my eyes to confront his. To face this truth.

When I do, *fuck me*... all I see is the man I love, the one who grabs my falling heart and won't let go of it.

"Look," Redix steps closer, "we haven't done anything. Just what you've seen and the acting we did at work."

"That shit ain't acting. You're into him."

He clenches his jaw. "But I *love* you."

"I know you do."

"Then what should I do?"

I shrug. "I got no fucking clue this week."

"About Charlie?"

"About her. About you. About my wife, who's so damn amazing, and I love her so damn much because all she wants me to do is *love* everyone else."

Redix grins. And dammit, it makes me smile. *Every. Damn. Time.*

He steps even closer, and I glance right, spotting Eily walking with Daniel and Charlie farther down the beach. Cade's to my left, talking to some locals. I got Redix all to myself, and fuck; I miss him sometimes.

"I haven't talked to him," he says, "because I wanted to talk with you first."

"Why me, first?"

"Because you'll always be my first. You know, like—"

"Like when you're with *other* men now?"

Fuck. Where did that jealousy come from? I'm not used to this emotion. And I fucking hate it.

He lowers his voice.

"I never saw myself with any man but you. And I don't know if what I'm feeling for him is from acting something out or if it's legit, but it's fucking with my head. And my heart."

I get the head part. I know actors can get so into their characters it changes them, sometimes permanently.

"How's it fucking with your heart?"

That's what's underneath the ugly jealousy—fear. This is the pain in my heart that scares me. I can't lose Redix. Take one of my arms, not him. And if you take Eily from me? Well, take my life, too, because I'd have none left.

"Because I love you, Silas. You mean everything to me, and I don't wanna hurt you. I *won't* do it if it hurts you."

Emotions strain his deep voice. He's trying to hide it, but he can't from me. That's how we got so close. Redix is my mirror, and I'm his. We look so much alike; even our souls match.

"But it's hurting you, isn't it? The wondering? The not knowing?"

Fuck, am I asking about him and Daniel? Or me and Charlie? Or both?

"Yes," he confesses, and looking into his eyes reflecting the ocean, I see the man who taught *me* how to love. The way he loves Cade like no other. The way he sacrificed himself for her. With no fear. The way he'd do it again for Cade. He doesn't know how to ever not love her.

That's how I love Eily now.

Redix showed me how.

And that's how I love him, too.

"If I lose you," I clench my teeth, the fear strangling my throat, "it'll fucking kill me."

He grabs my shoulder. "You'll never lose me. I promise. I belong with Cade. I belong with you and Eily. We have families to grow, and I'm not going anywhere."

"But I lost the first man I loved, and that's what he fucking said too."

"No, you never *had* the first man you loved because he

wasn't out. He wasn't proud of his love for you, but I am. I always will be. Silas, Cade is my soul, but you found my heart again." He glances around. "Hell, I'd kiss you right now. I'd prove how much I love you, but I don't know the vibe here, and I ain't getting in a fight and fucking up my pretty face."

I grin. "You ain't that pretty."

He grins back. "You ain't that smart."

Asshole. Making me laugh.

"So you won't fight for me?"

His blue eyes burn so bright, swearing, "I'd fuckin' kill for you."

I grab his arm braced over my shoulder. Can he be any sexier right now? Could I love him even more?

Yes.

I'm not a jealous man. Jealousy is a cancer for the weak, for the insecure. Why do people find it attractive? I guess they got a death wish because it'll kill love if you let it.

And me and Redix are too strong for that shit. We've fought too hard to get here.

"Then fuck for me, too," I tell him. "Talk to Daniel. Y'all figure it out. Fuck him if you need to. I don't want you always wonderin'."

He gives me that look. The one that's fucking scuba diving through my soul, searching for my truth.

"What about you? Do *you* wonder about him?"

Because he always finds it, and I shrug.

"It'd be easier to fuck him than Charlie."

Like my mirror, he shrugs back.

"Fuck them both if they want you to."

"It's more than sex between us. There's deep feelings and shit."

"Yeah, there's deep feelings between *all* of us. But at the end of the fucking night, you were made for Eily, I was born for Cade, and Daniel belongs with Charlie. That don't change."

"Dude, I know you're sober, but you sound high. Like me fucking my best friend won't change things."

He laughs, sounding just like Eily.

"You've given each other cum showers, and you showed her a lot of mouth love last night. Things *have* changed. Besides, if you don't finally fuck Charlie this week, the sexual tension between y'all will get worse. It'll be awkward as hell."

"Okay, echo chamber," I huff, "that's what *you* want to hear after your taffy-pulling contest with Daniel last night."

He winks. "You jealous?"

"While your wife was fucking my ass?" I chuckle. "Not particularly."

"So what are we gonna do tonight?"

"Seems you need to put words in your mouth before you find cocks in it."

"What words?"

Cade interrupts us, so I wrap my arm around her shoulder, pulling her into our huddle for an update.

"Our Mister Woody here is gonna have a chin wag with Charlie's Big Ben before someone gets their jolly bucket painted white tonight."

Cade gently kisses my cheek. She'll always be special to me, asking, "And you're okay with it?"

"I fucking guess." I trust Redix. I trust love. "As long as he always comes home to us."

"I CALL BULLSHIT."

The box of popcorn in my grasp tempts me. I want to launch it at the movie screen.

"Quit talkin'," Eily hushes me.

And it's her popcorn, well, a few pieces, that get launched back my way.

I grin at her sitting on the double-wide chaise diagonal to mine. She's curled up with Cade like it's a slumber party in our ship's movie theatre. They're cute, and teasing them is *my* favorite entertainment.

"How many of these damn teenage vampire movies did they make?"

"Five," Cade and Eily answer me together.

"Well,"—I recline beside Redix while Charlie and Daniel cuddle in the chair beside us, sitting behind our wives drooling over vampires and werewolves—"we're on the second movie now, and I'm just sayin'... The real story ain't the girl in love with a man who flat-out told her he *wants* to kill her. Like she ain't the brightest bulb in the box because the real tea is that Edward wants to fuck Jacob. *That's* the saga."

"Nuh-uh." Eily pelts me with popcorn again. "Bella and Edward get married. Then they have a baby who almost kills her because it's half-human, half-vampire."

"Sounds like parenting, alright," Daniel chimes in, "sucking the life right out of you."

He grins my way, and I smile back. *I like him on my side.*

"No, that sounds like breastfeeding," Charlie adds, making Cade laugh.

"Shhiiittt," Redix hisses, twisting his bare leg over mine, "now y'all got me thinking about sucking nipples. Let's watch porn. Forget vampires who sparkle and that tan dude who won't wear a shirt—"

"*Silas*," Daniel quips, and I flip him off, laughing, guilty as fuck.

"Y'all... " Eily pops up. She turns around, kneeling in her seat to inform us, "We have to watch 'til the end. 'Til Bella becomes a vampire, too, and gets to use her powers."

"What powers?" I keep egging her on. "Crying in a chair for months and screaming in her sleep?"

"It's romantic," Eily sighs.

"It's pathetic," I tell her. "Baby girl, if a woman wants a man, get the fuck out of the damn chair, and get him. And if he doesn't want you back, get some damn pride instead. Because the only man worth having makes you scream while you fuck, not *sleep*."

"He *does* make her scream," Eily sasses back. "The first time they fuck, he breaks the bed and wants her so bad he bites a pillow."

"Told you!" I laugh. "A pillow biter. Edward wants Jacob."

"Jacob winds up with their daughter."

"*Ahh, hail no*." Now, I'm throwing popcorn, making Eily giggle. "We got better things to suck around here than ten hours of vampires."

"Now, we're talking," Redix growls.

Leaning my way, he's been inspired, biting and sucking my neck while he grabs my cock under white boardshorts. The urgency in his touch and the heat of his mouth storm my body.

"See," Eily grins, "y'all are just horny for dick. That's why you think every man wants it, too."

But I can't fuss with her right now because I can't fight this—the sudden urge to be with Redix, too.

I know why he's grabbing me so tightly and doing this now. He needs me to be sure. In front of Daniel and everyone, he needs me to know that he's mine too and never leaving me. And I trust him. I trust our love, so I rip my shorts open.

"You want this cock?"

I guide his hand to it.

"Yes." He gets me so hard, so fast, choking my cock with his twisting strokes, just how I love it. Sucking on my neck, he's gonna leave marks on me, too, claiming me, and I fucking crave it.

"You love my hard cock, don't you?"

"Fuck, yes," he growls, biting my neck.

Those damn vampires have him going crazy because Redix leans down and starts biting my nipple next, tonguing and sucking it, too, while his thumb spreads my slick precum over my swollen tip, and I throw my chin up, groaning, "Fuck, I love you so much."

When I open my eyes, while Redix claims my flesh, I turn my gaze and...

Daniel's watching us.

Desire hoods his intense stare, which swells more blood to my dick so quickly I get light-headed. But I don't push Daniel. I don't taunt him. Fuck, yes, I want him, too, as I push Redix's head to my lap.

"Suck my cock," I tell him, "and show us how much you love it."

"Stand up," Redix demands.

He's doing this for me.

He's letting everyone watch while I rise between our chaise and Daniel and Charlie's before he surges beside me. Clamping the back of my neck, Redix pulls us into a rough kiss. His stubble bristles against mine as his hand grabs my cock again, and I groan at everything hard on him. How his lips are soft while his touch is strong, it's so damn aggressive as his tongue owns my mouth too.

"I love it when y'all kiss." I hear Eily sigh. "It's so beautiful and hot."

I growl into Redix's kiss. He does, too. *This is hot. This is beautiful.* Everything about him is as I tug at his white T-shirt. It's getting in the way when I need to feel his skin, his shredded muscles, as he rips it off between our kissing that won't stop.

"*Fuuucckk.*"

I hear Daniel groan, so I grab a breath, glancing away from our kiss to see Charlie stroking him. She's freed his hard cock from his navy bathing suit, and they're both watching us.

It makes Redix fall to his knees, ripping my shorts down before I kick them away. I'm nude, and all eyes are on us.

Cade and Eily are turned around on their chaise, leaning over the plush back of it. By the look on Cade's face, Eily's fingering her. They're doing something; I can't see it because all we want to watch is this...

How Redix's fist clamps down on my base, holding my dick tight while his tongue licks over my swollen crown.

"*Yessss,*" I hiss so loud, watching him, "that's it. Now, put your lips around it. Fuck yes, just like that. Do it. Come on. In your mouth. All the way. Yes, fucking take it. Take it. Damn, take it. My cock loves fucking your throat."

Redix groans, his deep voice vibrating down my shaft to my balls. I swear and, *goddamn,* I throw my chin up, grabbing his head tight, holding him here, wishing a million people could watch him choke on my cock because it feels so damn good.

It's different than when Eily does it. Or Cade. Redix is

bigger. Stronger. Able to take more of my aggression, more of me in his mouth as I start fucking it. I swear this man doesn't have a gag reflex; either that or he loves cock as much as me.

"Fuck yes." I fist his hair and look down at him. "I'm gonna fuck your throat, and I love it. You *love* it." His eyes roll back. "Yeah, you do. Now, take your big dick out and stroke it off to my cock fucking your face."

Ripping the velcro open on his boardshorts, Redix lifts his hefty cock out and starts pumping it with his other hand.

"That's it." I watch him. "Let them see you jerk that dick off, with my cock in your throat, until I come in your mouth and watch you swallow every drop."

We take turns; neither rules the other, top or bottom because we're too alike. We share everything: the same love and trust and desire.

We can make a trip to Home Depot the best day ever. The jokes Redix makes about wood and pipes. It's his easy company I need the most. He understands me. But when we have the chance, when we feel this love, too?

Like me, Redix is so fucking good at it. He twists his head with each descent and takes my length, as much as he can, before twisting back. We know how to make each other's thighs shake.

And when I look up to see that Charlie's stripped her sundress off. That she's nude and straddling Daniel, riding his cock, both turning their heads to watch our show...

"Yes," I grunt.

I get fucking lost. In gazing down at Redix. At the love and lust in his eyes. At his tall, ripped body kneeling before mine. Then I turn, seeking my way, to find Daniel and Charlie, their bodies moving like they belong together, her creamy cum coating his shaft, their cheeks touching, their lips barely kissing while they pant, their eyes watching us, and I groan, knowing they're sharing my pleasure too.

"God, y'all *gotta* fuck," Eily sighs.

Her voice. Her love. I'm pulled to Eily like no other as I find her jade eyes taking us all in, and I fucking love her. So goddamn much. I'm all hers as pieces of me light up, suddenly wanting it too—all that Eily wants me to have, to let myself finally feel it.

I can fuck Redix. I can fuck Daniel. I can fuck Charlie?

"Oh, fuck," I grunt, sliding my eyes from Eily's down to Redix, and he's watching my surrender. He's got me so close, in his mouth and on my edge, I'm thrusting harder toward it.

"Yes." It's always my answer for Redix before I lift my eyes to Daniel's, my lust making me ask him, "You want this, too? You want his cock? You want mine?"

Daniel's grip on Charlie's hips tightens, blanching her tan flesh. His lips shake as he finally confesses, "Yes."

His answer makes Redix groan over my cock, and I ain't fucking jealous; I want it too. I'll share Redix with Daniel and have him, too.

It's what we want, but there's another question in the room, and like he knows what I'm giving him, what I'll do for love, Daniel offers it. Desire strains his voice and corded forearms as he clenches his jaw, growling, daring to ask me.

"You want her sweet pussy like this? With your cock buried deep inside her? With her dripping on your dick and riding you so hard?" he asks, but I can't answer, I can't speak. Charlie's staring right at me. "She's shaking for you. She's clenching tight. She wants it. She's coming for me, for you, too, Silas."

"Yes," Charlie huffs, her body shuddering, her thighs

lifting, trembling over Daniel's hard cock as it falls out of her, her cum squirting over his lap for us to watch.

"Oh fuck."

It escapes my lips, and I lose my mind, my fucking sanity. It's everything I want and fear.

It makes me clutch Redix's head tightly to hang onto him. Because the sight of Charlie's cum, of Daniel's hard cock, the feeling of Redix's hair in my grasp, of the wet heat of his sucking mouth; *I'm coming so fucking hard.* I'm swelling so tight; the white fire at the base of my spine is blinding, but I find Eily's eyes because she sees my truth.

"Yes, fucking take me," I beg all of them.

My thighs shake, my knees too, but Redix grabs my ass, securing me here, so I let go in his grasp. I grunt, hanging onto Eily's gaze as I come in Redix's throat, my cock pulsing. Another grunt grabs my breath, and I can't help it. I look at Charlie next, my eyes hooded with lust, and I grunt again, more cum filling Redix's sucking mouth, shudders ripping down my flesh. My desires thrill and terrify me.

"C'mere," Redix growls, moving so fast. He stands up before his hands grab my shoulders, shoving me to my knees.

"Fucking show him." He aims his hard cock at my quaking lips. "Show Daniel how we love each other. How I'm never letting you go."

Redix fucks my mouth as brutally as I fucked his. The sound of my *glucking* throat, taking his pounding, has me staring up at him; *I love him, too.* And he's watching me, holding me tight before his eyes lift to Daniel's.

"You want us? You wanna fuck like this? Love like this?"

Redix demands and confesses; it's all in his deep voice

as I hear Daniel, that accent so distinct, barely able to grunt, "Yes," before he groans, so deep and loud.

He must be coming inside Charlie: I don't know, but I know Redix is. His shaft swells rigid, his swollen vein thrusting over my bottom lip. *Yes, give it to me.*

"*Fuuucckkk!*" he roars.

I don't know what he's letting go of, either. What desires and fears Redix has, too, but I taste them. I swallow them. I feel them, too.

Tonight will be new for us all.

Daniel

NINE

> **"Y'ALL ARE GONNA LOOK LIKE HOT ASS GLADIATORS AT AN ORGY."**

The sound of Charlie's muttered curses fills our stateroom.

I'm used to it. My wife is so bloody stubborn; it's cute—*most of the time.*

It makes me grin while I sit on our bed, scrolling through pictures our nanny sent this week of our kids. We FaceTime them every morning. Yes, we love them. We miss them. But my wife was right. *She usually is.* We needed this holiday.

It's not that I don't find Charlie to be the sexiest creature alive. She is.

Want to own a man's heart?

When you first meet him, glance at the bulge in his trousers, then look him in the eye and tell him his ego is even bigger. That's what Charlie did. It was love at first ego stomp.

And it was sexy as fuck.

She's owned me ever since. I worship her, I adore her, I love her... and... I love fucking her into submission.

What's even better?

That's exactly what Charlie craves.

She demands my love and respect, and she has it. She demands to be dominated, too, and I'm honored to oblige. She doesn't always want to be the strong one, and that's where I come in. Literally. It makes me come so fucking hard for her because she can take my strength when no one else can.

Yes, my life began when I met Charlie Ravenel.

But fine, I admit it.

I get so bloody busy, so bleeding knackered, I fall asleep every night reading to our kids. When I'm filming, I don't get to see them enough, and at the end of the day, I have to decide who gets my final waking hour.

My wife? Or our kids?

I've been choosing them lately because time is fleeting while they're young. Because I know I'm spending the rest of my years happily married to Charlie, so I've been giving my days to our kids.

"Dammit. Me-n-you are gonna mix!"

But now, my fussing wife has my undivided attention as I follow her threats into the washroom.

"What are you going on about?"

She's standing in front of the vanity, wearing a fluffy white robe and a stroppy face.

"This!"

She points to the round brush tangled in her long hair.

"Why'd you do that?"

"Yes," she stomps her foot, "I did on purpose, Daniel. I figured this brush knotted in my hair would look so sexy tonight at dinner. I was gonna add some lipstick on my teeth and crusty eye snot to complete the look."

The brush sways, dangling from her snarled blonde strands. Her beautiful face twists, all cheesed off. Her gorgeous eyes are so frustrated, while glimpses of her sexy, naked body peek from behind her robe, and I fight my smile.

Fucking hell, I love her but, quick, use the answer that saves your arse every time.

"You look fucking fit."

She rolls her eyes.

"Fit to be tied. Get this thing out of my hair, please."

I approach her like the alligators we find in our yard—something I had to get used to being married to a Southern woman who lives on an island. Charlie could snap any minute, taking me under in a death spiral, and yes, I'd die a million times for her.

"Babe," I inspect the knots, "how'd you manage this?"

She winces as I gently tug at her tresses.

"I'm distracted," she says. "I'm about as confused as a fart in a fan factory."

I laugh, reaching for the scissors in my dopp kit.

"What are you doing?"

"I have to cut it out."

"Like hell." Her eyes plead to mine in the mirror's reflection. "Just pull it out. I can take the pain but not a big chunk out of my hair."

"We'll be here all bloody night."

Tenderly, I pull at a golden strand looped in a mess, and she winces again.

"Fine by me." She sighs, "I don't know if I'm ready for tonight."

Focusing on the puzzle before me, I don't reply until she asks, "Are you?"

Am I ready?

After what I saw today of Redix with Silas? Of all I've felt this week? Bloody hell, since I kissed Redix before a camera and crew. I was sweating then, and I'm sweating now.

I didn't know this desire was inside me. I thought that time, so many years ago, with that bloke in Italy exchanging handjobs was a drunken fluke. I've always been drawn to women, *too many women.*

But men?

I'm man enough to admit when I find one attractive. They're everywhere in my profession. It's our job to look fit.

But I never felt that same surge in my cock, like when I kiss my wife until I kissed Redix.

Fuck, it shocked me.

I was focused on tilting my head left, aiming for his lips, and grabbing his neck hard with my left hand, as our director had instructed, remembering that my line after our first kiss was: "We can't. We fucking can't."

Then Redix was supposed to fist my shirt, keeping me close, delivering his next line before we kissed again: "We *want* to, and we will. Quit denying it. You fucking love me, too."

I knew it'd be an intense scene.

I knew we'd stream to number one and go viral.

I didn't expect we'd be nominated for our performances because while we were in it, while we were kissing, our almost naked bodies coupled like we were fucking under a white sheet, our eyes connecting while I thrusted my hard cock against Redix's barely contained by a modesty pouch, somewhere, deep inside, I knew...

We aren't acting.

This feels real.

It wasn't just in my stiff cock, leaking and about to explode. It was flooding my chest; every warm, friendly feeling I had for Redix was magnified by a thousand. It was so overwhelming I couldn't breathe.

I've never felt that with a woman actor. I hate shooting sex scenes. They're not personal. They're awkward as fuck. It's a forced performance in front of a crew staring at my naked, humping ass.

But not that scene with Redix.

Hiding behind a character, I let myself feel desire, emotions that would normally terrify me. Not the being with a man part. That doesn't scare me. I'm surrounded by all sexualities.

It's the feelings for my friend part.

Redix and I have become close mates. I like him. I respect him. He makes me relax and laugh. We have so much in common. I love working with him. And what?

I want to fuck him, too?

My body roared *YES*, and so did my heart, and that's the other part that scared me because I'm a happily married man. I mean, I have blessings and bliss beyond what I deserve. I'd never betray my wife again. I already hid a big secret from her once. Now, I'd crawl over glass for a thousand kilometers before ever hurting Charlie again, so I tried to figure out a way to tell her, but she saw my truth first. She always does.

Charlie loves me so much, and I live to love her in return until my very last day.

So now what?

Am I ready to be with a man? My friend?

Two friends, two men, actually, because I can't deny how Silas seduces me, too. Bloody hell, he looks like Redix's brother, but that's not how they act together. There's so much passion between them. It's trust, commitment, and respect, too. You can't deny when love surrounds you like an ocean.

And I can't fight it anymore. With my wife's blessing, I'm diving in.

"Yes," I answer her, almost freeing the knot. "I'm ready. Are you?"

I glance up to find her chewing her lip.

"I don't know," she answers. "For you? Yes. Daniel, I don't want you closeting how you feel. It only makes me love you more. But for me? Fucking Silas?" Her dark brows crinkle. "It's different."

"And yet," I grin, "the thought of it gets you off. It surely did this afternoon."

She grins back.

"Maybe that's what it should stay—a thought. Some things are better left to fantasy."

"Could say the same for me and Redix."

"Y'all don't have the same history."

"Maybe that's even more of a reason for you and Silas to try. With your history together, how does it end? Eily wants you to. She says you're like a burning question inside him."

Charlie's voice softens.

"She said that?"

"Yes. She loves him like I love you. We're not stopping you. You, of all people, know you only live once. So finally let yourself feel it, whatever it is between you two."

I used to be threatened by Silas. Fucking hell, he smiles, and ovaries burst. I knew he was in love with Charlie the second I met him. Then she and I survived *real* threats, and something shifted. Like a fucking earthquake, our hearts were rearranged.

It made us stronger. I don't question our love. Our future is together.

I just question my desires. And I'm so bloody stubborn, as well; I want answers tonight. *Am I into men, too?* Well, just two men in particular?

Let's find out.

Freeing her hair, I set the brush down as she turns to me, resting her hands on my chest. I've been sporting unbuttoned linen shirts all week because I love the freedom, this new side of me.

Whoever he is.

"Maybe tonight," she caresses my pecs, and yes, I flex them for her touch, "we just focus on you."

"Tonight is Cade's turn."

"I can convince her to switch with you."

Charlie winks a smile up at me like she can flip the world on its axis to make me happy. *Fuck's sake, I love this woman.*

"It appears you can convince Cade to do a lot of things with you."

"I told you years ago I was drawn to her. That I found her attractive. I mean, who doesn't?"

"So, it's just that easy, yeah? You're good friends and colleagues, *and* you like Cade licking your pussy, too? Evidently, Eily as well?"

"Jeez, Daniel." Smiling, she doesn't deny it. "It's not every woman. It's just them. I feel safe with Cade and Eily. I feel free. We're trapped on a superyacht with sexy people, making me horny as hell, and I'm not overthinking it."

"So what? After this week, it's back to friends and work? Like it never happened?"

"No, it happened. And it may happen again. Who knows? There'll be a mountain of laundry and emails when we get home. Life will take over, so let's just enjoy this now."

Is it a woman thing? They can compartmentalize like a ninja and set their pussies aside while ticking down a To-Do list? Maybe. But I can be the same way. I've been thinking with my bigger head for years now.

"How do you do it?" I smooth her hair where I left a nest. "How do you cross lines and not worry?"

"Maturity and talking. Besides, women didn't make those dumb lines. You men did, and they kinda suck, don't they?"

She rubs my bare chest, the spot where she always sleeps, the part of my body carved out only for her.

"Imagine," her eyes sparkle, "if you said 'fuck the lines' and let yourself fuck who you're curious about?"

A chuckle hits my chest.

"That door swings both ways. You and Silas. Me and Redix. What's the difference?"

"Huh." She wonders aloud, "Is that why they call it 'swinging'?"

Like destiny hears us, a knock on our door answers. When I open it, it's Cade and Redix holding hands as he speaks first.

"Dude, we gotta talk."

I'VE SPENT HOURS SITTING BESIDE REDIX ON SET. We're always talking. Joking. Going on about the best protein powder or way to work your calves. Fuck, we're such blokes sometimes.

But sitting across from him now on the L-shaped sofa in

our cabin—*I've stroked his big dick*—the thought taunts me —*and he's stroked mine.*

And I liked it.

A lot.

I can't shake the memory of him making me come in his fist, of what his warm touch felt like, as Charlie serves us cold ginger ales from the minibar in our room.

Cade's flopped on our bed, her head propped on her hand, watching us, and this is so bloody awkward.

Where the fuck do we start?

"I, uh—" Redix softly punches the throw pillow under his arm. "Dude, I don't know how to say this."

"Just say what you feel," Cade interrupts, and Redix slides a grin her way. "Sorry," she shrugs, "I'll shut up."

Charlie plops down beside her and keeps quiet, too.

Our wives are making us do this.

That whole maturity and talking thing.

But when Redix looks back at me, studying my gaze... he fucking smirks, all cocky like every camera loves, and every fan creams their knickers for.

"So, Daniel," he asks, "how you like them Falcons this season?"

Maturity? No. We're blokes using sports metaphors, and that's safer than feelings.

Mischievously, I grin back.

"Don't know much about American football." But fuck, his lips are so full. *I want to kiss them again. I want to wrap my hand around his big dick again. I have a hard cock in my trousers, craving him.* So fuck it. "But their quarterback is fit, and I really like their tight end."

He tosses his chin up, laughing like he's relieved. "Do you now?"

"Appears so. Who knew I'd be such a fan?"

A smile won't leave his sexy face.

"You ever play the game?"

"Handball. Twice now."

His eyes darken, desire swimming in their blue water. "And did you like it?"

Don't be a knob, Pierce. You're both exposed, so fucking say it with balls like a grown man.

"I liked it with *you*."

"I liked it with you, too."

Our tones change. We drop the act. My pulse starts thundering, feelings pounding through my veins, desire stirring my cock, the truth falling over my lips. "It shocked me that I did."

"Same," he shares.

"At some point, we weren't acting, were we?" I ask him. "Like we're actors, we're mates. I thought it'd just be another scene—"

"But it wasn't." He punches the pillow again. "And it fucked with my head."

"Sorry."

It pops from my mouth. I never want Redix to suffer over me.

"Don't apologize, man. We didn't do anything wrong," he says. "I just wanna know if it was acting or is it real between us."

Suddenly, my fingertips tingle. Every part of me does. Just like in our scene together. This is more than lust. More than me being curious. I care for Redix. He has a smile for everyone, and it bloody makes my heart flutter whenever it's aimed at me.

Do I really need to name this to feel it?

"Me, too." There goes that flutter in my heart again, but

I'm not afraid to tell him, "I need to know because it felt real, and that's never happened to me before."

"Does it scare you?" The rugged lines of his face soften. "The whole being with a man thing? Being bi? If you are? Is that freaking you out?"

"No." The answer feels true, from every cell in my being. "That's not what scares me. It's the being *friends* thing. Even more, the being *married* thing. I'd never betray my wife, but now," I glance at Charlie, who's gently smiling back at me, "I have her blessing."

"And us?" he asks. "Our friendship?"

Dozens of platitudes fire through my mind, but they're not true, not real enough.

"Do you remember that day on set when I ate something from craft services that had me honking in my trailer?"

"Told you not to eat that last Krispy Kreme."

"It wasn't the bloody donut." I laugh. "Whatever it was, it was you, not my PA, who sat on the floor with me while I hugged a porcelain bowl. You put a cold flannel on my neck and made jokes about me making pavement pizza until I felt better."

"Dude, you were white as a fucking sheet. I felt bad for you."

"Exactly. You felt for me, and I felt it, too. I have mates. I have guy friends. But"—now I'm punching the bloody pillow under my arm—"but when you touched me like you cared for me, it felt—"

"It felt like we were more than friends," he finishes my sentence and won't let go of my stare. "I ain't gonna lie, I felt it too."

If a pen dropped a kilometer away, we'd hear it.

Our wives keep their usually opinionated mouths quiet

while I'm so fucked. Because these urges inside, staring into his light blue eyes, tell me...

I want him. I want to kiss him. To feel him. To taste him. To fuck him.

I've let Charlie peg me before. I like the rare occasions when I give up my power. It's liberating. I have too much of it as it is. Usually, she wants me fucking her ass, and I love that more. I hump her like a feral animal, and we get off on me recording it too.

Told you I like fucking her into submission.

But now?

Everything about this week feels like when we left shore, we left reality. There's no plot to our lives, just pussy and pricks. We're floating in luxury and lust.

Maybe Charlie was right... again.

Don't overthink it.

Feel it instead.

"So whatdawedo now, Daniel?"

Redix's deep accent drips like honey from his tongue, just like Charlie's, Silas's, Cade's, and Eily's. I'm drawn to their sultry voices, to their steamy world. It makes my bloody pulse race, my pits sweating, my cock keeps twitching; I'm losing control, *so fuck it.* The metaphor works. It helps me to confess.

"Redix, I want you in my tight end."

His eyelids drop heavy with lust, his lips parting. "*Fuucckk,*" he sighs. "Fuck, are we really?"

Are we?

Or should we be like Charlie with Silas and keep it to fantasy? I have no bloody clue what will happen between them, which makes me remember.

"What about Silas?"

"I have his blessing."

It's too easy. It's too good to be true.

"What if we hurt him? What if we muck it up?"

"I'm never leaving Silas. I'll always be with him, and I'll always love my wife above anyone else." He gestures to Cade. "We work. The four of us belong together."

"What about us?" Charlie asks. "Do we belong with you?"

"Yes," Cade grabs her hand, "whenever you want. No pressure. You decide."

It's been so easy for Charlie, letting her desire for Cade become so natural. Same with Eily. *Typical.* The women are miles ahead of the men. They make it look easy, like it can work. But...

"We go back to set next week." I remind Redix, "For five months, we have to act like closeted VICE cops."

"But *we* don't have to be." Redix shoots his brow up, determined. "I ain't ashamed of who I am, who I love, not anymore."

"I'm not ashamed either. I'm not ashamed that I want you. Bloody hell, I want Silas too."

Instantly, his blue eyes ignite. At what I just said. At the part about me wanting Silas, too.

Redix has talked with Silas about me.

They both want to fuck me.

I can tell by the flame in his hungry eyes. It burns through my flesh, too, fire crawling up my neck, *and holy fuck,* it swells my cock. I'm getting stiff and aching for it, but I warn him.

"As actors, as number one and two on the call sheet, we have careers and crews counting on us. It's not the same as all the bloody men with women, shagging on set. We know it happens. But two leading men, who are married to women, who have kids, being out about our... " *Fuck, fuck, I don't want to admit it.* But I do. "Our *feelings* for each other? That story will be bigger than us. It'll destroy us."

Redix nods.

He plays the bad boy, the rebel who breaks laws and hearts. While I play the one who needs rules and control. It's not too different than real life, but he's also bloody smart.

"I get it," he answers. "I know how people talk about me, about who I love, and I don't give a shit. We're used to it. But y'all," he points to me, then Charlie, "y'all have been through hell with the press. It almost fucking killed Charlie, so I get it. You can be a tourist."

"It's more than that," I answer him. "I respect you, and I care for Silas. Yes, Silas and I have been through hell together, with Charlie's stalker and... "

I can't say it.

I don't know if Redix knows what Silas did for us.

"Dude," Redix grins, and there goes my cock again, my heart too, "it's all good. I know we're more than that. Whatever we are, we ain't gotta name it. We ain't gotta tell everyone. We just gotta... "

He leans forward, grabbing my thigh, and the heat of his hand over my flesh is incendiary. Bloody hell, it makes me grab a breath.

"I just gotta... " His grip tightens on my leg, his hand moving up, oh so close, his jaw clenching, my cock surging against my zipper. "We need to know if... "

He searches my eyes, searching for how to say it, too. He must feel the fire between his hand and my leg; it burns with need. Then he uses that cocky smirk of his, using the same metaphor, too.

"Daniel, I wanna fuck your tight end tonight."

I surrender. This is Redix's sport, and I want to play.

Grabbing him by the back of his neck, I crave his lips, for real this time, but he stops us, pressing his forehead to mine.

"Silas," he says, "we do this with him. Okay?"

My cock suddenly leaks for it. I'm so hard in my trousers, I nod. The lust for what's next is so intense I can't speak.

I wish I could say I wasn't nervous, but my bloody knee bounces under the dining table.

We've feasted on conch fritters and callaloo. Silas's chef has spoiled us with Caribbean dishes, and the whole table is going on about the shrimp mofongo, too, but I can't focus.

I keep glancing at Redix across from me, and he grins back, making my eyes dart left to Silas, waiting for him to catch us. To say something.

But Redix said we have Silas's blessing.

Hell, we must if Redix insists that Silas joins us, and when I imagine that... my palms sweat with anticipation. Charlie must sense my tension. She must feel it, holding my hand.

I don't want gourmet cuisine. I want to fuck. Fuck in ways I never have.

Since we've confessed how we feel, I'm a bloody champagne cork about to pop. The pressure is building; I've been curious about Redix for months. And for years, I've felt a pull to Silas, and now I know what it may be and...

Fuck's sake, hurry it up.

Or break the tension.

I can't bloody stand it.

Like Eily can read the "help us" look Charlie gives her across the table, she saves us with her blurt.

"What's the funniest thing that's happened to y'all during sex?"

Cade laughs. "The time Redix made my vag neon blue."

Charlie snorts her wine. "Blue?"

"Yeah, blue," Cade answers her. "My husband has a food fetish, so for my birthday last year, he thought it'd be a great idea to smear cake all over my pussy so he could dine at the Y."

Redix kisses his fingertips.

"Chef's kiss: pussy cake," he says. "All sweet and creamy and kinky."

"All *blue* icing," Cade declares. "It stained my pussy lips blue for a week. It looked like I'd been fucking a Smurf."

"Well," Eily toasts her glass, "blue *is* my signature color."

Redix chuckles, throwing it back to Cade.

"Well, how about the last time you gave me head while I was driving? I was gonna come and crash, so I pulled over. We parked at a gas station so Cade could finish her slob job, but a cop pulled up. He approached my window, so I rolled it down, but she kept going. She got off on getting caught, so I explained, 'Sorry, Officer, but as you can see, my wife really likes her lipstick on my dipstick.' She gave him a thrill, and I gave him an autograph, all while my raging hard-on and wife wouldn't stop in the face of the law."

Cade scoffs, "Like I'd get arrested by another cop for swabbing my tonsils."

They make us laugh again, and I relax a bit while Charlie feels free to share.

"Gotcha beat. One time, I visited Daniel on set. We were in his trailer, and he was feasting on his husband's supper before the PA started banging on his trailer door like it was an emergency, so Daniel jumped up from my pussy to answer it. But that poor PA got an eyeful, all shocked and worried, asking Daniel if he was okay, that his nose was bleeding because we didn't realize that I—"

"Hell, yeah, man." Silas fist-bumps me. "You earned your red wings too."

"Bloody right," I answer, "many times. But the worst bust was our twins. They were only three when Charlie and I dared to have a loud bonk. I was smacking her ass, making her scream like she loves, thinking they were fast asleep until we heard crying at our bedroom door. Thank fuck, we had locked it because Caroline, our daughter, was crying, "Daddy, quit hurting Mummy.""

"Kids," Cade sighs, "life's precious little boner killers."

"That's why we're waiting," Eily agrees. "I want nothing to come between me and my favorite boner for years."

Silas toasts Eily.

"Unless you break it again."

I wince. Every man does.

"She broke your dick?"

"Yeah, dude," Silas answers me. "My little horny cowgirl here was giving me a reverse ride—"

"Like a rhinestone cowgirl," Eily tips the imaginary cowgirl hat on her head, "with a matching butt plug, too."

"Yeah, well," Silas smiles at her, "bouncing Betty here was going to town on my saddle like a rodeo champ. But then she jumped so high; I fell out, and she came crashing down, bending my dick."

Eily giggles. She's the kind of cute that can get away with murder—even of cocks.

"I didn't *break* it." Eily corrects him, "I just *bruised* it."

"Lucky for you," he says, "I love you and your little pussy so much because I had to sit with frozen peas on my crotch. I was out of commission for a month. That's how my wife became such a Dill Doll collector."

"My favorite," Eily has no shame, "is my rainbow unicorn dildo. It's so twirly and cute!"

"It's fucking huge!" Silas exclaims.

She shrugs. "That too."

Cade taps her crystal water glass with a gold fork.

"Perfect time to begin our game tonight," she announces, "and I've decided to give my turn to Daniel. If he opens a gift with a rainbow horse cock, we'll know the horny culprit."

"Wait," Redix says. "Silas didn't share."

"I took my broke dick to a doctor," he replies. "Ain't that enough?"

"That one's on your wife." Redix grins. "Tell us one you gotta own."

"Dude, I got so many."

"Then tell us your first," Cade suggests.

"Oh, *I* know his first." Charlie jumps in.

"Ah, shit." Silas rolls his eyes. "Not *this* story."

Eily claps, jumping up and down in her chair. "What story?"

"Silas was what? Fifteen?" Charlie sounds too delighted to share. "Poor guy kept popping boners around me. Whenever we went swimming, he was sporting wood. I thought it was cute—"

"It was fucking embarrassing," Silas butts in. "My young dick wouldn't stand down at the sight of your tits. Or ass. Or pussy. Damn, you always wore that little red bikini, and it was torture for my trouser worm."

Eily snorts, "More like an anaconda."

Charlie grins. "So one day, I guess he couldn't take it anymore. We were swimming in my pool, and then he suddenly jumped out. It was weird, so I got worried and followed him to the side of my house. And I found him standing there with his back to me, so I asked what he was doing, and he said, 'Taking a piss.'"

"I was jerking off, and she knew it."

The way Silas looks at Charlie now, with his eyes sparkling, he's not embarrassed. He's amused.

"What was worse at the time but kinda hot now," he confesses, "was when she busted me; I guess I liked her knowing because I came so fucking hard. Man, I shot my yogurt all over her calla lilies."

"Bloody hell." A riddle's been solved as I query, "*That's* why you planted all those calla lilies for her years later, isn't it?"

I confront Silas, not angry. It's kinda kinky... and sweet.

"Yep," Silas pops his lips, "and like hell if I was gonna tell your ass because you'd fucking kill me."

"I always thought it was sweet." Charlie sounds all swoony.

"I think it's so hot." Eily does, too.

"Speaking of hot."

Cade points to the deck above, and we don't need encouragement.

Charlie holds my hand as we wind up the spiral staircase. The others go before us as she stops midway and whispers, "You can always change your mind."

Though my palms are sweating, I'm too sure.

"Even if it's only tonight, I'm doing this."

She kisses me, making me more confident before everyone settles in familiar spots on the sofas while I stare down three black boxes on the credenza. But as my hand reaches for one, Silas wants to know.

"Are we gonna talk about this or just go right to it tonight?"

I turn around, and all eyes are on me.

I perform for cameras. I have multi-million dollar projects resting on my shoulders. I lead franchises and stand in front of thousands of screaming fans. But this? Staring down two men I want to fuck? Three other women, too, especially my fit wife?

"No," I answer, "we go right to it."

Talking would only kill my boner. It'll dull my edge. I've had enough mature chats and fuzzy feelings. I'm a man of action, too.

"Whatever's in this box?" I pick one up. "I'm getting fucked tonight."

Redix licks his lips while Silas reasons.

"If that's the case, let's move this party to an empty stateroom. We need a king-sized bed for that kinda fuck."

Cade asks, "I thought y'all were moving a bed up here?"

"Not in the rain," Silas answers her. "You gotta move big items over the railings outside. You gotta use the crane and—"

"Ugh," Eily playfully backhands Silas's chest, "we don't need an education on ship logistics. This night is for fucking Daniel. I mean," she grins, "for fucking *you*, Daniel."

I laugh, grabbing the large box while Cade grabs a strap-on and Redix grabs bottles of lube and condoms.

Fuck, this is going down, and I'm already hard for it.

We form a single-file line down two flights of spiral stairs, and this seems so odd; it's normal. After three nights of erotic practice and sex games, it's like we're a six-person Olympic team, ready to win the fucking gold together.

The empty stateroom is like the others. Black, white, and ivory everywhere. Except the duvet in this room is ivory, all pristine and crisp.

"Uh-oh." Eily points to it. "We're gonna mess those fancy sheets up."

"I prepped myself."

I got a case of her blurts. It pops out of my mouth.

Clearly, ass is on my mind.

It makes Redix curious, laughing.

"Whatdaya mean, 'prepped yourself'?"

Is that a fire up my neck? In my bloody cheeks? Can the ocean floor please crack open beneath me and swallow me whole?

"I showed him," Charlie saves me, "how to prep for anal sex. You know, anal douche. Usually, it's me who does it, but—"

"*Buuutttt,*" Silas sings, grinning from ear to ear and taking the piss, "you mean Daniel got his butt clean as a whistle for us?"

I roll my eyes. *Fuck it.* No sense in being cheeky now. Pun not intended.

"Yes," I throw it back, feeling proud, "so you can toss my clean salad all night."

Eily jumps up and down, clapping.

"Well then, open your gift box and salad bar. Let's go!"

Like an audience to a bum chain, the wives plop down on the white leather sofa in the room while Redix and Silas remain standing. All watch with heavy anticipation as I open the box I set on the bed.

Once I figure out what all these black leather straps are, laughter bursts up my throat.

It's three sets of men's BDSM harnesses. Three for our chests with silver rings in the center of our pecs and three waistband straps with a center strap, offering a silver cock ring.

Destiny, meet Not-A-Coincidence.

I hold them up and turn to my audience.

"Which naughty little minx wanted to see the men in these tonight?"

"Don't know," my wife beams, "but y'all are gonna look like hot ass gladiators at an orgy, that's for *dayum* sure."

Eyes dart and dance. It's hard to tell who's guilty until Cade asks, "Anything else in the box?"

Is it her? She makes me turn and check, finding three black bottles, too.

"Yes," I answer, "it's flavored massage oil."

"Dude," Redix calls out, "better check if that shit's edible. Cade knows the hard way."

"So this is *her* gift?" I ask.

"Nope," Cade answers, but she's too stunning. With those plump lips, sexy purple eyes, and short brown hair with long bangs cloaking half her stare, Cade's a Bond woman, a seductive spy who could fool anyone.

"All I know," Eily chirps, "is I'm popping pics of y'all. No faces. But I want your bodies all oiled up in black biker leather. It'll be the screensaver on my iPhone." She pauses. "And my laptop. Desktop in my studio, too."

I grin, not opposed to the idea. So do Redix and Silas. Filming anything, especially sex, turns me on.

"Well, go on, Hollywood," Redix mocks, like the moniker doesn't apply to him, too. "Put on your wardrobe and pose for the camera."

"Bollocks," I scoff. "All three of us will be in wardrobe before you can snap pics."

Eily directs, "All three of you better be hard, too."

"Oh," Silas answers, "we *will* be. I've always wanted to be a Leather Daddy."

It's almost comical as I disappear into the adjacent washroom. I can't hesitate. If I do, I may change my mind, not about the sex, but about putting on this get-up. After I strip down, it takes a minute to figure out where all the bleeding straps go. I've sported a semi all night. With a few quick tugs of my tool, I'm stiff and sliding the cock ring down to my base.

When I examine my body in the mirror over the vanity, at my muscles bound in black leather, my hard cock, too, I either look hung or humiliated; tough call. But I won't be the bloke to back down.

Do it, Pierce. You got sod all to lose.

When I swing the door open, jaws drop while Charlie bites her lip, her sapphire eyes growing wide as saucers.

The status is HUNG.

It makes Charlie jump up like she can't control herself. Like she's a bachelorette, and my name is Mike.

She starts snogging with me. "My god, Daddy..." She's not teasing, caressing my biceps, and devouring my neck. "You have to wear this *all* the time."

Her hands shamelessly grope me, rubbing oil over my pecs and abs, my whole body shining, while Redix, then Silas, disappear into the washroom and return, looking equally Dom, I can't lie.

We're like catnip for our wives. They're all over us, rubbing oil on us, stroking our cocks, then snapping pics of our hard bodies together. I keep expecting dollar bills to appear until, finally, Redix stops them.

"Ladies, you'll have to do your own sexobatics for a while. The men promised Daniel a fuck tonight."

Suddenly, that promise makes my nostrils flare, my shoulders drawing up, desire raging through my veins. I can't believe I'm going to do this because... *I will.*

One night, right? Maybe one week? Don't overthink it. Just enjoy it.

I turn from Charlie's lips and reach for Redix on my left.

"Can I kiss him?"

I ask Silas because I'd never hurt him. He loves Redix, and I have to be sure.

"No."

But Silas answers abruptly. It makes my heart clench—*fuck, I've gone too far*—but he smirks. "You're not in charge, Daniel," he says. "We are, and we're kissing *YOU*."

I smirk back.

Cheeky, fit bastard.

Our wives recede. They cuddle on the sofa together, wearing sundresses and eager eyes while I swear my hand shakes—*it's real this time.*

Redix reaches for my neck, and I grab his back, weaving my hand into his hair. There's something so fit about long hair on a man. I'm used to it on my wife. Maybe that's why it turns me on.

But that's where the similarities end.

Because Redix is an all-powerful man, almost as big as me, his lips take mine, and it's different. His big hands are, too, seizing my naked ass and crashing our slick bodies together as his kiss dominates my mouth.

Fuck yes, he's aggressive.

He's as hungry as I am with his carved chest in that harness pressed against mine. *Holy fuck*, our hard cocks rub together as Redix takes my mouth like he's claiming it, rolling his tongue over mine, sucking on it before he bites my bottom lip, making me groan. It makes the sex scene we shot together feel like a cartoon.

Because this isn't an act.

It's in my body, my heart, desire cracking my skin open. It's lightning storming my every nerve. It's warm oil, soothing my mind. Knowing. Realizing. Feeling. *This is what I crave.* This is real, raw, and between us, until Redix grabs my hair and turns my head, and Silas takes control of my mouth.

Fucking hell, Silas is kissing me.

He's grabbing my neck so hard, too, and he's so fucking good at this, tangling his tongue with mine as I growl against his plush, dominating lips.

Was this always between us? Did I always want Silas? Like he's always wanted Charlie?

I can't answer because I'm overwhelmed. *Two men. Two mouths. Two cocks rubbing against mine. Holy fuck,* this cock ring strangles my swollen dick, making it feel like I can last all night because I want to. I didn't know it'd be so powerful, that it'd feel like this as they urge me back against the bed.

Redix nips my lip again before he growls, "Lie down for my fuck."

I fall back on the mattress, moving to its center. Redix stands at the edge of the bed, and Silas stands beside him.

Fuck me; I'm randy as hell, watching Redix slowly stroke his rigid shaft as he asks, "You sure you want this cock?"

"Yes."

I answer, feeling it so strongly, feeling myself grin because his cock is enormous. So is Silas's. I don't know if I can take them, but like fucking hell if I won't enjoy trying.

"Daniel, say exactly what you want," Redix insists.

"This ain't football. This is real. We can be whatever by day, but tonight I wanna fuck your ass so hard, but I won't make you. You gotta tell me the whole time that you want it."

Silas touches Redix's backside, and I've noticed it; the unusual scar Redix has there. I've never asked. It's not my place. But it must be the reason why he has to be sure.

Like Silas knows Redix's secret, he kisses him while I can't help it; my eyes dart to see my wife. Charlie's taken her dress off. All three women have. They're sitting nude, side by side, playing with their pussies at our show, and *hell, yes.*

We ALL want this.

All I feel coursing through my muscles is consent and permission and freedom and lust. Whatever they want to do to me, there's something liberating about not being the dominant one tonight.

Silas's lips lift from Redix's kiss as they look at me, waiting for my answer, so I spread my legs. The act and the words feel so foreign and right.

"Fuck my ass," I tell Redix. "I want you to."

"Roll over," Silas commands. "We gotta get your ass ready because his big dick ain't no joke."

I roll over, presenting my ass to them. I don't care. I want this. I want my wife to watch this, so I put my eyes on her.

She's fingering her pussy, watching me, then watching Silas as he strolls to the nightstand with his big dick bouncing hard in a cock ring. He examines the bottles from the gift box.

"What flavor you want?" he asks Redix. "Banana, pineapple, or mango?"

"Banana."

I can hear the coy smile in Redix's voice as Silas returns.

"Up on your knees." I love Redix's commands. "Give us that ass."

I comply, suddenly feeling manly hands on my cheeks, spreading me open as cool liquid drizzles over my asshole... and then... an aching, dripping nothing. It's a thrilling, vulnerable exposure to their gaze, to the cool air, to everyone watching, making me wait.... before... finally, a warm, piercing tongue rings my puckered hole.

"Fucking hell," I grunt.

I can't see who it is; I just feel tongues and fingers spearing me, my eyes rolling back. I feel rough hands rubbing my ass cheeks, spreading me as open as possible. My dick hangs so heavy and hard, but I'm suspended, forever on the edge of coming with a ring choking my cock. I'm not used to this, and I love it.

"That's it. Get ready to take it. To fucking love it."

That's Silas. That's his one, *oh, hell yes,* then slowly... two, then... *oh goddamn...* three fingers fucking me, pumping in and out and stretching my ass open. He uses so much lube it doesn't even burn. *He knows what he's doing.* It feels so fucking good.

"You ready for a big dick in your ass, Daniel?"

Silas likes asking me. He craves this role reversal. It's like he's been second all these years to me, and now he's first. He sounds in charge, and I trust him more than most can ever know.

"Yes," I mutter into the duvet because desire for this drips from my cock.

"On your back." It's Redix. "You're going to watch my eyes while I fuck your tight end."

Flipping over, I see them standing at the foot of the bed. Fuck's sake, their bodies in those harnesses; they do look like powerful gladiators getting ready to dominate me, to initiate me into some dark, secret manly rituals, and it makes my cock drip for more.

Fear hasn't set in. Only desire. Only trust. I'm all in, asking Silas. No. *I need to be sure he's alright with this.*

"You're going to let your man fuck me?"

"Yes," Silas smirks. "And you'll love his dick in your ass as much as I do."

"Then let me suck you off," I tell him, "to thank you."

He didn't see that coming. Bloody hell, neither did I. I don't know this man I'm becoming, the one with desire torching through my veins, wanting so much cock, but I'm right here and raging hard for it.

Redix kneels between my legs while Silas walks around and kneels by my head. He's facing our wives so they can watch it all. But when Redix picks up a condom, he pauses.

"Wait." He asks, "We've all been monogamous, right? I mean," he gestures to the room, "it's just been us?"

"Yes," I answer, never guessing a week ago when I could barely find time to have sex with my beautiful wife, that I'd find myself with my knees falling open for my costar's bare cock too.

Fuck me; I love that woman.

I love that she made us take this holiday.

That she set me free.

"Good," Redix says, tossing the condom aside. Grinning at me, he's not evil; he's the man I trust. The one I'm not afraid to want, not anymore, glossing his long, thick shaft in lube.

"We're going bareback, Daniel. Alright?" It's all Redix, half consent and half command. "I'm gonna feel my cock come in your ass."

"Yes," I confess, "I want you to."

Silas kneels by my head, leisurely stroking off while we watch Redix wedge his tip into place.

Then suddenly, I feel him pushing in, and I tense up, afraid of the pain. And like this is more than sex between us. Like Redix and I aren't some random raw-dog hook-up; we care for each other. He makes me laugh. He makes me trust. He makes me want to explore this new man I'm becoming, this new desire pounding in my heart. This is my first time doing this, and he doesn't abuse it.

He does it like it should be done.

"Guide me," he tells me. "I'll go slow until you say you want more. Or you can tell me to stop. It's okay."

"Don't stop." I feel him pushing in. "Don't stop. Just go slow."

And he does. Redix goes so slow that it makes me sweat. It makes me pant. I exhale, making my body relax, stretching to receive him, and the pressure is immense. It's incredible, burning to the tips of my ears, shoving the breath from my lungs, and I want more. I lock to his penetrating eyes, watching Redix as he watches himself claim me, his lips parted like he's as enraptured as I am. Like he doesn't believe it either, so I demand, "Yes, more. Fuck my ass, Redix."

He bottoms out inside me, and stars shoot across my vision, sensations ripping across my flesh. My legs start shaking, so he grabs them, holding them open and steady.

I thought my cock would go soft to this, but it doesn't. Redix can see it, reaching to stroke my stiff shaft, too, and *oh fuck, it's too good.*

"You like this, don't you, Daniel?" He lifts his gaze from the act to be sure. "You like my cock in your tight, virgin ass. You're so hard for it."

His abs flex; he's holding back, but I won't.

"Yes," I keep huffing. "Yes, go on. Fuck me. Take my ass. Give me all that cock."

"Then suck my man's cock, too."

Redix nods toward Silas, and I turn my head.

It's like gazing up at the sun. Silas shines over me, and I've never seen him in this golden light, and now I know why everyone wants him—*even my wife.*

"You wanna wrap your lips around my cock, Daniel?" Silas grins, hovering his fat tip over my mouth as if he loves this and can't believe it either. "You wanna put my hard cock in your mouth while my man fucks your ass?"

Redix is *his* man. And he's Redix's.

I can feel it between them, and I don't know my future with them, where I'll fit in, and I don't need to. I want this night; I'll sort the rest later.

So I don't answer Silas. I just crane my neck, wrapping my fist around his wide base, and I do what I want, what I desire. I let two men inside me. I let them take me, fucking my mouth and fucking my ass. I've never been here before, and I groan; *I fucking love it.*

"God." I hear Charlie sigh. "God, he's so hard for y'all; he's loving it."

The praise in her voice. How I must look to her with Silas's hard cock thrusting into my cheek, with Redix's massive dick stirring in my ass, grinding deep because he doesn't pull out. My dick surges in a cock ring, hard and straining with pleasure.

Fuck, I'm going to come soon and forever.

"C'mere," Redix says, and to whom, I don't know at first. "C'mere and fuck your husband's cock while I fuck his ass."

I groan from depths I've never known with Silas in my mouth, my mind blitzing for what's next. Feeling the mattress sink on my right. Feeling my wife's hands. I'd know her touch among millions; it's the only one I want to die with.

I plop my mouth off Silas's cock, my spit trailing from his tip to my lips. It's shameless, and I only crave more. More of watching my gorgeous wife straddle me as Redix moves my legs so she can lean forward and fit between us. So she can glide my aching cock through her slick pussy lips before she slowly sinks her tight, wet heat around it.

"HOLY FUCK!"

I roar, and the whole boat crew, the whole world, can hear me. I go blind, losing my mind, and finding a new one, loving a dick in my ass and my cock in a pussy.

"Fuck! Fuck! Fuck!" I swear it. "This feels so *fucking* good. FUCK!"

If this is death, don't be afraid.

Because it's freedom, too. It's liberation from every pain because all I feel is pleasure, is pure white light, white heat flaming through my nerves, across my heart, through my flesh and cock and ass, to the truth—*we're born to fuck and love and die. It's all worth it.*

"You like this, Daniel?" Charlie leans forward, grabbing my shoulders while she rides my cock so slowly. "You like fucking my wet pussy while Redix fucks your ass?"

"Holy fuck." I can't stop saying it, feeling it. "Holy fuck, yes, babe," I huff, grabbing her hips, finding my vision and staring up at her. "Don't stop."

"I'm gonna fuck with your wife's ass, too." I hear Redix. "I'm gonna play with her while I fuck you until she does that thing, squirting all over your hard dick."

Smack.

It cracks the air.

It must be Redix spanking Charlie's bum. Only when

he fucks is he like this, so Dom, which is just like me and right where I belong.

"Ride him," he commands her. "Fuck his big dick until you come on it. I'm gonna finger your ass like a good little whore until you do."

"Oh god," Charlie gasps, staring into my eyes, with me inside her. She's right here with me, sharing this desire, surrendering to it, too. It only ignites my lust more as she tells another man, "Oh my god, yes. Use two fingers. Yes, Redix. Make me a whore. Fuck my ass harder."

"Suck my cock."

I hear Silas growl, and I turn my head, taking his fat tip again, swirling my tongue over his crown. I close my eyes and groan, sucking him how I like, tasting his salt and making him moan like I am.

"God." I hear Charlie sigh. "God, Daniel, you look so hot with Silas's big dick in your mouth."

I groan again, feeling the stretch of it, what she sees, and sensing what she can't, which is Redix stirring harder into my ass. There's no pain, only blinding pleasure. There's only our bodies losing time, sweating, and moaning for more.

"You want my big dick too, don't you, Charlie?" Silas's voice growls wild with lust. "I can see your little mouth drooling for it."

I open my eyes, lifting my mouth off his shaft to witness this.

How Charlie's lips are parted. How they're so close to Silas's hard cock hovering between our mouths. How Silas is looking down at her and how she's staring up at him. The desire between them is excruciating.

What do they want?

I don't know, but I want Charlie to let go as I have. We should share this, so I grab her neck.

"Suck his cock. Be my naughty little wife and suck Silas's cock with me."

For a moment, she pauses as Silas gazes down at her. His eyes are bent heavy with lust, with a silent word on his parted lips. It's like he's in pain; he can't take it anymore... *please*... his whole body is begging for her.

So she anchors her stare to his. I watch her eyes answer his plea as she slowly parts her lips for Silas's cock.

"Oh fuck!" he shouts, watching as she slowly glides his cock into her mouth, taking him as much as she can until he hits the back of her throat, making her gently gag and lift away.

"How you like my calla lilies now?"

She plays with him like they always do, smiling up at him with spit drooling from her lips to his swollen tip.

But Silas isn't smiling.

He isn't playing.

He fists her blonde strands, his hazel eyes narrowing.

"Suck me again, Charlie," he demands. "Fucking suck my goddamn cock right now."

His length is so swollen, his veins straining. It's like he'll come in a second because he's wanted her forever. With her nipples pearling hard before my eyes, she's suddenly not playing either.

She wants him, too.

I squeeze her neck; that's my permission as Charlie does it to him again, right in front of my face. Her lips plunge down Silas's rigid cock, gagging, his mass *glucking* in her throat. I can feel her shameless, ardent efforts in my grasp, watching Silas's dick fuck her beautiful face over and over, dragging spit over her lips.

"Fuck, Charlie, fuck. Fuck!" Silas cries out. "Fuck, I'm coming."

He comes so hard in Charlie's mouth, his thighs shaking, his lips too, watching the sight. He can only grunt while he spurts over her tongue and open mouth, wanting more.

"Yes," I taunt her. I taunt them, "Yes, my naughty wife, taste Silas's cum."

I make him grunt again as more spurts from his dick, filling her mouth, and she shakes. It makes me shake, too, feeling Redix's vigor, his cock fucking my ass harder.

With my free hand, I grab Charlie's hair, too. Silas hasn't let go of her, and I won't either.

Yes, we got her right here.

"Now, fucking swallow," I demand. "You'll look so beautiful swallowing Silas's cum. It'll make you come, too."

I squeeze her throat as she obeys, and I know her body. I live for it. I know her sounds when she's panting like that, her thighs trembling against my torso, so I command her, watching her eyes roll back.

"Now, fucking make that cunt squirt on my cock while you taste Silas's cum dripping down your throat. You fucking love it, don't you, babe? Such a naughty girl while Redix pounds your tight ass too. Come on. That's it. Show us. Come for us, my wet whore."

Charlie bucks in my grasp, screaming, her eyes frantically searching mine, then Silas's, as we grab her hair so tight. Her quaking thighs lift, but they're not strong enough through her orgasm to move, so I help her. I let go of her neck and hair, and lift her hips while, *yes,* she shakes, showering my dick with her watery cum.

"Fuck!" she screams again, but her body flips off mine.

At first, I don't know what's happening; then I realize it's

Cade. She's grabbing Charlie, resting her on her back beside me as Cade kneels beside Redix. Spreading Charlie's thighs, Cade starts fucking my wife with a strap-on, and I groan.

"Me, too."

I hear Eily's Tinkerbell voice, but her actions are bold. She straddles Charlie's face, presenting her pussy to her mouth while Eily turns, facing Cade. She leans forward and licks Charlie's clit while Cade fucks her pussy and...

"Holy fuck!"

I shout at the sight, at the sensations, entering another world. Their world. The best kind. The one of forbidden sex for an eternity while the room spins, but I feel a strangling, perfect choke of my cock, holding me here, and I look to see it's Silas.

He's jerking me off while Redix's fuck becomes brutal, his muscles straining along his neck, his voice.

"Look at y'all," Redix says, every emotion filling his eyes, staring down at me and Charlie. "Look at my wife fucking your wife. Look at me fucking your ass. Are you with us now, Daniel?"

"Yes," I huff, hearing Charlie's moan, muffled by Eily's pussy on her face.

Redix starts pounding my ass. "Suck his cock. Finish him off. Make sure he fucking loves it and comes back for more."

He's commanding Silas, who's eager to comply.

And when Silas's mouth takes my cock while Redix's cock claims my ass, "Fuck," I roar, searching for Charlie, grabbing her arm beside me, needing her, making sure this is real and not the most erotic dream.

She moans, grabbing me back, and *yes, we're here, we're together forever, so I let go.*

"*Dammnn*," Silas growls, licking my shaft and praising, "your dick tastes like Charlie's cum; it's so fucking good."

It ignites his hunger, his vigorous suck of my cock, tasting my wife on it, and I slip into a blinding light, dropping into an orgasm like my body's never known. My ass clenches around Redix's dick, feeling my cock throb, pulsing and bursting into Silas's mouth. I come so hard and have no control. No breath. No voice. Only pleasure shaking my bones as I can barely focus, watching Redix growl. His eyes lock to mine, and I feel his fat cock jump in my ass—*he's coming inside me*—and I grunt, shaking, coming even more.

Yes, I love this.

Yes, we're coming back for more.

Yes, we're with them.

Now and forever.

Redix

TEN

DAMN, THE PLOT KEEPS THICKENING, AND SO DOES MY COCK.

My dick is sore, and I love it.

Proudly, I grab a couple of frozen gel packs from the small freezer hidden in this buffet furniture thing in Silas's dining room.

Man, this ship is sick. It's got everything you didn't know you wanted and more.

What I love about Silas? Of a million things? He didn't even feel guilty about buying it because it wasn't for him. It was for us, and what can I say?

We like sharing.

Yeah, Silas is the kinda man who wears flip-flops until they blow out. Or the same jeans for years, loving the rips he earns like memories. He only spends his billions on others, like the island he bought for Eily, the indigo farm he had planted for her, and the impressive Lowcountry home he built for her, too.

I love visiting them.

Their porch with those rocking chairs and that view from their island? It's magnificent. We spend some evenings watching the sunset over the water, talking about everything and nothing. All while my daughter climbs from my lap to Cade's, to Eily's, then to Silas's. She calls them by their names, but they're so much more.

They keep me grounded. They keep me sane.

Fame can go to your head if you let it. But I don't. I do my job; I love that part. I take the selfies with fans; I don't mind it. I work long hours, and it's not a sacrifice.

Just as long as I have my weekends.

Usually, it's me, Cade, and our daughter, Glory. I live for my weekends, to wake up and make them pancakes. But some weekends, we spend with Silas and Eily. My favorite part is watching them take over, like practice parents. Silas loves making Glory laugh, usually by blowing bubbles in his milk. And Eily always looks happy finger-painting with her, even when it winds up everywhere.

They'll make great parents one day.

But not yet.

Me and Cade need time like this, too. We don't get enough of it. And since I've danced with death twice, I know time is all that matters.

Best spend it with the ones you love.

So this week is for adults only, and I ain't got an ounce of guilt about it.

Every day, I live to treasure Cade. At home, I take care of her like she saved my ass so many times for so many years. Taking a week off to take care of her in a kinky way on Silas's fancy ship?

Well... you had me at an orgy.

"Hey, dude,"—I tap Daniel's shoulder with the extra gel pack I grabbed for him—"need this for your tight end?"

Goddamn, I had to hold back with Daniel last night.

I got my answer, alright.

It's not an act.

It's real.

Hell, yes, I want to fuck him. Hell, yes, I feel something for him, too.

And no, it's not how I love Silas.

Silas is the first man I loved. The first one since... well.... he taught me to trust men again. He's the one who made me feel safe. He's the one who got me and Cade back together. No man can ever replace Silas.

But there's something about Daniel, too.

Yeah, he's a global panty-melter, stirring millions of dicks too.

But I admire him. All the shit he's survived with Charlie. The kind of father and husband he is. The kind of man he is on set; how he respects everyone on the crew.

We have so much in common.

Daniel's an alpha, a gent, and a top man. He's such a Daddy. *But he wasn't last night.*

That's another thing that's got me hooked: how he trusts me, too. I've never been a man's first. I wasn't Silas's, and that's okay. More than sex connects us forever.

But for Daniel to share that with me? To not be afraid of his feelings? To let go and just let us take him like that?

I'll never forget the sight of his perfect, hulking muscles bound in black leather straps. The sight of his hard body and piercing eyes softening to let me inside. His dick was dripping for me. Hell, yes, we made it kinky, too, but there were feelings as well. There's no denying it.

Damn, I guess we got us a bromance.

Well, one with fucking and sucking, too. It's not as

strong as what I share with Silas, but it's here, and I'm damn lucky to have both of them.

"Cheers, but I'm fine," Daniel answers me, sipping from his mug, but I see his satisfied smirk. *Sexy, English motherfucker*; he even makes drinking coffee hotter than hot.

"You sure?"

I plop down beside him at the dining table, shamelessly resting the ice packs over my crotch covered by my black boardshorts.

His eyes follow my gesture.

"You ain't gotta be shy or tough it out," I tell him. "Ass fucking and aftercare are legit. It ain't like I don't know. Sometimes, Silas plows my backyard so hard; I wince when I sit the next day."

He nods, appreciating my wisdom, his half-grin sexy as fuck before he shares.

"Charlie gave me ibuprofen, and we took an Epsom bath together this morning, and you, uh.... I could tell you took it easy on me last night, and thank you. I feel *very* fine. Guess you could say I feel crackin' today."

I laugh and, fuck, his English accent. I can listen to him all day.

On set, Daniel stays in his American accent. I almost forget it's not real. He's even picking up our Southern drawl, which helps his character. Our show is set in Atlanta. Cade and I rent a house there when we're filming on location, and now I'm glad it's down the street from the one Daniel and Charlie are renting, too.

Who knows what we'll do now on weekends off? Go back to our home on Hilton Head Island together? Or Charlie's house on Daufuskie? Or Silas's island—Indigo Island, he's named it for Eily.

I'm curious what's next for the six of us, but I'm not

pushing it. I could live satisfied with what we've done so far. But it makes me wonder.

"You got any questions?" I ask him. "Or regrets?"

"No regrets, no. I just wonder... "

His deep voice trails off, along with his thoughts. We watch our wives and Eily chat over breakfast at the other end of the long table while Silas talks to the bridge captain.

"Dude," I lower my voice, "you can ask me anything. We're kinda there now. Like no holds barred... or holes."

I make him laugh and comfortable enough to ask me questions.

"How do you do it? How do you balance being attracted to women and men too?"

"Is your brain trying to catch up with your dick?"

"Yes," he sips his coffee, "and my heart. I don't want to feel guilty about it."

"Do you?"

"No," he answers, "as long as no one gets hurt."

"Well, I can't answer for anyone but me. Guess that's lesson number one. We're all different. But for me, there's no balance. It ain't even close to fifty-fifty. Cade's my priority; our marriage and family come first. Silas says it's the same for him and Eily, and that's how we work. I got a hunch it'll be the same for you and Charlie. Y'all got a good thing, too. She's your priority. What the six of us do after this week; it's just ribbons and bows."

Daniel grins, turning his stare my way.

"So you'll be fine if we never, uh... "

His voice falters, and it's kinda cute. *Is he getting shy with me now?*

"Fuck?" I help him.

"Yes, fuck. You'll be fine if we never fuck again?"

"Yeah."

And I mean it. Only a fool has love like I do and dares to demand more. I'm very content... until Daniel cocks his dark eyebrow, lowering his nose, using that wolf look that made him famous.

"And what if I want to fuck *you* next?"

"Well, now... " I give him my famous smirk right back. Like I don't know how to throw my cocky around too. "That'd be even finer."

"What about Silas? Would he be okay with it?"

"Clearly, he's a hard supporter of whatever we three do together."

But the mention of Silas makes me wonder again. I care about Daniel and Charlie, too, so I gotta ask.

"What about Silas with Charlie? Will you be okay if he fucks *her*?"

Circling his fingertip over the rim of his mug, he pauses, and I get it. I caught all kinds of feelings when Cade and I broke up for a while, and she was with Silas. Funny, none of them were jealousy, and it doesn't look like Daniel feels that either.

"Yes, it's alright with me. I know Charlie and I are strong," he answers. "And we love Silas. It feels right if that's what she wants."

"Does she?"

He chuckles. "She doesn't know yet, and I value my twig and berries too much to tell my wife what to do."

"Oh," I start laughing, "you married one of those too?"

"Hey, y'all." Silas bounds down the spiral steps, joining us late for breakfast. "We gotta head into Nassau this morning."

"Where are we now?"

Eily's curious, peeling a croissant and dropping flaky

layers into her mouth while I look around and see a turquoise paradise outside the open glass doors.

"I wanted to take y'all to Eleuthera for New Year's," Silas answers, grabbing a strawberry from Eily's plate, "but we gotta turn back real quick."

"What's going on?" I ask him.

He rolls his eyes, chewing his fruit.

"We're out of toilet paper," he answers, and Cade starts howling.

"One hundred and sixty-seven million dollars for this ship, and you're out of *toilet paper?*"

I can't believe it either, laughing too.

"Who's been filling up the shitter with all that paper?"

"A crew of two dozen," Silas answers me. "Us and all our fucking too, I guess. We stocked up, but what can I say? We gotta make a supply run."

I huff, "Someone's got the runs, alright. Go check the Captain's guilty log."

"Talk about a shitty situation."

Daniel throws it out, and I start laughing harder. We all do.

"We can make a day of it." Silas ignores our jokes. "We're docking in Hurricane Hole, and there's a bunch of shit to do there."

"Sounds like shit's been accomplished already." Daniel keeps going.

"Yeah," Charlie jokes, "it sounds kinda *crappy* to me."

And we can do this all day, folks. Toilet humor is number two on my list of skills.

"I don't know," I add. "After last night, I'm feeling kinda *wiped* out."

Cade grins, sitting across from me. "You do look *flushed.*"

Dammit, I love my wife.

Eily shrugs, giggling. "Y'all. Come on. We gotta do the doodie together."

"Ah, hail no." Silas pops his neck. "You're gonna play this shit all day?"

He hears it; his dumbass slip... *again.*

Charlie smirks. "You're making this too easy. Like taking the Browns to the Super Bowl."

"Silas, quit being a party pooper," Cade chirps, "even though it runs in your jeans."

Eily snorts. "Like diarrhea."

"Hang on, hang on." I hold up three fingers. "I got a turd one." And Silas growls. "Fine, I was gonna tell you another shitty joke, but it'll be corny."

"Yeah," Daniel nods, "and it'll stink."

Silas snarls, "Y'all can go kiss my ass," but his eyes laugh.

"Hell, no. Not while we're outta toilet paper." I raise my dick-freezing gel pack to him. "But I'll kiss your ass for New Year's, I poopie... I mean... I prick promise."

And we're off to Nassau.

Once we're on dry land, Silas tosses the keys to the six-seater buggy he's rented to Daniel.

"Here, dude," he says, jumping into the passenger seat, "I can't drive on the wrong side of the road."

"It's not the wrong side." Daniel sits beside him while we pile into our seats. "It's the left side."

Silas buckles in. "Exactly, it ain't *right.*"

"Hey, Little Shit." Charlie's nickname for Silas fits like a glove today. She points to her back seat with a grin. "Is this stool taken?"

"Charlie Girl," he points right back at her, "keep joking, and I'll tell 'em about the time you ate a whole bag of corn chips and couldn't shit for days. And when you finally did—"

"Yeah, yeah, yeah," she mouths back, "I gave birth to a turd baby and showed it to you."

Cade shakes her head, laughing.

"Damn, you two. What haven't y'all done together?"

Whoops, we know the answer, but no one's saying it. Eyes dart, and lips zip. Thankfully, Eily and her mouth can always be trusted to pop off at any second, filling the silence.

"I wish we could get a day pass to the Atlantis water park."

"Sorry, fun size," I answer her. "That's the cost of fame. We'd get mobbed. Besides, going down a giant waterslide would only be a giant enema after the fucking we did last night. Talk about a shart attack."

Daniel shakes his head, laughing at our candor.

"See how open we are?" I ask him.

Cade snorts, "In every way."

"Alright, kings of comedy, we got four hours to kill." Silas turns our way. "Ann, my bosun is from here, and she said we should check out the Bat Cave."

Eily groans, "Why are you determined to torture me with little creatures that bite?"

"Baby girl," he pats her knee, "all creatures bite."

"No, they don't. Some suck."

I flip Eily's long ponytail. "Those are my favorite kind."

"Yeah, well," she swats my hand away, "bats bite *and* suck your blood like flying vampires. It's gross."

Daniel turns on the engine. It revs to life as Silas teases her.

"It won't be gross if we find Bella there, getting bit by Edward while Jacob sucks *him*."

Eily kicks his seat, sassing back.

"I'd rather find Batman sucking Superman."

She's sorta joking, but I swear the reference makes Daniel blush. I thought I had to deal with celebrity bullshit with my movies, particularly my male-stripper ones, but Daniel's got me beat superhero style—*poor bastard.*

But once we arrive, I don't get the big fuss about the place while Cade reads aloud from some page she pulled up on her phone.

"It says a Bond movie was filmed here."

And it gets worse for Daniel, rolling his eyes like he can't escape his fame while Eily holds her nose.

"It smells in here."

Silas wraps around her, teasing her more.

"That's bat poop. Told you—your vampires stink."

"You know..."—Eily gazes up at him, batting her lashes, craning her neck for his lips while she swoons—"I love you like diarrhea; I can't hold it in."

He chuckles through their kiss. "And I love your jokes. They're cute and corny, just like your poop."

Then he snatches her up so fast, making her squeal as she wraps her little lop-sided legs around his waist. *And damn, they're cute.* I don't think they'll ever stop kissing and teasing each other, which makes Silas so damn happy. He's at his best with Eily. And with Cade, he's so relaxed.

But with Charlie?

That's a situation I can't clock.

Daniel's given them his blessing, permission, whatever

the fuck. Eily has, too. Hell, she keeps taunting Silas with Charlie's pussy every chance she gets.

She sees what we all do; there's something between them—Charlie and Silas.

It's way more than friendship, and yeah, they're messing around this week, like playing with fire and loving the burn.

Because damn, when Silas licked Charlie's pearl, and she squirted an ocean in his mouth, it was so fucking hot I almost came too. But I wanted to give that honor to Daniel, and hell, yes, to finally feel his big hand wrap around my cock; it was intense. I swear his touch gave me butterflies when I climaxed.

We're on a voyage, alright.

All six of us are sharing a superyacht and a sea of feelings.

Because, last night, I've never seen Silas come so fast. It's like the second Charlie plunged her lips down his dick, he blew in her mouth. Guess after twenty years of fantasizing about her, his joy juice was finally set free.

Don't get me wrong; Silas loves Eily. More than anyone else. He won't make it if he loses her. He was ready to give everything up to get her back. His life. His money. Me and Cade, too. But Eily wanted to join us, not split us apart.

I don't question his love for her because Eily's amazing. She makes Cade happy, too. They're so close, and yeah, I love our little horny Tinkerbell, too.

Damn, we won the lottery when our wives married our dumb asses.

I know I told Silas to do it, to fuck Charlie. The sexual tension between them takes a seat at the dining table.

But should they actually fuck?

Would it ruin their friendship?

They don't act like brother and sister, and they don't act

like Charlie does with Daniel either. That woman is a badass. The whole world knows some of what she did. I've noticed the bullet scars on her gorgeous body. They only make her more breathtaking.

It's obvious why my wife's been creaming her panties for Charlie for years.

But it's like Daniel's the only man who can take Charlie on. Like I'm big and Dom, too. I get off on it. So does Silas. But Daniel's a Sir, a Master, and a Daddy Dom rolled into one giant creamsicle.

But underneath all the kinky fun the six of us can have and the intense sex, too, there are friendships.

Truth is, I value those more.

I know, deep down, we all do.

"Hey," Cade wraps around my waist, "what gutter is your mind playing in?"

"Wondering about Silas and Charlie," I mutter so no one else can hear.

Charlie and Daniel hold hands, inspecting the little black rats hanging from the ceiling. Silas has Eily standing beneath the dark cloud, too, but she won't look. She's buried her face in his neck, begging him not to bring the bats down on them.

"What are you wondering?"

Cade pulls my stare back to her, and when I look at this beautiful woman, who's all mine? It's like my porch light's on, but no one's home because I lose my mind for Cade. Air and water? You can have them, too. I only need Cade to live, our daughter, too.

"I wonder," I whisper like a gossipy teen, "if they should fuck?" Cade blinks, her hot lips frozen. "Got an opinion on that?"

"It's none of my business," she answers, and I laugh.

"*Puh-lease.* You're the CEO. The Walmart of opinions. They fall like prices from your sexy lips."

Again, she doesn't say anything, so I gaze into her violet eyes, waiting for gravity to work.

"Okay, fine," she huffs, glancing at them, making sure we're not overheard. "Yeah, I think they should. The tension's so hot it's painful between them. What do you think?"

"I'm not sure. At first, I told him to do it. To fuck them both, but—"

"But what?"

"I can see me and Silas with Daniel. Hell, last night I thought Daniel was gonna pop blood vessels; he came so hard with us."

"Well, then, why can't Silas fuck Charlie too? It only seems fair."

"It ain't about fair. It's about friendship. Men and women can just be friends, you know. I have women friends. Men friends, too. And yeah, some are hot as hell, but that's not our vibe. We don't always want to fuck."

"Yeah, I got 'just friends' too. But Charlie and Silas are more." She reaches, gently brushing hair off my face. "They vibe way different. They got itchy pants for each other."

"Don't mean they should scratch it."

"Scratch what?"

Fuck, busted.

"Nothing," I answer Silas, who appears with Eily beside us.

Twisting his face, he silently calls "bullshit."

"Fine," I confess, "we're talking about you and Charlie."

"What about us?"

That's Charlie's voice, stepping out from behind Silas

and Eily. She's holding Daniel's hand and, *fuck, busted again.*

Dammit, I'm staring down the Spanish Inquisition, minus the Spanish part, and Cade, who's got no fear, confesses for me.

"He was asking me if I think y'all should fuck. If it'll mess up your friendship."

Charlie darts a nervous glance at Silas, and he volleys it right back.

"And?"

But Daniel's seeking opinions, too.

"And I told him it's none of my business." Cade takes candor next level. "But if it were me, I'd do it. I'd fuck Silas."

"Moot point," Silas mutters. "You already have. Many times."

Cade shrugs. "Exactly, and we're still friends."

Charlie shuffles her sandaled feet, looking down at them. "But you and Silas don't go way back like him and me."

"Yeah," he says, "you're talking about the girl who taught me how to surf and do armlocks and a rear naked choke."

"Sounds like her calla lilies really loved the naked part," Cade teases, trying to keep the mood light.

"Har, har." Silas half chuckles. "She taught me a lot. That's all I'm sayin'."

"But you taught me how to shave my legs," Charlie adds.

"Yeah," Silas joshes, "and you said I needed to shave mine to show you how to do it, and like a fucking idiot, I did."

Charlie tosses her head back. "I didn't think you'd actually do it!"

"For you, I fucking would," he says. "Then I had to do both legs, so I wouldn't look like a dumbass."

"Well, you got me back." Charlie laughs with him. "You showered me in shaving cream. We got in a big fight with it and ruined the wallpaper."

"Exactly," Eily says, "and you sucked his dick last night, and he loved it. And you fire-hosed his face the night before that. Clearly, y'all want to fuck each other."

Even if they made mouth filters, I never want Eily to wear one. Her blurts are always a breath of fresh, awkward air right when you need it.

"And that's okay," she soothes. "It's really sweet and hot, actually. You don't have to feel guilty about it. I want y'all to finally fuck."

But I watch deep questions twist Silas's face. Charlie's, too. They look at each other with mixed emotions, half wanting, half worried, and Daniel's silent. He's not weighing in. He knows his wife too well.

It's their decision, and they don't know what to do.

"Y'all," I say, "nothing kills a boner like pressure. So let's just end this convo now and explore some more shitty destinations."

But the tension is with us all afternoon while we bounce around the island. We visit Clifton Hill Park and then the Pirates of Nassau experience, which becomes a shitshow.

It seems to be the trend today.

Because Daniel and I get spotted.

Fans with phones corner us in the Blackbeard exhibit. Thank fuck, I wasn't sneaking a kiss with him. As costars, it's already extreme the press we get, given the romantic plot twist in our show.

Now we'll be all over socials "vacationing together," and

our PR reps will shit themselves with the rumors we're starting.

I should've known better.

The tension weighs heavy on us, silent but unmistakable, as we wind our way back to Silas's ship, and the couples disappear for some R&R in our cabins before dinner.

"Fuck." I flop on our bed. "I fucked up," I tell Cade.

"No, you didn't."

She flops beside me, knowing exactly what's stressing me out.

"I should've kept my damn mouth shut."

"You love Silas. You care about Charlie. We all do, and it's okay. They're the last remaining piece in our six-person puzzle this week. It's obvious, and they'll figure it out."

I turn, propping my head on my hand, lingering my fingertip down her belly. When Cade was pregnant with our daughter, she looked so damn beautiful: I was in awe of her body every day. And now, she's looking too damn sexy in this white bikini top and jean shorts.

"Maybe we should just cancel tonight," I suggest. "Keep it just between the couples."

"Hell no," she answers. "It's finally my turn."

"But now they're gonna feel pressure, and that's not how we roll. No one does anything they don't want."

"And they won't." She flicks my nose. "You underestimate how stubborn they are."

"Silas ain't stubborn."

"He is about Charlie."

I keep my dumbass mouth shut this time. It already caused enough trouble today.

"Look,"—Cade sees it across my face—"I'll do something tonight. I'll break the tension somehow."

That gives me hope. "How?"

"Depends on what gift I open. But I got an idea, either way."

A couple hours and a shower later, Cade leaves for dinner upstairs early, and I don't know what she's cooking up. I just know how fucking smart my wife is. How she already crafted a plan to get away with murder.

So right now, I have to trust she'll fix our sixsome situation because my boss, our showrunner, just texted me. And when Lorraine Morris texts, you answer.

With a call.

"Happy almost New Year," she greets me.

"Yes, ma'am," I reply, standing outside on the deck of our stateroom. "You too."

We've left the port, and I'm staring down the perfect sunset smearing corals into the indigo ocean while I suspect what this call is about.

"You know what's happened," Lorraine says.

And talk about a friendship I value, one I'd never fuck up? Lorraine's had my back since the day we met in Hollywood at a burger joint.

"We're viral," I huff, *"again."*

I don't have to check socials to know the pictures of me and Daniel, hell, all six of us, vacationing together in Nassau spread like wildfire.

"Yep," Lorraine answers. "And I just want you to know —whatever's going on—I support you and Daniel. I always will."

I want to lie and tell her not to worry. That it's nothing.

But I don't do lies and secrets anymore. They almost killed me.

"Thank you," is all I can say.

"Do we need to release a statement?"

Lorraine ain't got a judgmental bone in her body.

Hell, she loves me. She loves Daniel. She was our boss on previous shows, and this show was Daniel's idea. He pitched it to her, and I was the only person they wanted cast as his costar. I'd never say no to her and wanted to work with Daniel. Every actor does.

I just never would've guessed we'd wind up here, with the world gossiping that we're in a polycule... and... I wonder...

Are we?

"No," I answer her, hearing laughter booming from two decks above.

Dinner is outside tonight and good. I hope everyone's mellowed out after my fuckup this afternoon. The six of us can do some kinky stuff, and damn, it's fun. But still,... some lines you don't cross.

Like fucking over a friend.

Or fucking a friend.

Question is, what if you're meant to be more than friends? That's how I feel about all of them now.

I care for them.

I want to protect them.

"We don't need to release a statement," I tell Lorraine. "It's private. We know our responsibilities to the show, and we won't fuck it up."

"You wouldn't be fucking it up," she answers. "You'd be adults who aren't ashamed of their love." She chuckles, her deep voice rumbling. "Hell, it'd only soar our ratings, like that's even possible."

"It may help our ratings, but it'd be hell on our lives and families. We're not doing it."

"Gotcha." She pauses. "Just know I got your back. Always."

"Just cover Daniel's," I tell her. "I'll be fine."

I'm used to this. I'm known as Hollywood's bad boy, and I earned it. It only helped my career. But that was years ago, before I had a wife and a family to consider.

Now?

I won't let anyone get hurt but me.

I can take it.

But Lorraine's quiet, which means she's cocking a wisdom bullet to fire my way. Seems women are loaded with them.

"Redix, you don't need to sacrifice yourself for the people you love. Not anymore. You're not alone this time." Lorraine knows my past. She helped me to survive it. "All *six* of you will be fine—*together*," she soothes. "It sounds like there's genuine love and respect, and that's all you need."

"I love you, Domina."

I use my nickname for her, and I mean it. Lorraine's a sexy, beautiful boss with all the respect she's earned, *and* she's my dear friend, and I'd never fuck that up.

"And I love you, too, Mr. Horner."

I laugh because I deserve that nickname; I was a promiscuous drunk.

Now, I'm a proud, sober man in poly love, and I have no shame about it. I love the life I've chosen, and I'll fight like hell to protect it, too.

"If it gets bad," Lorraine adds, "I'll let you know if the studio insists we say something—"

"Fine. We'll deal with that shit if it happens," I tell her.

Because I ain't stressing anymore what I can't control. I

wish her a Happy New Year, and I know mine will be because, dammit, I got so much love in my life.

Ending my call with Lorraine, I see two missed calls on my screen. Both from another friend who's been there for me.

Luca Mercier.

Calling's not like him. He's a text-me-whenever man, so I dial him back.

"Hey, dude," I greet him, surprised he picked up so quickly. "What's going on?"

"I'm checking on you, dickhead." In Luca's European accent, American slang sounds highfalutin. I love it. "It seems someone's having a *very* Happy New Year's trip."

My fist gently pounds the chrome railing.

"Fuck man, I can't go anywhere without it going viral."

"You sure as hell can't go anywhere with Daniel Pierce and expect it *not* to."

Luca's a billionaire hotelier, a single dad, and my close friend. He also doesn't blow sunshine up my ass. So, I gotta give him a little hell.

"Is someone gettin' jealous?" I tease.

"Of you with Daniel? Or with Silas? Or wait... with your gorgeous wife *and* Silas's? No, we're good. But please, spare my heart if you've been with Charlie Ravenel, too. Because I really will hate your ass. I'm her client, you know, but I have very admiring eyes."

Luca's a confident man, private about whatever sex life he does or doesn't have but fully in support of mine.

We all love him; we just wish he'd find his love. His wife died years ago, and it's long overdue.

"I'm a gentleman," I answer. "I don't fuck and tell."

"You're a gentleman on a superyacht having an orgy

with five hot people. There's nothing to tell.... only to watch."

"So, you *are* jealous."

I know my friend's a voyeur. Luca's watched our foursome at the club before. Like that's the only pleasure he'll allow himself to feel.

Except one night at the club.

I saw who he was with.

Then, never again.

"Maybe." But suddenly, his tone changes. He sounds playful, which ain't like him. Luca's always serious, but now he's suggesting, "Maybe next time, *I'll* join you?"

What the fuck-my-hot-man-friend?

Shock punches my heart. It makes me sway on the teak deck. Luca's suggestion makes me start to sweat, but not in a good way.

Talk about ruining a friendship.

Yes, I'm attracted to Luca Mercier. Everyone with a pulse is. If I'm famous for being Hollywood's sexed-up, wild Romeo for so long, then Luca's equally famous for being the world's most wanted and celibate bachelor.

Is this what Silas fears with Charlie?

It's one thing to be attracted to your hot friend. It's another thing to fuck them.

Truth is, I don't wanna fuck Luca. I love him like a close friend. I'm no horn-dog. I meant what I told Cade—some people are just friends. Close friends.

Hell, sometimes I have more fun cooking in the kitchen as friends with Silas and Eily than we have in bed. We're just a rare combo that can make both work.

But me fucking Luca?

Yeah, it wakes my dick up. It has its own head at the

sight of hot bodies, and Luca's is mouth-watering. He makes "tall, dark, and handsome" an understatement.

He's massive, mysterious, and magnetic.

But my mind, my heart that values his friendship screams a hard, "Hell-to-the-never-stick-your-dick-in-him no!"

My bigger head always wins nowadays.

"Relax, man." Luca chuckles, reading my racing thoughts. "Yes, you're very sexy. Your whole foursome is. Well... sixsome now. I'm sure it's a sight I'd thoroughly enjoy, but I don't want to join you *that* way."

"Dude,"—I puff out a thousand pounds of pressure—"I mean, I'd do anything for you. I'd fuck you if you really needed it. Like if we were the last ones on earth, but I'd have to close my eyes and think about golf the whole time."

He chuckles again. "You'd have to think about my dark holes and your long stick sinking your balls deep in them?"

"Okay, wrong sport. But you get the idea. I want you to be happy, but why do you wanna join us now? And in *what* way?"

"Well, don't you make a gentleman feel welcome."

I laugh at the sunset.

"It's not like that. You know you're welcome. We fucking love you, man. I'm just... surprised, curious, is all. You're usually a vault about who you fuck... or never fuck."

"That's just it," he confesses. "It's time for me to open up."

"And you need my help?"

"I need you to help me make it right."

"Who did you wrong?"

I ask him what we never talk about, but I have my suspicions.

"I'm a gentleman, too," he answers. "I don't fuck and

tell. But I want to finally show you and everyone I care about... *who* I love." *Ah, who knew Luca's romantic?* But then he taunts, "And I want you all to watch... *how* I love them."

Alright, press pause.

My mind's gotta catch up.

I gotta remind myself that I run in seductive circles. I don't know how it started, but I find myself here, in this life, with sexually adventurous friends who are very public about it.

Me and my poly of love. Maybe Charlie and Daniel, too. Definitely Stacey and her men at Delta's. Her adult store is full of kinky stories. And apparently, Luca is, too.

Then again, why should it surprise me?

We don't judge. We don't shame. Everyone is safe with us. Thinking back, each of us has been through hell. So alright, yeah, fuck it. The more the merrier in our kinda heaven now.

Because I know how kinky we are, but I can sense Luca's about to school us all. And for the first time in my life, I'll be an A-student.

"You want Silas to send the chopper for you?" I ask him. "You can show us tomorrow."

Because I'm damn curious now.

"No," his chuckle is deep, "I've waited this long. Let's find a weekend this month when you can join me as my guests."

"At your golf resort?"

"No. At my Charleston hotel." He coyly answers, "There's something I want to show you there."

"Show who?" I ask. "All six of us? You want Daniel and Charlie there, too?"

"Yes, Charlie Ravenel definitely needs to be there. If

her husband wishes to join her, that's even better. It will only add to the scene."

Damn, the plot keeps thickening. So does my cock.

Because even though I'll never fuck Luca, I want in on this kinky action. He's sat on the sidelines of my love life for so long, I'm ready to cheer his on, whoever he's with.

"Until then," he asks, "do you think you can survive this latest scandal, or do you need my help? You know, I know some people."

"Nah, man. Thanks, but I got this. Me and Scandal go together like a prom date. The kind when you look so pretty at first, but you're fucked by the end of the night with pictures to last for decades."

I make us both laugh because fuck it.

People will think what they want, and now, some of it's true, but let them wonder about the rest.

I sure as hell do.

Cade

ELEVEN

"THIS IS GONNA BE LIKE THE SUPER BOWL OF FUCKING."

R edix joins us late for dinner, looking like he's seen a
ghost. A sexy-as-fuck ghost, and he can't believe it.

"Y'all," he says, "clear your calendars when we get
home."

He's shaking his head, making Daniel suck his teeth,
tossing his napkin onto the table.

"Fuck," Daniel snarls. "We have to do press after those
pictures in Nassau today, don't we?"

"*Pfft,*" Redix scoffs. "Lorraine don't give a shit. Nah,
we're good for now. This ain't for our show. This is for Luca
and something kinky he wants to show *us.*"

Eyes get wide, in particular, Charlie's. Cautiously, she
says, "But Luca Mercier is my *client.*"

Redix shrugs, dropping into his chair and telling Charlie, "He says he definitely needs *you* there."

"Where?" Charlie asks.

"At his Charleston hotel, where he lives."

Redix starts slurping his conch chowder while Eily muses, twirling her ponytail.

"Luca Mercier could ask me to get my wisdom teeth pulled with no pain meds, and I'd grow another set just to do it for him."

She sits in Silas's lap, her usual spot after dinner, and he kisses her cheek.

"The only thing that gets pulled," Silas says, "is Luca's cock whenever he watches me fuck you. We're working our way around the world with him in his hotels. He has a thing for watching balcony sex."

"*That's* what Luca's into?" Charlie sounds shocked. "But I thought he's a grieving widower? That all he cares about is protecting his daughter?"

"Oh," Redix answers, "that's the side of Luca we all know. He's got another side he's never shown us, but it sure sounds like he's ready to *now*."

While Redix catches up, finishing his dinner, and we devour coconut ice cream for dessert, I wonder what I should do.

Should I try to fix this whole Charlie and Silas thing? Is it even my place? Their friendship runs deep; the feelings are so strong between them. With all their sexual tension, it could go either way.

I'm not sure, either, but my plan feels right. It's our fifth night, and I'm more than ready for this kinda action. I know Eily is, too. She begged me to do this.

And we adore Charlie. Yes, she's starting to feel like one of us. But every woman wears her slut pride in a different fashion.

But tonight, I plan to show Charlie what she can have. How good it feels, and it's okay if she wants it. If Eily and I show her, there's no shame if she secretly desires it, too. If she wants Silas the same way Eily and I do tonight, here's her chance, and I'll go first... because a slut's gotta do what a slut *wants* to do.

With three men.

And a proud smile.

Once we're done with dinner, we wind our way up the stairs, and I'm starting to get bummed. Like my whore parade is gonna end too soon. But with teases of something with Luca next or witnessing how much Daniel loved last night, this isn't our last trip. The six of us are just getting started.

I can feel it in my happy kitty.

Grabbing the second to the last black box, I pick it up. It's got some weight, but it's not heavy.

"I hope it's a spreader bar," Eily blurts, "one with cuffs so you can bind my wrists, too, and take turns with me."

With the gift, I turn around, laughing at her cute fantasies. How Eily went from the quirky virgin to the boldest of us all, and she deserves it. Our group is comfortably sprawled across the ebony sofa as Silas kisses Eily's neck, reminding her.

"This is my pussy,"—he lifts her sapphire minidress, skimming his fingers over his claim while she sits, exposed in his lap—"first and last. They'll get turns with you if *I* say so."

And that's exactly what Eily loves to hear, how Silas will never let her go, his possession making her softly moan into his kiss while he teases her folds open, and I inform the room.

"Whatever it is, we're going up on the sun deck. It's a gorgeous night, and we'll need the platform."

That turns heads, raising eyebrows because the sun platform is like one giant bed across the width of the deck.

It's covered in plush white cushions with a mountain range of black and white pillows. It's meant for a crowd to enjoy, lounging by the pool and soaking up the rays.

But I have other plans tonight.

And when I set the black box on the ivory sofa, opening the gift, peeling back the gold tissue paper... clearly, someone wanted to add to the cheer.

"What is it?"

Even Redix sounds impatient, asking while I stare, revising the game in my mind.

"Three matching naughty cheerleader outfits," I answer, holding one up.

In one hand, I have a black micro skirt with red and white trim, and in the other, I reveal a matching, skimpy halter top that reads *Daddy* in red.

"It also has a red blindfold, adding to the score. And... " I set the cheerleader outfit down to pull out a man's black, silky, pouchless brief. "It's got three pairs of these."

"Oh my god," Eily sighs. "When you stick your huge packages through the holes in the front of those tight briefs, your big hard dicks will enter the room five minutes before you do."

She makes Daniel laugh, and she's not wrong.

"Are there pom-poms?" Silas asks. "Because I can think of dirty games with those."

Eily squirms in his lap. "Do tell."

"You're the one who likes butt plugs, baby girl," he answers her. "Imagine the cheer you'd feel with a pom-pom as one."

Daniel growls, "Fucking hell, I'd blow right there."

Charlie kisses his cheek, whispering something in his ear that makes him grin, probably promising him that performance while I regret to inform my horny friends.

"No pom-poms, y'all. But here's the game. While the ladies get dressed, you guys take some supplies to the sun deck, put these briefs on, and wait for us."

Redix grins at Daniel, so I add, "And no starting without us. It's my night, my game."

Thankfully, it doesn't take long to freshen up in our cabins and slip on role-play lingerie. Tonight, I grab my phone that's been charging by our nightstand, too.

Daniel's kink has inspired me.

Told you it's contagious.

Gathered in the corridor, the women giggle. We really do look like cheerleaders. Eily and Charlie have their long hair stacked in high ponytails, and I pinned my long bangs to one side with a sparkly clip. We look so nice; we're naughty, pinching each other's exposed butt cheeks as we climb the stairs, stepping into the starry night above and coming to a screeching halt at the sight.

All three men face us, beefy arms crossed like a football team, standing tall in black briefs harnessing their proud cocks jutting out to greet us.

Talk about scoring touchdowns. Or hang time. Or ball carriers. Or tight ends. Or wide receivers. *Oh, we'll be receiving alright.*

Too many men on the field is not an offense tonight.

I know they played around to get hard like that and fine. But now, I'm in charge. Like we're a squad, and they're the players, I coach them.

"Guys, the game tonight is you have to prove how long you can last. All three of you, the team, will take turns with each naughty cheerleader, however she desires, while the other two cheerleaders watch and record it. All while you have to last until the end of the game."

"*Fuck.*"

The three men huff in unison. They're really a team now.

"Is that a yes?" I ask them. "Do you think you can play that long?"

"Is that a challenge?" Redix grins at me. "You wanna bet on how long these dicks can last without busting a nut?"

Silas elbows him. "I'll bet on who busts first."

Daniel scoffs, "I'm the oldest. It's not fair. I've had the most practice."

"Y'all," Eily sighs, "this is gonna be like the Super Bowl of fucking."

Charlie laughs. "And when the men are done playing, who says the women have to stop?"

Redix pops off, "Fuck yes. We'll record that, too."

"What's the order tonight?" Charlie asks, and it warms my heart.

I know how fearless she is. She's proven it. But this is new. She's still unsure about her desires, and like her Fairy Godmother of Fucks, I shall grant her wish.

"It's my night, so I'll go first. Then Eily. Then you. And then, the goal is for all husbands to return to their wives and finish with her. *If* you can last that long."

Silas smirks, raising his dark eyebrow.

"Fine then," he says. "The first dude to squirt his seed pays the crews' tips this week. That's at least a hundred *K*."

"Easy," Daniel answers. "I no longer have seed. I've been nipped."

Eily claps. "Oh, bless your empty balls."

"Oh, they're not empty." Daniel winks at her. "They're just very full of blanks."

"So, wait." Charlie asks, "Everyone's raw dogging?"

"It's how we usually do it," Redix answers her. "We're

all clear and protected. It's just us, but it's up to you. We'll do whatever you want."

And I melt. My husband is the king of consent, and why he is makes me love him with the deepest ache.

"But I'm not," Charlie says. "I'm not protected since Daniel got snipped."

"Well, then," Redix grins, "me and Silas will wrap our willies if we fuck you."

Eyes dart again. The question returns, hanging heavy in the air. The longer it goes unanswered, the bigger it grows.

We're all wondering—*will Charlie fuck Silas tonight?*

They keep doing it, looking at each other with lust in their eyes. The desire between them is intense, like a hungry animal in the room. I can feel their passion, too. Hell, it makes me wet, wishing they finally would; it'd be so damn hot.

Eily wants them to do it. She doesn't want Silas always wondering. Questions like that become more powerful than they need to be.

And Daniel looks eager for it, too. He's changed this week, and he's not going back. It's as if he wants Charlie to join him fully, and ironically, I know she's the one who suggested they join us, and Daniel clearly has. He's all in. He'll partner with us in any way we desire, but Charlie?

Everyone has their boundaries.

I love that about us, too.

How Redix will only kiss me. Even when he kisses Silas or Daniel now, it's not the same. When Redix kisses me, he cups my face and drinks from my soul; it's like I'm the air he needs to breathe.

Silas is so generous with his sex, but his heart belongs to Eily. He only sleeps with her, wrapping around her tightly.

He only wants to wake up to her. Like she's his sunrise, she gives him life.

It's obvious between Charlie and Daniel, too. Yes, they're exploring new things with us this week. And there are feelings, too; we all have them, but I see how Charlie folds into Daniel's embrace. How when he holds her, pressing her cheek to his chest, she drops her defenses, as if only with Daniel does she trust all will be okay.

I get why Redix worries. He respects the friendships we have, too. But I believe there's so much more we can share.

So I'll fuck first.

One, because I want this so bad, my pussy is purring for it. And two, I love my ladies so much, I'll take three for our team any day.

I point to the massive cushion in the middle.

"Eily, you sit there, and here's my phone. Record the action." I hand it to her before pointing to the lounger on the far right. "Charlie, you wait there and watch us. You'll record Eily when it's her turn. Then I'll record your turn if that's okay."

She grins, crinkling the long scar down her cheek. "Hell, yes. Daniel will die a happy man with empty balls to that video."

"Bloody right," he mutters, kissing her cheek.

"Alright then." I aim for the deep cushion on the left. "I'll start."

I lie back on the comfy platform, propped up on my elbows, and face the guys. They start stroking off to get hard again while Eily climbs onto the plush cushion to my left, and Charlie sits on the other side of her.

We're like a row of cheery pussy, lined up to be worshipped by the three hot players looming above us.

"Guys,"—I spread my legs for them, exposing myself,

showing them how I'm already so slick for this—"I want to reward you for your game tonight. You did such a good job; you deserve to be bad now. So why don't you take turns with my pussy and fuck me so hard until you make me come on your winning cocks?"

Redix and Silas grin. They know how I love getting railed. Daniel? He looks feral for his first team fuck, and I wonder if he'll last.

"Put on your blindfold," Redix commands me, "turn around, get on your knees, bend over, and show us our trophy to fuck."

Hell, yes, my husband came to play.

And I obey, tying the blindfold on before turning around and touching my cheek to the cotton cushion before spreading my knees, exposing my pussy to the warm night air.

This sporty skirt is so short it skims my bare ass. The shameless show I'm giving sparks lust through my nerves. I can't see what they do next, but I hear things, bottles snapping open, I think, and then... I feel it.

Fingertips, different ones slick with lube, tickle my hard clit, and I shudder, a mewl purring up my throat. With no sight, in such a vulnerable, wanton pose, every touch they lavish my sex with is electric.

"Let's get this trophy nice and wet." I hear Redix. "She's gonna need to be for how we're gonna fuck her so hard tonight."

Then I gasp, sensing a mouth on my tingling pussy, a tongue licking through my wet slit, split open for them, lips sucking on my clit. I rest my cheek on the cushion and can't stop moaning into it as three mouths, three tongues devour me, taking turns until I can't take it anymore.

"Fuck me now," I demand. "Fuck me hard and punish me for being the team's whore."

"Oh yes, we will."

It's my husband's familiar bourbon voice while the cushion beneath me sinks to a man's weight, and a new pair of hands, big hands, grab my hips. I know Silas's touch, too, and it's not him. It's Daniel, the fat tip of his cock teasing my aching entrance, his sexy accent making it obvious it's him first.

"You want this, Cade?" he asks. "You want me to fuck you like our whore?"

"Yes," I shout across the ocean, and he answers with a grunt.

But his first thrust is too gentle. He doesn't want to hurt me, so I tell him, "Harder. I like it real fucking hard, Daniel, so do it. Fucking rail me with that big cock."

"Do it." That's Silas. "Her pussy fucking loves it, trust us."

So Daniel listens. His fuck becomes brutal. Grabbing my hips, he delivers the force harnessed in his massive glutes and powerful hips. You can't deny the power in his body, in his hefty cock, and now I feel it pounding all the way to my throat, my body absorbing the lush shock, my blinded eyes seeing stars, and I can't stop screaming in ecstasy. My clit, my entire sex, my every nerve ignites with fireworks.

Even though I'm blindfolded, heightening my other senses, I know Silas's touch. On my left, the cushion sinks beside me, too, and his hand reaches under my top so he can pinch my nipple while the other fingers that start strumming my clit are woven into my soul.

It's Redix's touch. "That's it, Daniel," he taunts. "Fuck

our beautiful whore. Fuck her sweet wet pussy. She feels so good, doesn't she?"

And I lose it.

I scream, coming so hard, pulse after pulse, seizing my sex, and it happens so fast. I can't even come down from that orgasm before the cushions shift, bodies move, and another hard cock starts pounding into me. It's unrelenting, hammering my pussy, and I fucking love it; the spasms don't stop.

"Yes!" I cry out, recognizing Silas's girth next. "Yes, fuck me more. Give me more cock."

Smack.

Silas spanks my ass; I love the sting of it.

"Such a sweet whore for us, aren't you, Cade?" he asks. "Cheering us on and wanting our cocks all the time. Don't you?" Cool spit drizzles over my ass before a fingertip circles it. Whose? I don't know. "Don't you want our cocks fucking you all the time?"

"And our pussies, too."

I hear Eily, remembering that she's recording this—my gangbang fantasy—and now it's fulfilled. Taboo becomes a reality we'll be able to watch forever, making another orgasm crescendo through my nerves with someone's tease of my asshole, too. It shakes my thighs, the lips on my face trembling, my clit sparking again.

"That's right, our whore," Silas taunts. "Your pussy loves this. It's creaming my dick fucking you so hard. Come on. Come on this dick, too. Show us how much you love it."

My body obeys; my desire can't deny it. I cry out, coming again as the cushions quickly shift beneath me. The sudden exit of Silas hits me; it's almost painful, leaving my spasming pussy open and pulsing for more.

"C'mere." Hands I was born to love grab my shoulders,

yanking me into his grasp until his touch wraps around my neck, his lips pressed to my ear. The heat of his body is my home. "Whose whore are you?"

Redix drives his cock into my clenching walls, satisfying my ache, my groaning throat strangled in his grasp, barely able to answer, "Yours."

"Damn right, you're mine."

He yanks my blindfold down. I'm kneeling. I'm getting fucked in front of Silas and Daniel, who kneel on the cushions after their turn with me, my milky cum glistening on their hard cocks.

"This is *my* pussy," Redix swears it to the world. "This is my beautiful whore to fuck forever. Show them." His free hand smacks my swollen clit. "Show them how this pussy was made for me, for my cock."

It's true. It's singing through my flesh that vibrates to his touch. Redix doesn't hold back. He knows how hard I like it. How I can take it. How his body belongs inside mine so he can claim it as ruthlessly as he wishes, and I fucking love it. The painful smacking of his hips against the tender flesh at the crease of my thighs and ass; I'm designed for him. He invades me in every perfect spot.

"That's it," Silas taunts, watching us. "Fuck her good."

"Show the camera, Cade." Daniel's piercing eyes and daring accent make me groan as he directs me, "Look into the camera and show them what a beautiful whore you are. How you love getting gangbanged by three men."

Oh my god, we'll be doing this again.

It's so fucking kinky and getting me there so fast as I glance right and see Eily. She's kneeling with my phone in her hand, recording the sight, the whole thing, while she fingers her pussy and Charlie's behind her, tickling her clit to our show, too.

"This is how we fuck our whore."

Redix taunts me and the lens. He lets go of my neck to rip my shirt up, exposing my bouncing tits for the camera too. The lewd act, his control I trust and crave, his fingers pinching my clit, his others pinching my nipple, his massive cock driving inside me, and his deep voice in my soul; it's the annihilation I crave.

"Come for me, Cade," Redix growls in my ear. "Now and forever."

And I do. I have no voice. No truth but this, my body seizing in his grasp with everyone watching the pleasure he kills me with, delivering the sweetest orgasmic death of my shame. I have none. Not with him. Not while I rest my convulsing body against his and collapse safely in Redix's loving arms.

This is exactly where I belong.

Eily

TWELVE

"**Dude, she *is* our dirty little cock princess.**"

By the time it's my turn, I know what I want. My body
can take it. My desire demands it.

I'm a slutty little princess, and I shall reign tonight.

The problem is...

Silas will resist at first. But he can't refuse me. He grants
my every wish like I'm all his to spoil, and I let him because
I spoil him right back. There's nothing I won't do for him,
with him, and we can do this too.

I pass Cade's phone to Charlie, smooching her an air
kiss. She smooches the air back, and her gorgeous cheeks are
as flushed as mine. Watching Cade get banged, how she
came so many times, has Charlie and me ready, too.

I don't know what Charlie wants, what she'll do. I hope
she lets herself feel this. I hope she shares this with us. I
hope she'll feel free now. Free to fuck Silas, to fuck all the
men, because I am.

I love our life. There's something so amazing about the
love we share.

When you know you have this many people to play with, to laugh with, to lean on when days are rough, or to fuck when nights ache with need, it makes life rich with joy I didn't know was possible.

I spent too many years hiding and alone.

I spent too many days trapped in the nightmare of what I survived.

But now, my life is a dream. I live in technicolor every day because I live it with no shame, only love.

Silently, the men line up in front of me, their perfect bodies glistening with sweat. Silas has his hair back in his usual knot. Redix leaves his dark bronze strands hanging to his shoulders, and Daniel's coal waves shimmer in the night.

And those big shiny cocks...

Damn, Bella. My husband was right. *You should've stopped crying, gotten out of that chair, and fucked both Edward and Jacob. You didn't have to choose.*

Because I won't.

I can't believe our men's boners have lasted this long, but then again, don't bet against Silas on anything. He or Redix. They're too competitive, and Daniel looks the same.

"Well, hey, boys." I lean back on my elbows, letting my naked legs fall open, spreading my cheery pussy for their stare while I love this role-play. "You know, I've been a very naughty girl. I've been playing with my pompoms while you were busy. I've been wishing they were your big cocks the whole time. I'm such a naughty, horny little virgin. I really need some big dicks to fuck me. Think you can help me?"

Three grins and cocks surge before me.

Touchdown: it's their fantasy, too.

"Who will be your first?"

Daniel asks me with a sexy grin, and damn. I never imagined that man in a cape on the big screen would be right here, with his superdick, ready to fuck me with my husband and his best friend.

This is the trilogy women really want.

"I want you," I answer Daniel, "to fuck my pussy like a dirty little girl while my husband fucks it too. And Redix punishes my mouth for being so filthy."

"Baby girl,"—suddenly Silas looks worried—"don't you mean your ass and pussy? You want a DP?"

"No." I spread my lips, showing them how wet I am, just waiting for it. "I want a double vag. I want two dicks in my pussy."

"Hell no." Silas starts raining on my slutty parade. "We'll break you open. You're too tiny."

"No, I'm not. I've been practicing with two dildos. It makes me come so hard, and you've watched me do it. You liked it."

"Dildos aren't the same as dicks."

"Yeah," I agree. "Dicks are even better, so I want two of them."

Silas starts stroking off to stay hard.

"Your little pussy can't take it," he says. "Daniel's fucking hung, and so am I. We won't fit, and it'll hurt you if we try."

With that big tempting cock in his grasp, he's losing this fight. It only makes me want it more.

"So," I remind him, "you say you wanna put your baby inside me, and with as tall as you are, I'm sure it'll be a ten-pounder. But you won't give me two big dicks, too? Like, doesn't my little pussy deserve some fun first? You need to let my kitty play."

Redix starts stroking off, too, trying to stay hard. So does Daniel while I conduct smutty negotiations with my husband.

It's not the first time I've had to convince Silas I can take it. That, yeah, I may be small, but I'm a grown woman. I know what I want.

Go ahead and empty an ocean. That'll happen before I don't get my way. Especially when my horny pussy is involved.

"Let's just try it," I assure him. "Let Daniel in first, then you can try slowly, too. Don't worry. If it hurts, I'll tell you."

"But why?" Silas looks puzzled.

"Because she *wants* it," Cade answers him. "Just like you want a dick in your ass while you fuck her pussy. We all want what we do. We don't have to defend it."

"It's her body." Charlie defends me, too. "She knows what she can take. It sounds like she's gonna love it."

"Yeah." I strip my top off, doubling down, knowing Silas can't resist my little tits either. "I'd take three dicks in my pussy if I could, but I'd like to *not* feel like the Grand Canyon tomorrow, so I'll start with two for now." I point to Silas, warning him, "But that doesn't mean I won't try for three later. We'll build up to it."

Redix chuckles. "Dude, she *is* our dirty little cock princess. Double-dick her if she wants. I'm jealous. It's gonna feel fucking amazing for you and Daniel."

Lust shoots across Daniel's eyes. It ignites in Silas's, too.

See, he hadn't considered that. What it'll feel like to rub his dick against Daniel's while they share my pussy.

His hazel gaze can't deny he's curious now. I can tell he's almost convinced.

"Look," I tell him, "it's Daniel. You've known him forever, and he'd never hurt me. Right?" I ask Daniel.

"Never," he swears to me.

"Exactly." I nod, telling Silas, "Now, hurry up and fuck me like a dirty little slut taking two dicks in her pussy, and tell me I am the whole time and make me come before I lose my lady boner fussing with you about it."

Like she's got my back, Cade hands them bottles of lube. Not that they'll need it because my pussy is dripping for this.

While they gloss up their dicks for round two, I'm full of instructions.

"Daniel, get under me. I've seen it in porn. Sit me on your lap, lie down, and fuck me from behind. Keep your dick in my pussy while Silas gets between my legs and enters me too. And you," I tell Redix, "wait until they're both in before you let me suck your cock. And you," I glance at Charlie, "film it so you can see them both fucking me."

Gently, fingers grab my chin. Silas lifts my gaze to meet his.

"Someone's being a bossy little slut again." He's smiling, taunting me, "Is this what your pussy wants? This pussy that belongs to me? You want it to be double stuffed with dicks?"

"Yes," I assure him, offering him a kiss. "Please, it'll feel incredible."

And it does.

I'm always right.

Once Daniel's hulking body is beneath mine, lifting me like a rag doll into his lap with my legs dangling in the air, spreading my pussy wide open. Once his giant dick slides slowly into my excited cunt in front of Silas's eyes that glimmer with lust, sparking with possessiveness, too, at the sight. And once Daniel starts fucking me, taunting Silas while his cock slowly thrusts inside me, "Fuck, Silas, you've married a naughty little girl," I come so fast.

Oh my god, I'm so horny I can take five dicks.

Silas kneels between my legs and Daniel's. He grabs his

cock, and I sit up in Daniel's lap, bracing with my arms beside me to watch us, too. But Silas is reluctant, pressing his fat tip against Daniel's thick shaft, slowly straining into my tight pink entrance, but I'm not afraid.

"Do it," I urge Silas. "Please, Daddy. I want your cock so bad."

Because I do. And that word. That tease ignites Silas. He loves it, gently pushing inside what is his alone, and it makes me tremble with pleasure. It cracks through my bones; the insane stretch, the sweet burn, the lush pressure, feeling my walls resist at first. But I want this too much. I gradually open, wet and wanting to receive him, both of them and only demanding more.

"Oh fuck, mate," Daniel grunts beneath me like he's about to lose it. "I can feel your hard dick sliding against mine in her tight little cunt. Fuck, she's so fucking wet and tight for us."

"A hundred *K*," Redix warns him, standing beside me on my right, with his dick hovering over my lips. "Don't blow yet," he warns Daniel.

And he doesn't. Daniel finds his careful rhythm with Silas, who watches where our bodies are joined with parted lips in awe, and I do, too. It's so taboo and perfect. It's what we both desire. Two big, slick dicks, parting my bare, pink lips, pistoning into my pussy like a perfect fuck machine. The pleasure is overwhelming. The only thing I fear is that I'll stop breathing; it feels so good. Too good.

"*Fuucckk,*" Silas sighs.

"Oh my god." I'm stretching into a new woman, begging Silas, "Daddy, don't stop."

This is nothing like a DP. It's so damn intense. It's so incredibly intimate for Silas and Daniel, too, and that's why I wanted it as well. The look in Silas's eyes staring into mine, he's lost. He loves both cocks and cunts. His pleasure is getting me off just as much as mine. I love pleasing Silas, too.

"Oh my god," I gasp again, needing more, and Redix fills my open mouth.

"You got three daddies fucking you now, little princess."

Redix thrills me, too. Gently, he thrusts over my lips, glazing his drops of arousal over my tongue, but he stays shallow like he knows my body can only take so much. Like his cock barely in my mouth is just a tease while the real storm is in my pussy about to unleash a hurricane.

"Look at my little slut." Silas takes me there, rubbing my swollen clit with his thumb in perfect, maddening circles. "Let the camera see you taking two cocks like a good little slut."

When I open my eyes, I see Charlie standing by Silas, filming it all. Forever capturing my swollen pussy, creamy and sliding, glossy with two dicks stuffing me beyond what's allowed; I moan at the forbidden, loving it and the dick in my mouth too. *Oh my god, what I must look like.*

I'm so shameless and happy. I don't know where the pleasure originates because it's everywhere. It owns my body and mind. Nothing exists but this ecstasy.

"Yes, our little slut, fucking come." Silas sees it taking me. "Come with two big dicks fucking your tight little pussy. You're so bad for your daddies, aren't you? Feeling me rub against Daniel's big cock as I let him fuck my beautiful wife with me."

Daniel grabs my hips harder. "Fuck, you're a naughty little girl wanting all this cock."

I moan to that, my eyes rolling back to Daniel's accent and taunt. To Silas thumbing my clit harder. To my sex so overwhelmed it can't even clench. It has to surrender to the spasms that are coming. To the orgasm my legs are shaking for.

Daniel growls over my shoulder, his thrusts getting harder as Silas's do, too, with his thumb rattling my excited nub. *I'm right there.* Pleasure's coiled so tight in my body. My pussy's dripping, loving it. I'm stretched and about to explode into a million gorgeous pieces, and Daniel's, "Fucking come on our cocks, you naughty little girl."

"Ahhhh!" I scream over Redix's tip, my mouth open and gasping for air. My body jolts with ecstasy while Silas grabs my legs, letting the massive orgasm quake through my sex.

"That's it," Silas taunts, his dick not stopping. He keeps pumping against Daniel, pumping inside me, too. "Keep coming for your daddy, baby girl."

And I do; I come again, letting wave after wave rush through me. This new sensation in my pussy, the two incredible dicks fucking me, they make my walls spasm and not stop. All I know, all I feel is a blinding pleasure and wetness, my cum. It's dripping over my cheeks, wetting Daniel's thighs.

"Fuck," Daniel huffs. "Fuck, we have to stop, or I'll come."

Silas gently pulls out before Daniel does. They leave me open but so satisfied. I'm trembling over Daniel's body before Silas lifts me into his arms. Standing, he cradles me, my limbs, my heart, my world, wrapping around him. I bury my face in Silas's neck, inhaling his smell, pressing my lips to his glistening flesh. *I love this man more than life itself.*

"Are you okay?" he asks me.

"Yes," I sigh to him. "I think I can take three next time."

And I love his laughter, too.

Charlie

THIRTEEN

> "We're gonna set your twat water free."

I wished for something new in my life, but this is another world.

And I'm not leaving.

Send for my things. My kids. My job. My house. Everyone and everything I love, this is where I belong.

I can't handle this pleasure every day or every week. Hell, maybe only once a month, but this is my life now.

It makes the hell I've survived worth it. It makes the mundane, cozy, the routine comforting. It makes quick, vanilla sex a nice little break when you're fucking like this every so often.

I hand Cade her phone. It's slick from my sweaty palm watching Eily get a double vag fuck that inspires me. Or do I want the hottest train run on me like Cade just did?

The choices are endless as I strip off my naughty uniform and sit on my cushion, nude and watching my husband stand to catch his breath and composure at the sight of me. He almost came inside Eily, losing his wad and a hundred *K*.

The money's not the issue. If he didn't save himself for my chance, that would be the real loss.

All three men look like they're struggling. Like their cocks, surging in those sexy black briefs, are swollen and begging for release. I stare down a trio of hard, slick dicks in my face, and I'm not sure.

"Can you guys handle more?"

"I'm not losing." Redix glistens in front of me. "I can keep going."

"What about you, Energizer Bunny?" I ask Daniel. "You gonna make it?"

"The bet says we have to wait until it's our wife." He lifts his left hand, showing off his platinum band. "Bloody lucky for me, you're next. "

"No, no," Cade says, standing beside them, phone in hand and ready to film us. "You have to wait until it's just you and your wife."

So Daniel shakes his limbs like he just finished a tough workout and is returning for more. When he starts jumping up and down, his hard dick bouncing too, I can't even.

"I'm not a prize fight to win." I laugh. "This ain't Vegas. You're not going for a gold belt."

"Bloody hell, we're not," he says. "This is the best workout ever. My dick will retire after this."

"The bloody hell it is," I warn him with a grin. "We're fucking at champion level from here on out."

"Alright then." Daniel leans down, softly kissing my cheek. "We're all yours, babe. What do you order?"

"What am I? A drive-thru fuck?"

"Hell, no." Redix smirks, all sexy-like, his gaze combing my naked flesh. "We wanna fuck you, too."

But I sense him to my left.

Silas is staring down at me with a hard dick but soft eyes, and I put my stare up at him, seeing his fierce desire and yet so many tender memories shared, too.

It's heavy, this question between us. It's aching, simmering in the air, and making my flesh prickle with anticipation.

I've been asking myself, "What should we do?" I'm trying to be rational.

But right now, gazing back at him, at every perfect flexing muscle on him, on all three bodies looming over me, three hard cocks wanting me, reason is gone. Lust pulses through my body. I can't find the right answer. I'm wet with need. The hunger overwhelms me. The only question I can answer is, *what do I crave?*

The only answer I can give is, "I want a DP."

Instantly, lust rips across Silas's eyes. His reaction is so fast. The idea of fucking me this instant changes his breath. His intensity makes me softly gasp. He's so damn hard looking at me, he won't even speak. It's like he's about to be unleashed on me, and it makes my stomach flutter, my pussy clenching. Fear races against desire through my veins.

My god, I've never seen Silas like this. I've never wanted him like this.

And now I do. I want him so much, too... but...

Silas took me to my prom because no boy would date me. I intimidated them, but Silas proudly asked for the honor. He even bought me a corsage. I was proud he was my date. He was young but bold and handsome, insisting he'll take care of me like the man he is now, and...

Not like this.

Maybe not ever.

I suddenly want Silas so badly, but I fear it so much. I can see it in his eyes, too. The same emotions consume him.

"With Daniel and Redix," I say, saving us the worry, buying us time. Turning to my husband, I tell him, "You love my ass so much; why don't you have a go at it while Redix gets my pussy."

When I turn to Silas, relief softens his face but not his cock. He still wants me, anyway I'll take him.

"And you," I tell him. "You water my tongue like lilies again. Talk to me like you do the other cheerleaders. I'm no different. I want a dirty team fuck, too."

A thousand years ago, when Daniel and I had time to get kinky, we explored sex with him inside me and toys, too. I'm not afraid of the sensation. I want it.

It's the real men, the real cocks joining the party, that thrill me to the point of almost being shy. It's kinda hot like I'm a virgin.

I'm a little nervous as Redix lies down beside me on the cushion. Cade hands him a condom, and he makes quick work of rolling it on.

Straddling Redix is sexy as hell. Lifting his sheathed cock to my entrance and holding it here is so dirty. And the upward curve in his long dick, it's going to strike my G-Spot like a church bell, making me sing, I know it. And when Silas steps up on the cushion, hovering over me with his eager cock waiting for my mouth, too, and Redix, with his daring dick, is waiting for my pussy...

Oh my Slut Goddess, am I really doing this?

Were those "Just a Tipsy" rosé bottles magic potions? I drank all three of them, and now I get all the dick I wished for?

I'm ordering cases of it when I get home.

Because Daniel kneels behind me, straddling Redix's

thighs as he fists my hair. Looping it around his hand, Daniel yanks my neck open like I'm on his leash, and I love it.

"Are you ready to be our next whore?" he growls.

Praise the Pussy, my man is back.

"Yes, sir," I reply to my husband, and it widens Silas's eyes.

He's never heard me this way or seen me like this. I'm usually so strong, so in charge. *I am.* But not when I get fucked. Not usually. This is how I like it.

"Put his dick in your sweet pussy." Daniel steams over my ear. "Show Redix how my whore loves riding a cock so hard."

"Yes sir," I reply, glancing left at Cade sitting with Eily. She's smiling, holding her phone up and recording my turn, while Eily, our insatiable fairy slut, is playing with her pussy again.

I love how these women are so free with me. It lets me feel so free to do this.

I glance down at Redix, and though he's hard as hell and prone for my fuck, I won't take him. I care for him, too. Like me, Redix has scars. He's survived, so I have to be sure.

"Can I fuck you?" I ask him, and his blue eyes deepen with my request, filling with care and lust.

Grabbing my hips, he coaxes, "You fuckin' better," and we do.

I take another man's cock inside me. I fuck him while my husband kneels behind me, fisting my long hair like reins while I start my shameless ride. While I can't believe I'm doing this, and I am. It feels so damn good, and I take him so damn hard.

"Fuck," Redix huffs at my strength. "Fuck." At the power in my quads. "Fuck, yes." Squats in a gym pay off when you fuck. That and an even stronger, slutty disposition. I grab Redix's pecs and revel in this taboo, taking his cock with all my might. "Goddamn," he groans.

"He likes your pussy. How I've trained you so well." Daniel's in my ear, his concrete chest pressed to my back, his hard dick poking between my ass cheeks. "Do you like fucking his cock for me?"

"Yes, sir," I sigh, bracing myself against Redix's body.

Damn, this man is hot. His dick is impressive; that curve in it is maddening. It's making me crazy. Redix is so shredded and perfect. They all are.

Daniel cups my breast. "My sweet, Charlie," he sighs in my ear. "You're going to be my dirty wife and whore now." Slapping my tit, he thrills my nipple and Silas's gaze. "You're going to keep fucking that cock while you take a hard dick in your mouth too."

Silas steps up to the plate, keeping my gaze locked to his. Dragging his thick thumb over my bottom lip, he taunts me.

"You said you wanted to be our cheerleader, too?" I nod while I start sucking Silas's thick thumb. "Then say it," he demands. "Say it like our other sluts do."

"Daddy, please let me suck your big cock."

I can play, too, and Silas didn't expect that, not from me, and it cracks his veneer. He sinks his fist in my hair, holding it intertwined with Daniel's grasp like my sex is in their dual control.

"Take it, Charlie." Silas presses his velvet crown to my lips. "Take this dick in your mouth like a good little whore."

Oh shit, I love this.

Sliding my lips, stretching them over Silas's thick tip, and tasting his arousal, makes me shudder. That and Redix under me, moving his hips like a god. Like he's dancing into my slick sex. *They're so fucking good at this*. I moan at their skills controlling my pleasure. I don't have to seek it; they deliver.

"*Yeah*, she likes it," Redix taunts me too. "She loves all this cock."

Reaching up, Redix starts tugging on my nipple, and I moan with my tongue sliding down Silas's length. I can't take all of him, but I can take this, all the ecstasy they're killing me with.

"Are you ready, Charlie?"

Daniel's rolled on a condom, too. I heard him do it before he lubed his fingers, stretching me, getting me ready, and I am. I'm moaning for it, knowing Daniel's going to have his way with my ass before he snaps off that Magnum and comes in my pussy last.

"Are you ready to be my whore with my dick in your ass?" He's so hungry for it, too, asking me, "Are you ready for me to share you with my friends?"

I gag on Silas's dick before I lift away, spit webbed from his tip to my lips while I stare at Silas and answer Daniel, "Yes, sir. Please, share me. Make me your whore and fuck my ass, too."

Silas gives me a lewd grin, watching as Daniel knows how to do this. It's his favorite sport as I return to my new one, sinking my lips down Silas's shaft while he keeps guiding me, tugging at my hair with just enough pressure.

But then it's suddenly intense. I start panting over his cock, feeling Daniel urge into my ass while Redix stretches my pussy.

This isn't like toys.

This is so damn real.

"Oh my god," I gasp, and Redix stills inside me.

"Do you want this?"

He asks while Daniel waits for my answer, his dick barely inside me, too, and I know I'll never be the same, and I don't want to be. I want to change. I want to be freer than ever before. I want this with Daniel and the ones I love, each in their own way, and yes, fuck me too.

"Yes," I gasp again. "Yes. Don't stop. I want it."

Daniel goes slow while Redix doesn't move, and Silas waits for his turn, caressing my cheek.

"Say it feels good, Charlie Girl," Silas coaxes me. "Tell them how you love it. How you love them fucking you."

"Yes," it's my constant refrain. "Yes, I love it. Don't stop."

Pleasure shocks my body, igniting my nerves, sparking goosebumps across my flesh as my body slowly receives Daniel. It makes me shake, feeling the exquisite pressure as Redix holds my trembling shoulders, his cock not moving until Daniel's fully seated inside me.

But he can't help it. Daniel's fucked my ass so many times, but not like this. Not with another man inside my pussy. Not with a man that's fucked Daniel too, and *oh my god, this is our kinky life now, and thank you.*

"Fucking hell." Daniel kisses my shoulder. He's in awe, too. "Fucking hell, babe, I can feel his big dick inside you, too."

But this isn't a tender moment for me. No, I glance left again, and Cade's still recording us, Eily's still getting off, and I am, too. So fucking hard and with no shame.

"Fuck me," I insist. "Use me and fuck me now like a whore, all three of you, and don't stop until I come."

That's all Daniel needs to hear. Redix too. It feels too good for them. They start fucking me, sharing me, grunting, and using my body to get me off while thrilling their swollen cocks too.

And when I take Silas again into my mouth, gazing up at him, he unleashes. Like he wants this for me. For me to join his forbidden world forever. His dick glides over my swollen lips, his words taunting me from above.

"Yes, Charlie, look at you now. Fuck, you're our sweet slut, too. Just like my wife. Just like Cade. You look so hot, loving all these dicks using your holes."

I moan, tears leaking from the corner of my eyes to his fuck of my throat. To the dick curving inside my pussy. To the cock filling my ass. To my clit about to combust. My edges blur. My boundaries cease. I give it all away, and I don't want it back.

"That's it, babe." Daniel's in my ear, one hand grabbing my shoulder, the other in my hair with Silas's. They're filling every part of my being. "You said you wanted cocks and cunts and all the kink, Charlie, so fucking take it now like a good whore. Take it. Fucking take it."

I moan, trembling, feeling Daniel drip more cool lube over my crack, coating his dick; he loves watching it too. He gets off on a shameless, glossy fuck, and I crave it, too, panting at his lewd, stretching penetration. It's everywhere.

"Fucking take these cocks." Daniel's thrusts become feral, like every time he fucks my ass, but this time it's next-level with Redix inside me too. "Fucking suck Silas's cock and take Redix's dick." Daniel growls, "They feel so fucking good inside you, don't they, Charlie?"

I groan. *My husband and I have shared a dick, two dicks, and pussies too,* and I sink my fingernails into Redix's pecs to hang on to the truth as I fall into the fantasy, making Redix groan too.

"Fuck, she's loving this. Fuck her ass harder," Redix urges Daniel. "Make me feel your dick inside her, pumping against mine."

They thrust in obscene unison, and it's here. The wave is cresting. It's rising so high in my body, eclipsing everything I've ever felt before, and I don't want it to stop. I won't be able to stop it. Redix is hammering against my clit, Daniel's taking my ass, making the pleasure more intense, and I can't stop staring into Silas's hungry eyes, witnessing what a slut I am for him, too, sucking his big cock with no shame.

Oh my god, I never thought I'd be here, and it's about to crash over me. My new truth. My new world. I can't control it. It's inevitable, the orgasm that'll destroy the woman I was and goodbye. I shake, I moan, I suddenly can't move, and I want this change. I let three men fuck me into the woman I want to be next. I growl for her arrival, my clit crying out for her to come.

"Oh fuck, she's coming." Silas reads my eyes trapped on his. "Fuck yes, make her squirt all over you."

"Fuck," Redix huffs, feeling my pussy clamp down. "Fuck, yes, do it." He's deep inside me, grinding circles against my clit, and I swear I'm going to come *and* cry; it feels so good.

"That's it, Charlie." Daniel buries his cock deep in my ass, and I'm a prisoner. I'm shaking, caged between their bodies, trapped by the orgasm about to obliterate me.

"Fucking squirt, babe. Fucking come for us," Daniel's in my ear, in my heart. "Look at Silas and tell him how you're gonna fuck him next while you come on our dicks."

But I can't.

I can't answer. I can't move. I can't do anything but come so powerfully that even my eyes can't roll back. They're anchored to Silas's hazel gaze wanting my answer, his heart and body open and asking me with his cock hovering over my gasping lips, and I'm helpless to tell him, to know anything but this.

Anything but pleasure so overwhelming, so safe with my husband, that I wake up in a new world.

DICK DRUNK.

It's a thing.

It's a legitimate condition for which I seek no cure. I wanna be dick drunk forever.

I hardly had anything to drink last night as I lounge in the morning sun, still feeling intoxicated. I'm in a haze, remembering how, after three men made me come like a banshee, my husband made me do it again.

Daniel snapped off his condom, flipped me on my back, slung my legs over his shoulders, and dove so deep inside me that he made me gush for more. It was so hot. It was beyond erotic. Watching Silas fuck Eily right beside us, he was like an animal with her too. The same goes for Redix. He had Cade screaming. The men finally got to come, and they made it a helluva loud show.

I'd almost be mortified that the whole crew could hear us, but it felt too good to give a damn.

Who cares when you're coming like that?

"Don't tell Silas... " Eily reclines beside me on the lounger where it all happened, the scene of our orgy crime. She looks cute in her blue polka-dot bikini. "But my kitty's so sore, she ain't purring this morning."

Sipping a peach smoothie, Eily confesses all to me. From behind our dark sunglasses, we watch our men standing behind the bar on the sundeck. They're making a big mess of the smoothie station the chef set up for us—something about a healthy New Year's Eve breakfast.

But I don't give a damn about breakfast. I'm hungry for something else today.

"You mean," I giggle with Eily, giving her my full attention, "you feel like two loaded freight trains crashed inside your tiny tunnel?"

She smiles with a straw in her mouth.

"Ka-boom," she says. "And it was so damn worth it. After I recover, I'm going for three trucks down my Venus highway next time."

Cade laughs on the other side of me.

"How are you gonna manage that?"

Cade's not embarrassed. She's got a gel ice pack on her pussy. It's resting over her black bikini while she wears sunglasses and a satisfied smile.

"I'm an artist." Eily shrugs. "I'm creative. I can get the guys to lie down naked, like intertwine their legs, and get so close. Then, I can stroke their dicks together and get them hard; they'll make a tower of three cocks for me to sit on."

"Talk about a three-way split." Cade warns her with a grin, "You're gonna have to go up *two* tampon sizes after that. But wait. I don't think Tampax makes a super plus, plus, plus. If they did, you'd be walking around all bow-legged and on your tippy-toes like you got a giant pillow shoved up your puss."

I laugh. I love how open we are as Eily swats the air.

"Don't worry," she says. "Pussies bounce back. You've seen what mine can do with a jade egg. And I Kegel daily, like an Olympic weightlifter. Watch: I'm doin' 'em right now."

Eily makes a cute face, barely twitching her pixie nose. Images of her pussy doing a daily workout, like it's lifting dumbbells in the gym, fill my mind before she grabs my arm, all excited.

"Charlie, is this how you squirt so hard? You do your Kegels?"

"I mean," I chuckle, answering her, "I have my pink jade eggs, and yeah, I use them when I remember to, but I've always come like that. At first, it embarrassed me. I didn't know what guys would think—"

"They fucking love it!" Eily blurts, "It's so hot. You squirt like a pressure washer!"

I start rolling.

"I do not! It's not that much."

"Yes, it is!" Eily admires. "And I wanna do it too. It gets Silas off so much."

"But he makes you squirt, too." Cade proclaims, "We've all made you squirt."

"But not like Charlie does!" Eily exclaims. "I just trickle, but she's the Goddess of the Gush, the Leader in Ladyjuice, the Empress of Ejaculation, the Queen of the Cumshot."

I'm dying. I can't breathe. I'm grabbing my empty stomach and laughing so hard if Eily doesn't stop, I'm gonna queef too.

"It *is* damn hot," Cade adds. "You gotta tell us your secret."

"It's no secret." I wipe the happy tears from my eyes. "It's just my body, but I guess if you really let the arousal build inside, it helps. And I was so frustrated before this week. Like Daniel and I rarely had time to fuck, and now—"

"*Girrrl*," Eily interrupts, nodding in deep understanding, "I gotcha; you're the Hoover Dam, holding back all that sexual tension. I'm buying you more of those cum blankets for your birthday because now we're gonna set your twat water free."

I clench my bare thighs, laughter cracking my ribs.

"Dammit," I tell her, "you're making me laugh so hard, I'm gonna pee, not squirt."

"Well," Cade smirks, "at least we're getting you wet."

"Speaking of getting wet," Eily sticks her hand out, "lemme see our video again from last night. I wanna make some highlight reels. Then I'll organize them in a Google folder by our nicknames."

"Nicknames?"

"Yeah," Eily answers Cade. "I'm Princess Horny Pussy, Charlie's Queen Cumshot, and you're the Duchess of Dicks."

Cade hands Eily her phone while I can't stop laughing, taking it all in, bliss bubbling through my veins. I can't believe my new normal now, and I love it.

It's a gorgeous sunny day. From where we're anchored, I can see the pink sand of Lighthouse Beach. We're supposed to play on Eleuthera Island today. It's New Year's Eve; I'm in a bikini, reclining beside my two new... *girlfriends*, I guess? I don't know what to call us, and I don't care.

Because I glance back at my sexy husband with his two... *boyfriends*? Hell, are Silas and Redix my *boyfriends* too?

I don't know. But they sure are mayhem with that blender, whipping up fruity concoctions. Redix squats down behind the bar; I guess to wipe up some of their mess while I ask Cade.

"What do you call Silas? Like Redix is your husband, but how do you refer to Silas and Eily? What do you call each other?"

"Friends."

"In my book, friends don't fuck."

Cade shrugs. "Then 'partners,' I guess. We don't care about labels." She tilts her head, studying me with a grin. "Why? What do you *want* to call us?"

"I got no clue. I just know I'm having fun and don't want it to end."

"It doesn't have to," she tells me.

"But we gotta be careful," I reply. "You and me at work. Redix and Daniel on set. They have to be *damn* careful because millions are watching them."

Eily mutters, "I sure love watching them like this." She's staring at Cade's phone, watching her XXX-rated performance. "Damn, y'all are right," she says. "How *did* I fit all that dick in me last night?"

"Well, my kitty ain't sore," I tell her. "She's purring and happy to take all the *D*s again for Team *V* tonight."

Eily snaps her gaze up at me, her face beaming. "Does that mean you're finally fucking Silas?"

"You're forgetting we have three willy clones, too."

That's my answer because I'm still not sure. I don't know if I'll ever be certain about Silas because I can't forget the way he looked at me last night while all the men were taking me; the memory clenches my sex now.

Like when Daniel's inside me and looking at me, there's so much love in his eyes; our emotions run so deep, so powerful; we both feel it. I mirror it back.

The way Redix looked at me last night? It was desire, like our bodies couldn't deny the pleasure we felt. There was no guilt, just erotic euphoria.

But when Silas looks at me? When our bodies are exposed like that, when sex is in the air, his eyes get wild with lust. It's like he's a caged animal, and I fear his release. Like we'll lose control, but I crave his freedom, too. The bonds holding us back are painful. I never want to hurt him, and I want to be free, too.

But if I fuck Silas, Daniel's right, there's no going back. I just wish I knew what was on the other side of our friendship if we do. Will it be okay?

"Y'all," Eily clicks the phone screen off, her voice excited with a plan, "it's my turn tonight, our last night, and it's New Year's Eve. We have six dicks, three real ones and three that vibrate. What do we wanna do?"

"I thought you were too sore?" Cade asks, sucking down the last of her smoothie, and my stomach growls. I haven't had one yet.

"That's what they make Tylenol for." Eily embellishes, "It says so on the bottle. It's for sore pussies that want another night to fuck."

"I don't know," Cade sighs. "After last night, I'm kinda satisfied for a while. And tired. Let the guys play in *their* backyards."

"But it's New Year's Eve." Eily almost whines, and it's cute. "And it's my night. Don't wimp out on me now. Can't you rally your red snapper for one more night?"

"My red snapper? Are you calling my pussy fishy?"

"You know I love your clam," Eily says, "so wake it up. For one more night."

"It is our *last* night," I add.

Cade shakes her head, tossing the ice pack aside. "Fine," she sighs, "we'll empty the wank tanks tonight, and then this bitch gets two weeks to recover."

Eily snickers. "Perfect. That'll be just in time for Luca Mercier's kinky show. God, I can't wait to see it. He's so sexy and mysterious. Who do you think he's—"

"Charlie Girl!" Silas shouts across the sundeck, getting

our attention. "You want a smoothie before we clean this up?"

"Yeah," I shout back, climbing off the cushions. "I'm starving."

Daniel and Redix pass me on the deck, smoothies in hand.

"Try the banana with whipped cream," Redix teases, his eyebrows dancing. "It's our favorite this morning."

"I bet it is," I answer, stopping for a sweet kiss from Daniel before my growling stomach can't wait anymore. I join Silas behind the bar and survey the mess. "It's a smoothie bar," I tell him, "not a frat house. Damn, y'all made a mess."

"Like this?"

Silas pops a squirt of canned whipped cream on my chest. It splatters my bikini top, so I swipe a dollop off and fling it on his face.

"You little shit." I laugh. "You really wanna go?"

"We can't." He licks the milky blob I threw off the corner of his mouth. "Redix used all the whipped cream. That's the last of it."

He throws the can in the trash bin under the bar, and I'm curious.

"How the hell did y'all go through a can of whipped cream in one morning?"

Silas grins, his dark eyebrows dancing with delight.

"Ask Daniel's sweet dick."

Oh my god, why does that turn me on so much?

"Is that what y'all were doing over here?"

"You don't mind, do ya? Redix was just showing Daniel his food fetish and wanting me to watch them. He sucked down all the whipped cream and Daniel's cream, too. Hell, you should see what Redix likes to do with eclairs."

I imagine it, the three men together again, and it soaks my pussy, filling my heart too.

"I don't mind. I'm happy for Daniel."

Silas nods, the smile gently fading from his face but not his eyes.

"I'm happy a lot is changing this week," he says, slowly handing me an empty pitcher for the blender, his fingertips brushing over mine. "We're changing too. What's happening between us?"

I can't answer him. I don't know what to say. His gaze pins me down, and the butterflies in my body make it impossible to speak. Normally, I feel them in my heart. I feel them for Daniel. But with Silas, they suddenly alight between my thighs.

I take the pitcher and look away.

Silas is too hot, and this is too intense. It makes my pulse triple, so I have to focus on something else. On making my smoothie.

Silently we work together, and Silas knows me too well. He hands me my favorite fruits: strawberries, a banana, then orange juice. I fill the pitcher with the ingredients while he leans over, his bare chest brushing my shoulder, his touch making me gently gasp as he adds two drops of vanilla. Then he grabs a handful of frozen cubes, plopping them in, while all I feel is fire.

All the times we've hung out. Doing nothing on the beach to almost everything on the water. This feels so familiar and yet so different. We've always been so close like this, standing right beside each other, but now...

I feel Silas inside me.

For the first time, my flesh blooms to his body heat so near, his muscular arm innocently brushing mine, making my clit tingle. The woodsy powder of his deodorant wafts up my nose, his enticing man musk, too. Out of the corner of my eye, I notice how his nipples are erect, his bare chest kinda beating hard, his breath changing around me.

I put my focus down, studying the buttons on the blender, but it's right there in my side vision, too, the heart-fluttering bulge growing in his white boardshorts, and my pussy clenches on instinct.

Pressing a button, the crunching whirl of the blender fills the air, but I can't drown out this tension between us. It's never been this strong, and what did I expect?

That I could let Silas taste me, or that I could taste him? That we could go from being best friends to making each other come so hard, and this wasn't going to happen?

That we weren't going to drive each other insane with a tease so powerful that it's bigger than us now? Like a tsunami, it's cresting around us and *will* crash.

We can't control it.

We can't stop it.

It'll take our bodies down with it.

Because my best friend is standing beside me and making me sweat. The boy I grew up with is a very big man now, looking down at me in *that* way—the way I witnessed last night. Like I'm his prey, and he's been starving for years. And though I'm not naked now, I feel so exposed. I'm just standing here, my body swaying dizzy with lust while I watch our partners relax on the loungers, laughing and having fun in the sun while this is torture.

Denying ourselves.

It's tightening my nipples. It's wetting my pussy. It's sizzling over my nerves that ache to just finally let him devour me. Silas has wanted me for so long, and now I think I want him even more.

The blender stops while my mind keeps whirling, and he mutters, "You're killing me; you know that, right?"

I can't face him. "What?"

"You're wearing a red bikini again, and I'm gonna fucking lose my mind."

I glance down. I was so focused on trying to ignore the allure of his body that I forgot mine. I honestly did. I didn't put two and two together when I dressed this morning.

"I didn't wear it on purpose."

It's the truth, so why do I feel guilty?

"That's just it, Charlie Girl." He stalks behind me, gliding his firm, silky flesh over mine, making a soft gasp seize my lungs. "You don't *have* to do anything."

Like he's helping me with my smoothie, his warm arms reach around my body, and it steals my breath. I'm drowning in his thirst as he lifts the lid to the pitcher, adding a splash of almond milk.

"It's too thick," he sighs, and so is his hard cock pressing into me, pressing all the buttons. The ones on the blender that make it whirl again and the ones inside my body that arches open for him. It's instinct, and I can't stop it.

While the machine whirls, he lowers his lips to the shell of my ear, his words shooting straight to my aroused sex.

"I don't know if we *should* fuck," he says, his lips tickling my flesh, "but can you feel how goddamn bad my body wants to fuck the ever-living hell out of you right here?"

His thick dick is rigid against my ass, with nothing but my tiny bikini bottoms and his board shorts stopping us. It's the same thing we've worn for years, but not the same between us anymore.

He stops the machine. He doesn't care if the others hear him, but they're too busy laughing and wouldn't care.

We have their blessing, so it's up to us now.

"Charlie Girl," he murmurs in my ear like he's in pain, his hard body urging against mine, "all the fucking times I came for you like this, to you in a red bikini. So many times and every day, I'd imagine it. It'd drive me crazy, wanting you so damn bad, it fucking hurt. You'd lay beside me on the beach, and I was in pain. My dick ached, my hands twitched, and my mind wouldn't stop telling me to do it."

His desire is intoxicating. In the haze of it, I sigh, "Do what?"

"This," he whispers, trailing his warm fingertip down my ass cheek, skittering goosebumps over my flesh before he gently wedges it under my bikini, dragging his touch down to between my trembling thighs, where he pulls the fabric away, exposing my pussy.

"Silas," I softly gasp, staggering back into him.

It's the slightest exposure, uncovering my newest desire, and *oh my god*, I'm getting so wet for him.

"Charlie," his fingertips barely dance over my bare lips, "all the times I wanted to roll on top of you and pull your red bikini aside like this. So I could bury my hard dick deep inside your pussy. I could see the outline of your lips. *These* wet lips." I moan at his fingertip, barely parting them open. "I memorized them. I wondered for years what your pussy looked like, what it would taste like, what it would feel like to come inside you. To make you come like you were the first to make *me* come." I'm glossing his fingers. My legs tremble as he grinds into me; he's as hard as I am wet. "You know that, right?"

I can't hide it as I watch Eily smiling back at me like she can see it across the sundeck. She can see Silas standing behind me, whispering to me. He's making my nipples so hard, and she raises her glass like *finally*. And Daniel's smiling my way, too. Like *it's about time*.

But is it?

"You know you were the first person I came thinking about it?" His middle finger glides between my slippery lips, reaching my clit, tickling it, and I can't control my moan. He leans down, looking over my shoulder, his gaze taking in the landscape of my aroused body.

"First, I was obsessed with your tits. Look at them. Look at how your nipples get so hard around me. I'd have to go to the side of your house and jerk off. I even did it in the ocean, standing right beside you. I did it so fast and so many times, and you didn't even know. But then I got older, hornier."

His fingertip teases my entrance, swirling through my wetness and making me shake, his lips still pressed to my ear.

"My fantasies about you got kinkier, darker. I wanted to tie you to your bed so I could eat your pussy out, and you wouldn't be able to stop me. I wanted to make you come so hard like that and so many times until you wanted me, too. Until you desired me, until you loved me, until you begged me to fuck you so hard, the way I wanted you so damn bad, for so damn long. I know it's wrong, but it's true."

"Silas," I gasp, "I did love you. I *still* love you."

"I know you love me. But you never wanted me *like this*." His fingers slowly enter me, penetrating my sex, making my knees weak, a deep moan escaping my lips. "You feel this?" He gently pumps them in and out. "How you get so damn wet for me now?"

He presses his lips hard against my ear. Like, we'll never kiss. Silas will only share that with Eily, but we can share this.

"And I still want you, Charlie. I don't think my body will ever stop wanting you." He pulls his fingers out, leaving my pussy aching and open. "But I don't know if we should.

I can't lose you. Maybe you should remain my teenage fantasy. My Charlie Girl."

He nuzzles his forehead into my hair, pausing for breath before he grabs my hips, grinding into me. *Fuck, his dick's so hard.*

"Or maybe," he growls, thrusting into my backside, "I should finally fuck you like a man right here. Fuck you until I make you scream for me. I'll make you squirt so much, and they can all watch me make you do it. They want us to fuck, and—"

"Yes," my body screams, but "Let's wait," I barely huff aloud.

We need air. We need sanity. We need a condom. I'm flooded with lust and logic.

"Silas, let's wait. Let's think about this first."

I turn around in his grasp, and I'm staring up at a new man. One I've known forever and one I've just met. Either way, this attraction is confusing. It's painful what our bodies want, but what about our friendship? Our hearts?

We both take a deep breath and a step back, letting our minds take over, not our desire.

"Let's wait until tonight." With panting breath, I tell him, "If it's a good idea now—"

His huffing breath matches mine, finishing the phrase I've said to him for years. "It'll be a good idea later."

We've often said it right before our biggest decisions. We've always been there for each other. We've shared so much, and the comfort is here, too, making his shoulders drop. Dragging his hand down his face, he slowly relaxes and grins, looking down at the surging tent in his shorts, pointing right at it and my soaked pussy, half exposed.

"What am I supposed to do with this chub?" he asks.

"You don't need my calla lilies anymore. You're damn

lucky to have a beautiful, amazing wife who can take care of you far better than me."

His face falters.

"Charlie, you know I don't love you like I love her, right? Eily has my soul. She's my everything. I'll die without her. That's not what this is between us."

"I know. Same with me and Daniel."

"You just make me so fucking horny. I wanted you for too long." He's always so honest with me; he's so crass it's cute. "It's like my dick is dying to finally fuck you, and I don't know if I should listen to it."

"Same." I wedge my bikini bottoms back to where they belong, and he proudly watches the gesture. "I'm not used to wanting to fuck you either. And today, I gotta finally decide if it's a good idea."

"Oh," he steps back, chuckling, "so I don't get a say? It's up to *you* if we fuck tonight?"

"Yeah."

I say it just to piss him off. It doesn't. I always amuse him.

"Ah, hail no, Charlie Girl." He adjusts his erection as it deflates. "You may have been in charge of me when we were kids, but I'm the man in charge now. This is my boat, my world. You're in Silas Land now."

I laugh. "Silas Land?"

"Yeah."

I put my fists to my waist. "And just what do we do in Silas Land?"

"We build some motherfucking sand castles."

Cade

FOURTEEN

"I THINK WE'RE ALL SOUTHERN PEAS IN THE SAME
HORNY POD."

"Damn, Silas," I sigh, taking in the view. "You're our tour guide from now on because this is perfection."

It is.

Some of his deckhands and servers took the tender, the inflatable boat, out first and set up a giant picnic on the beach for us. We have a cooler full of drinks and champagne, a basket loaded with yummy goodies, two umbrellas to shade us, a giant soft blanket, and a pile of enormous throw pillows to recline.

They've taken the boat back to the yacht and left us for the afternoon on this pristine, remote beach. We have the pink sand and clear water all to ourselves.

"So, is this gonna be our thing, now?" he asks while Eily reclines between his legs. Propped up on his chest, she sips champagne while Silas proposes, "Every New Year's Eve, we'll all come back here to Lighthouse Beach?"

"I'm game," Daniel says, mimicking him with Charlie resting between his legs.

"Speaking of games," Redix says, "you said you wanted us to play one this afternoon." He squeezes my waist, spooning me in the shade. "Though me and Cade learned the hard way about sex on the beach. Too much sand in the cracks. Talk about fucking sandpaper."

"We're not fucking, you horn dog." Silas laughs. "We're building sand castles. The women versus the men, and the winners get a one-hour massage."

Eily snorts, "That's only a punishment for our spa staff."

"Nah," Silas replies, "y'all gotta massage *us*. We got all that flavored oil to use before we go home tomorrow."

"Us?" Eily sits up. "The women aren't losing. You men are."

"Who's gonna judge?" Charlie asks.

"It'll be obvious," I answer her. "Our women's castle will crush the men's."

"Let's make it interesting," Eily suggests. "Instead of castles, let's build cocks and cunts."

"What?" I start laughing, and Redix does, too.

"Yeah, like an homage to our vacay." Eily pops up, brushing the sand off her legs. "The women will build a giant sand cock, and the men will make a big sandy cunt."

"Baby girl, that ain't fair." Silas pinches her butt. "You're damn good with a cock, *and* you're an artist. You'll beat us all."

"And *you* sure know your way around cunts." She shrugs. "You guys may surprise us."

"It's on." Daniel pops up, too, grabbing a bucket and shovel from the basket of supplies left for us. "Come on, mates," he says. "Let's have a go at a cunt."

Eily points at him.

"No *mating* out here. Keep it in your pants. Tourists can come by with kids."

"But we're building giant genitals in the sand," Daniel protests, laughing. "How G-rated is that?"

"It's art," Eily fusses back. "But three men fucking on the beach? Now that's just hot, triple X porn."

I love her so much.

I love US so much.

Eily had us cracking up this morning on the sundeck. We all witnessed that moment between Silas and Charlie behind the bar.

It was so hot. It tented Daniel's bathing suit, which got Redix going again, tenting his shorts, too. Even I got wetter than the ocean because desire steamed through the air.

And then Eily muttered so Silas and Charlie wouldn't hear us. So that we wouldn't disturb them.

"Hey, y'all, look," she whispered. "Look, they're doin' it. They're *finally* doin' it. It's like we're on a safari, and we're about to watch two rare animals fuck. Look, look, look." She slapped my thigh over and over. "It's like Charlie's in heat, and Silas can smell her horny pussy. He's going wild. He's mounting her. He's gonna hump her so hard. They're finally gonna mate right there at the smoothie bar!"

"They bloody better not. Not like that," Daniel whispered back. "His willy's not wrapped, and that's all kinds of drama I'm not acting out."

"Don't worry," I side-whispered back. We sat in a row like spectators watching the feral show. "They're stopping. Look."

"Dammit," Eily whined. "I really want them to fuck."

"Jeez, Ms. Eager Beaver," Redix chuckled low, "why do you want them to fuck so bad?"

"Because they wanna *fuck* so bad."

Eily sassed back with the obvious, making me quietly giggle.

But something broke the moment between them, and they started laughing. Charlie started sucking down her smoothie while I could overhear her and Silas talking about their mutual friend, Rob, his husband and their daughter.

There *is* history between them, and maybe Redix is still right. Some friendships are too precious to risk.

Or maybe Eily's right. Silas and Charlie need to fuck; they need to get it out of their system. It's obvious they want to.

But will they?

Whatever happens, I believe in Silas and Eily. They'll be fine.

No matter how Eily pops off with the funniest shit or the wildest ideas, deep down, she's the wisest of us all. The smartest, too. She's so past caring what others think because all she feels is love. And the love between her and Silas is powerful. God, how I cried at their wedding because the moment he saw Eily coming down the aisle in her indigo and white dress, Silas was crying. So was she.

It's like we all have our soulmates. How Silas finally found Eily. How Daniel fought for Charlie. How Redix sacrificed himself for me. That's love beyond what bodies can express.

But when I only consider our bodies? We all seem happy, satisfied except for the last two—Charlie and Silas— pulling like magnets held at that urging spot of natural tension, desperate to finally join.

"Alright, y'all." Silas hands out buckets and shovels before pointing to the east side of the beach. "You ladies, go down there and build your cock castle. And we'll build a sandy cunt down there." He points to the west. "And no peeking. We have two hours, and then we'll judge whose is best."

"It's no competition," Charlie says. "Cocks are best."

"Hey,"—playfully, I smack her arm with a pink shovel—"way to betray Team Pink Flaps. Pussies are great too. You're just dick drunk today."

"Right!" Charlie's eyes get wide. Like I just read her innermost thoughts. "Damn, I thought it was just me because I'm still high from all that man-meat filling my holes last night."

"Bloody hell." Daniel grabs the crotch of his navy board shorts. "Stop. You're giving me a stiffy again, and the Nun Nookie," he points to Eily, "says we can't shag out here."

Eily twists her face.

"Shagging is a dance old people like my parents do."

Daniel laughs. "Indeed, that's how you got here. Because shagging is fucking where I'm from."

"Ewwww." Eily scrunches her nose. "If you knew my parents, just... yuck."

Silas mutters, "Ain't that the truth."

"Okay," I start walking toward a good spot in the sand, "let's do this. Let's kick some cocky castle ass."

The women really do have the advantage because Eily's creative imagination is endless and pornified.

"Alright," she says, "let's start with two giant balls, like domes in the sand. And then, Charlie, you start filling your buckets. Let's make the cock at least four buckets thick and build up. I'll gather some seaweed, and that can be pubic hair, and Cade, see if you can find some thin reeds up towards those trees. We can turn the reeds into veins on the shaft."

"Holy, cock creations, this is so crazy it's perfect!"

I'm so impressed with Eily. No way the guys can beat

us. Though they look like they're having way too much fun farther down the beach.

I watch as Redix gathers buckets of water while Silas shapes a pussy in the sand, and no telling what Daniel is searching for in the surf.

Charlie starts pounding the mounds of sand she's gathered, shaping one into a testicle while I do the other.

"Whose cock are we building?" she asks.

"I think we have our limitations with sand and seaweed," I answer.

"Let's do Redix's." Eily fills her bucket with sand. "He's got that signature curve. No wonder you fuck him every day," she tells me.

"Okay, hang on." Charlie pauses. "First, if we build Redix's dick, the curve will make it fall over. And second," she asks me, "y'all fuck every day?"

"Yeah." I start shaping the base of a penis, smoothing four sandy bucket piles into one thick shaft. "I mean, we try to unless we're sick or something."

"Man," she huffs, "I guess I gotta set our alarms earlier to make extra time to fuck. Though, my lady juices don't really flow in the morning."

"Silas wakes me up with a woody almost every morning," Eily proclaims. "Talk about cock-a-doodle-doo. And we *do*."

"Y'all are newlyweds, though." Charlie stacks the dick higher. "But we have three little kids who always want to know where we are. Our nanny is amazing, but she's not a miracle worker. She can't make them forget about us while we have a quick fuck in the laundry room, and trust me, we've tried."

"But me and Redix have been fucking since we were eighteen," I answer her. "We're not a newlywed thing. I think you just gotta make the time. After I almost lost Redix several times, I won't take our connection for granted. Even when I don't feel like fucking at first, I rally."

Eily points her shovel at me. "Like you're gonna rally your rubyfruit tonight. I got plans for us."

Charlie teases, "Please tell me your plans involve all six crack hunters, real and rubber."

"Girl," I warn, jumping up to grab some reeds now that our dick is three feet tall and growing, "I know you're all dick drunk now that you've sipped our favorite love liquor. But if you stick six dicks in your crack, it'll only crack your back."

Eily snorts, "Trust me—it sure is fun trying, though. "

While I scour the beach's edge, where it disappears into a tropical forest, Charlie and Eily work like a machine, stacking the sandy cock until it's almost four feet tall.

The guys can see our creation, but they aren't giving up. I can see them laughing and working hard, too.

"Look," Eily points to the rounded tip she's sculpting once I return with long, thin reeds in hand. "We're making Daniel's cock."

I'm confused.

"How is this Daniel's cock? It kinda looks like Silas's, too."

"Because Daniel's uncut, so I can round off the tip and sculpt it. I can make it look like a turtle head hiding in a tube sock."

Charlie bursts out laughing while I argue, "But when Daniel's dick is hard, you can't tell he's uncut. His foreskin disappears into his thick-ass shaft."

"Oh my god." Charlie falls back on the sand in happy hysterics. "I can't believe y'all are debating how my husband's uncircumcised dick looks, soft or hard."

"I've never been with an uncut dick!" Eily exclaims. "I can check it off my list."

"Just how many dicks are on your list?" I ask her. "And does Silas know about it? Because I suspect after this week, you've met your quota."

Eily puts the finishing touches on our statue of Daniel's cock, and though it's not anatomically correct, the tip really does look like a sandy turtle head in a tube sock.

Now that's talent.

"I don't want any more real dicks," Eily says, gently pressing the reeds into the shaft, making them look like veins. "I'm in love with Silas's dick. Redix and Daniel's are like bonus dicks. And when I'm horny for more, Delta's has all the dildos I desire. Stacey shares all her new stuff with me. Did I tell you she just ordered a new line of glow-in-the-dark monster spacecocks? I can't wait. She wants me to try them because I write the best online reviews. I give five stars if I come in a minute. One star if it's too small."

"Does she really give sex toy demonstrations in her store?" Charlie sits on her knees, decorating sandy balls with seaweed pubes, asking us in awe, "Like her three men join her? They're all together, and they'll give you a private show?"

"Yep," I answer, "I love that lucky bitch."

"Stacey's amazing!" Eily blurts. "She even mailed a sex swing to the yacht for us." Her eyes widen. "Whoops! I didn't say that. Bleach it from your mind."

"*That's* the sixth gift tonight?" Now I'm the one jumping up and down for cocks and cunts. "It's a sex swing in the sixth box?"

"Quit being a detective." Eily sounds like Silas.

"If the sex swing is Eily's gift," I turn to Charlie, "which dirty gift was yours? It wasn't the Clone-A-Willy's. You were too surprised by that one."

"Y'all,"—Charlie stands up, dusting the sand off her ass while the guys walk our way—"let's keep some things a secret. That's what makes it fun."

What's also fun is how hard the guys laugh at our realistic cock castle, its pubic hair, uncut tip, and woody veins. Call the Smithsonian. It's a national treasure.

But what's even funnier is their sandy cunt. They stole our idea for seaweed as pubic hair, but they got creative with double pink sandy lips and pearly shells for a clit.

Charlie hugs Daniel's waist, admiring their work.

"It's good," she says.

"Yeah," Eily adds, "it's pretty pussy art."

Daniel grins at Silas, telling him, "Show them what our pretty cunt can do."

Silas pours a bucket of salt water into a well they dug at the base of the pussy, making it look like their favorite hole to fuck. Then he smacks the puddle, shouting, "Who's your Daddy?"

Water splashes everywhere, squirting our feet.

"Okay, okay," Charlie blushes, "it's a tie."

That means no one gets a massage, which is fine. By the time we're back on the ship, all we crave is a refreshing plunge in the pool. Splashing around as the sun starts to set, Eily climbs out, announcing, "I'm going to work with the Chief Stew and Engineer to set up for our party tonight. Y'all stay here. No peeking."

"Engineer?" Silas cocks his head. "Baby girl, what are you putting on my ship?"

She cocks her head right back. "*Your* ship?"

He grins. "*Our* ship."

"Smart man." She winks. "And it's a surprise. And y'all never complain about my surprises, so hush your fuss."

"Bloody hell." Daniel wraps around Charlie, asking her, "Is she your twin?"

"I think we're all southern peas in the same horny pod," Redix answers.

Minutes later, the sound of an electric drill is undeniable. The lull of ocean waves can't hide it.

Silas dunks one last time, his hair falling in a wet sheet to his shoulders as he emerges, declaring, "Watch: she's having them install a stripper pole in the salon. We already got one at home, and she twirls around that thing like it's a biblical drought, and I'm gonna make it rain for her."

"Do you?" Charlie asks him.

"Hell, yes," he answers, the tan muscles across his back rippling as he jumps out of the pool. "I keep my woman *very* happy. I always got a stack of bucks for that role-play."

Watching Silas drag a towel over his face, Charlie looks dumbfounded, asking him, "Do y'all ever work? Like, when do you find time to fuck all the time?"

"We make the time," he answers her. "We'd rather fuck at night than stream shit on the flatscreen." He nods at Redix. "No offense."

"None taken," Redix answers.

"Me neither," Daniel adds, his big arms squeezing Charlie tighter. "Don't worry, babe. I promise, after this week, we'll make the time. We're not suffering another drought again."

Silas aims for the snacks the chef has left on the table by the loungers. We're all hungry, so we climb out, too. While we dry off, Silas has work on his mind now.

"I'm kinda jealous of y'all," he says, going for the fresh guacamole and chips. "Eily and I don't work together. I only get to see her at night. But now y'all will be working together, and think of the fun you can have."

He juts his chin toward Daniel. "Think of how you can glaze Redix's donut in your trailer. Talk about a Krispy Kremey lunch break."

"Bollocks," Daniel scoffs. "We'll be under a microscope now. With all that viral shit, I won't be able to smile at Redix without starting more bloody rumors. Let alone be alone with him in my trailer."

"Are they rumors, though, if it's true?" I ask, claiming a seat in Redix's lap while we scavenge the guacamole and chips like it's the last meal on this planet.

"It's a truth we can't afford to expose." Redix's usual jovial voice drops. He's serious, and he's right. "It's not like we're ashamed of what we have now, the six of us, but we ain't stupid either. There's too many uptight, judgmental people in this world. All of us, we gotta work together to protect each other. To protect our families, too. Imagine what the press will do to us if they find out."

We don't need to. I dart my eyes to Charlie, who winces, and we know damn well the worst that can happen. She survived it.

"Well, what about you working for Charlie Girl?" But Silas lightens the mood again. He's always teasing us. "Y'all can meet privately in her office now, where you can give her a new kinda debriefing with your strap-on."

Charlie throws a loaded chip at Silas. It smacks his cheek, sliding off and leaving a trail of guacamole and a guilty smile on his face.

"What?" He laughs. "Like that ain't hot as hell. Like we men ain't imagining it. Both of y'all in naughty secretary outfits, but one of y'all is packing hard heat under your skirt. *Dayum.*"

"First of all," Charlie arches her brow, "I'm the *boss*. No offense to my secretary, he's amazing, but he doesn't wear a skirt. And the only heat I pack under mine is my .380."

"Yeah," I get her back, "I pack a 9, not a nine-incher. Get your horny head out of the gutter."

Silas laughs, gesturing to the tranquil water around us.

"We're floating in the horny gutter. All week on my ship, we've been playing dirty fuck-games, and *now* you wanna act offended?"

"What's offensive," Redix studies the bowl we're devouring, "is all the damn double-dipping going on. Gross, y'all."

Daniel sits beside him, giving him an elbow.

"You've fucked my ass," he says, "and licked whipped cream of my cock. Half of us are married, and the other half have double-dipped the hell out of each other's holes. Clearly, we're sharing everything but manners now."

"See," Silas nods, "I don't give a shit what y'all say. I got a hundred that says someone's fucking at work within the month."

"Well, what are *you* doing this month?" I ask him.

"I got new initiatives to launch with my family's foundation," Silas answers. "And if she'd let me, I'd like to initiate getting Eily pregnant."

"Be patient with her. Y'all got time." I tell him before I turn to Redix, informing him, "But we don't. You're getting me pregnant again this year."

Redix's eyes grow wide, reflecting the ocean and his surprise.

Shit, I should've saved that for a private moment.

But it's been on my mind and in my happy heart lately. I wanted to tell him during our New Year's kiss in a few hours, but whoops, there it is. Now, I've ruined the surprise, regret twisting my face.

But he cups my cheek, his lips leaning to dust over mine. "Are you serious? You're gonna give me another little reason to live?" And it doesn't matter. Having another baby is so special to Redix; he makes this moment count.

"Yes." His tenderness has tears biting at my eyes. "One more blessing for us, if we can."

His kiss makes up for my blunder. It's full of passion and hope like he wants to go for it right here on the cushions, and it's not like we haven't fucked in front of our group, but...

"After the New Year," I huff over our lips. "We'll start trying when we get home."

"Congratulations, mate."

Daniel grabs Redix's shoulder, and Charlie smiles, but I know Silas too well. He's happy for us, but the wish wells deep in his hazel eyes. He really wants to start a family with Eily. But I get why she needs to wait a bit longer. They went through hell with her family, trying to tear them apart. She needs more time with just Silas.

It's like Charlie can sense Silas's longing, too. She considers his silence before telling him.

"Don't worry. You're gonna make a great dad one day. And since I saved half of the childhood shit you threw away, you'll have some keepsakes to share too."

The light returns to Silas's eyes, asking her, "What else did you save? I hardly remember what I threw away; I was so angry."

"I didn't bring it all with me," she answers. "Just your baseball mitt and... " Charlie pauses. It's as if she knows this is gonna punch Silas's heart. "*The rope*," she says.

Silence falls over us.

The only sound is the drill, the secret Eily is working on in the salon. I'm sure it's the sex swing we aren't supposed to know about, a stripper pole or god only knows her naughty plans. It'll be a fun night, but that's not this moment.

This one is as deep as the water around us.

Silas swallows hard. "*That rope?*"

It's like he doesn't believe it. He and Charlie share some story; whatever it is, it's powerful.

"Yes," she answers him. "*That* rope."

I don't dare ask. Neither does Redix, but Daniel does. He has more history with Silas than he reveals. He and Charlie share a secret with him they'll never say aloud, and I suspect why, and I've got no right to judge.

"*Which* rope?" Daniel cautiously asks.

Charlie blinks back tears as Silas stammers, answering Daniel, "The rope my dad used to teach me how to tie nautical knots."

"But babe," Daniel gently rubs Charlie's thigh, "why does that upset you?"

"Because," tears spill down Charlie's cheeks, "my dad was there too. Our dads taught me and Silas together how to tie a butterfly knot."

"And a bow line," Silas adds, tenderly smiling, trying to get Charlie to smile back. "And a rolling hitch, which I *still* beat you at."

I smile, too. The tears they fight threaten me. But it ain't working. One escapes since I just told Redix I want another baby—*our* baby.

It seems we're all swimming in feelings because I also remember what happened after Charlie graduated from our high school; it was in the news. Her parents were killed in a small airplane crash. It left Charlie alone, and now I understand why her memories with Silas mean so much. It's like he's all she has left of that life.

"Shit, Charlie Girl."

Silas reaches his arm around her shoulder, pulling her into a side hug. His kiss of her blonde strands is loving; it's gentle. It's not sexy. It's a million tears and smiles shared.

"Thank you," he mutters into her hair.

Gently, she punches his chest. "Told you, I'll always protect your ass."

Daniel's smile is genuine, regarding their connection, their history. And I'm starting to love that about Daniel. Yes, he's Charlie's present and future, but her past doesn't threaten him. She wears it on her stunning face, which makes my throat tight whenever I notice how he often kisses her scar.

"Do you want me to get the rope?" Charlie asks, lifting her head off of Silas's shoulder. "It's in our cabin."

"Nah," he grins at her. "I'm sure Eily's bought plenty of rope for our adult games tonight. Cuz' like hell if I don't know how to tie a sexy figure 8, too."

"Now, we're talking," Redix chuckles, helping Silas lift our moods again.

"I'd like to see that." Daniel helps. "Surely, someone wants to be roped for New Year's."

And I swallow the small lump in my throat.

I don't need to know what sexy gift will be shared tonight or what games our bodies will play. I know that the six of us have forged even deeper bonds in our hearts.

A year from now, there'll be even more to share, to celebrate together.

Eily

FIFTEEN

"Oh, I'm opening my box, alright."

"Get his nipples, too."

Silas throws his chin up, moaning at my command. He loves it when I take charge and clearly loves my instructions now. His excited dick tents his tuxedo pants while Redix and Daniel rub mango oil over his bare chest. They're already shiny from the same slick torture.

"Do you want us to take his trousers off?"

Daniel asks me since it's my night, and they follow my wishes. I even told them how to dress, each wearing black pants and bowties but no shirt.

Yes, they look like male strippers about to dance for us. And as tempting as that show is, I have a smuttier one planned.

"No," I answer, sipping champagne, "your pants stay on for now. We want you all shiny and hard, all oiled up like our sex machines. Keep rubbing him."

Cade chuckles beside me, her violet eyes agreeing. The short black fringe chemise dress I bought her looks delicious. The thin, silky ropes drape over her ample breasts, her excited nipples poking right through.

My dress and happy nipples match hers, but my dress is white, while I bought a red one for Charlie. It looks incredible on her, and the guys about lost it when they could see through the fringe of our dresses to the rose pearl thongs I bought us, too.

Daniel and Redix keep rubbing Silas's abs, covering him in oil, their cocks surging as their fingertips linger under the top of his pants like they want to rip them off. They look like three glossy love-gods about to take the stage or go viral on #muscleman.

Their sexy show has me sitting on the sofa, rolling my hips over the pearls of my thong. The string of pea-sized pearls starts under the silky white rose above my pussy. It disappears between my lips, thrilling my clit and teasing up my crack to the back of the thong.

Yeah, I'm buying more pairs of these.

I glance left at Charlie beside me, and she's rolling her hips, too, at the show.

"Who needs a necklace," she sighs, "when your pussy's wearing a string of pearls and your eyes are watching shiny, hard men?"

"Good god, Eily," Cade purrs. "You've outdone yourself."

"I think I've found my side hustle," I agree. "It's organizing New Year's Eve orgies."

Cade chews her lip at the glistening display. At Daniel and Redix swirling more oil over Silas's pecs, flexing with tension. He's so turned on and tortured he keeps rolling his hooded eyes, a deep growl crawling up his throat.

"Talk about ladies' men," Cade murmurs.

"Oh, I'm *not* being a lady tonight." Charlie's eye-fucking Daniel while she asks me, "What's next because I'm dying for it?"

She sips champagne, looking equally aroused, and I almost feel guilty. I'm not playing fair tonight. We have four hours until midnight, and I know how we're spending them.

It's time to do this.

I'm not one to run, not anymore. This needs to happen tonight, one way or the other. There's one last question between us—Charlie and Silas. All the others we've answered this week.

I may be the youngest, and my mouth may fire faster than my mind, but I've also earned some wisdom—the hard way.

I know if Silas and Charlie don't have this talk tonight. If they leave this ship tomorrow with the same aching question between them, it'll get so awkward it *will* hurt their friendship.

They're already talking less than they usually do. They're acting shy when they've known each other forever. They won't look at each other when they used to laugh so much together.

The only thing that can hurt their friendship now is silence, not sex.

So, I've moved our festivities into the ship's parlor. It's an interior room with no windows. The walls and ceiling are embossed with black damask velvet wallpaper and soft uplighting that glows with seduction. With the help of our crew, I've turned this room into a sexy salon and not the kind for getting your hair done.

No.

This is a room designed for sin.

Our new sex swing dangles in the corner. The sex chaise has been moved down here as well. It awaits our next romp in another corner. A new red and black lover's bondage bench teases from the opposite corner, and a black strapped banging bench sex stool tempts in the other.

Yep, I got lots of holes punched in my Frequent Fucker card for my purchases from Delta's. I'm adding "Sex Room Decorator" to my résumé. Trust me, it's an art form, too. Because this room is now the kind of place where you'll do forbidden things you never would outside of it.

Stacey sent everything to our ship, and I tipped our ship's engineer to hide it from Silas. I made the poor man blush, setting this all up, but our Chief Steward has a crush on him. They got so hot and bothered helping me decorate this room; I'm sure they're hooking up tonight.

"Shit, y'all are getting me so goddamn hard. Eily, how much longer?"

See? Silas is clearly affected by the room. That and two men rubbing oil over his body have him losing his mind.

Grabbing Redix, he's not waiting anymore. He pulls him into a kiss as his hand blindly searches for and quickly finds Daniel's hard cock in his pants. Stroking it, he makes Daniel moan. His hungry touch drives Daniel to return the pleasure, grabbing Silas's stiff shaft in his hungry grasp, his mouth devouring Silas's neck.

"Is this what we're doing tonight?" Cade sighs, watching them. "The guys will fuck for us again?"

"You haven't even opened your gift," Charlie adds.

"Oh, I'm opening my box, alright."

Sitting on the long ivory velvet sofa across the room's back wall, it's like a deep spectator's bench as I spread my legs open for Silas's hooded gaze. He licks his lips at my exposed pussy, and the guys don't know where to stare when Charlie and Cade do the same.

Do they look at each other getting so glossy and turned

on or at the half-naked women on the sofa, watching them with strings of pearls teasing between our glistening lips?

I have some serious fucking talent.

Now that the men are lathered into a frenzy, Redix can't help himself. He looks around the room at all the temptations.

"Alright, our porno princess," he tells me, "you've designed a room for fucking, and we better start soon before I strap someone to that bondage bench and have a Happy New Year in someone's ass."

I laugh. "Jeez, Mr. Full-of-Fucks, slow down." I rise from the sofa, the white fringe parting over my little nipples, my white rose and pearl thong trapping Silas's hungry stare as I sashay past them. "Wet your whistles with champagne or sparkling cider while I open this last box."

The gift gleams on the white marble console table by the door where the ambient up-lights cast a sultry glow. The white and black rug at the center of the room is half hidden by the black vinyl bed sheet I put on the floor as I step around it, seeking the final gift.

Ripping the luxe black paper away, what stroke of lusty luck did I get to roll the six because I know what's in here? But the real surprise is what I've planned.

With that game?

I have no idea what's next.

"Okay,"—I present the gift, the stack of black and gold cards, to the group—"each person draws a black scratch-off card and a gold one. The black card reveals the sex act, and the gold card reveals the person to do it with."

"Hang on." Cade asks me as Redix settles beside her, "You had a sex game custom-made for us?"

"Yep." I fight the urge to start bouncing up and down. "Etsy and Eily go hand-in-hand. Told you I'm creative."

Daniel sits beside Charlie. He can't resist tickling his fingertip over her nipple, exposed by the thin red fringe draped over it as he compliments me. "You're an amorous artist, indeed."

"Baby girl," Silas adds, taking his seat beside Redix, draping his arm over his shoulder, "I don't even *want* to know how much money you spent on this sex furniture. Or the hot nuts you started with our crew setting this fuckroom up."

I answer him, "Name me something better to spend your billions on than a sexroom, especially when we share it with our friends."

"She's got you there."

Redix agrees before Charlie adds, "I'm inspired. We're making one in our house, and I'll pay you to decorate it."

"Oh, I'll do it for free. Just pay me in fucks."

I answer her as I pass the cards to everyone sprawled across the sofa.

"So whatdawedo, again?"

Silas considers the black and gold cards in his hand, so I show him the golden coin that came with them.

"You scratch each card to reveal your surprise."

"What if it's a surprise we don't want?" Redix asks.

I shrug. "No one has to do anything, but given our week so far and the toys in this room, I dare you not to enjoy it. I'll go first, then we'll go in order down the sofa. Like this..."

Standing before them, I demonstrate, rubbing the coin across the black card first. Who doesn't get thrilled by scratch-offs? Especially when it's a guaranteed win of the lusty lottery.

"It says FINGER."

I show it to them before I rub the golden card next. The

first letter that appears is a C, and I show them, teasing with that too.

"Is this even a game?" Silas challenges me with a sly grin. "Because you made these cards up, and I bet you've done all of them already."

"How could I?" I stomp my foot, not mad, just annoyed by the obvious. "I didn't know weeks ago if Charlie and Daniel would be down to play with us?"

"*Really?*" Charlie teases. "Like we'd be able to resist all the dirty games and hot temptations you put in our faces all week?"

"Hell," Redix chuckles, answering her, "I was putting my finger in you the *first* night."

"And my tongue," Cade coos.

"Was there ever any doubt we'd join you?"

Daniel wonders, but we all know who's left. Who hasn't decided if they'll join.

"Well," I grin, informing them, "this card says CHAR-LIE, so I guess it's my turn to join with her."

Thrill lights across all eyes, and I knew this game was a winner. Especially when I tell Charlie to bend over and grab Daniel's shoulders. Excitement raises goosebumps on her flesh while I gloss my fingers with the lube sitting on one of the several black lacquered end tables in the room. She moans as I slowly roll her pearl thong back and forth over her clit. Her hips can't keep still until she's begging me to get her off right in front of her husband, her body writhing at my touch.

Desire storms across Daniel's eyes, Silas's, too, while he watches me do to Charlie's pussy what I know he wishes he could. While he watches me make Charlie come, dripping over my hand with her lips kissing Daniel's.

The tension builds in the room as Silas takes his turn.

"My cards say.... TASTE and... " He scratches the next one and smiles. "EILY."

I love this game. I love how all our boundaries are crumbling. How I'm not shy with them. How it turns me on for them to watch this.

Eagerly, I lie down on the black vinyl sheet so everyone can see as Silas kneels over me, thrilling us when he pours champagne over my pussy. Rolling the pearls back and forth over my dripping clit, he makes me moan before sliding the pearls aside.

"Spread open for me, baby girl," he demands, smiling and admiring me from above. "That's it. Show them the beautiful pussy I love. The pussy that's mine. The sweet pussy I fuck every day." I spread my legs, and Silas moves aside so all can see. "Look at her. Look at how wet she gets for me. How swollen and pink her tight little pussy gets, waiting for me. She's all mine to fuck, now and always."

I'm so open and beyond wet, four people watching while I'm begging Silas to do it. Moving back between my thighs, he wedges his hands under my ass and lifts my pussy like a cup to drink, slurping through my sex with his talented mouth.

Silas always does this. He's so big, and I'm so small, dangling in his grasp. He loves doing it this way, drinking me like I'm the last drop of water. He keeps his face buried in my pussy like his final breath is inside me. I don't know what's hotter, our passion, our love, or our sex, as he makes me come on his tongue, screaming, "Silas!" with everyone watching us.

There's no soft dick in the room, the anticipation building as Cade goes next.

"SUCK," she reads her card aloud with glee. "REDIX," she reveals, and even though they've done it so many times, it's new when they do it in front of us. Because this time, she climbs into the new sex swing, face down so she can fly like Supergirl, saving Redix's world by giving him head at the perfect height.

Even with all the kink and toys, I love watching how their bond is so natural. When their bodies connect, it's palpable, their love and desire.

"Fuck, yes, Cade. Yes, baby, take it." Redix grabs the straps of the swing, controlling her drooling effort. Her spit starts dripping from his swollen dick, making his thighs shake. "Oh fuck, yes. Look at you. So beautiful with my dick fucking your throat. *Fuck,* you always make me come."

Then suddenly, he holds her there, gently gagging her, while he grunts and grunts again. He fills her mouth before letting her go as she swings away, grabbing a smiling breath, his cum dripping from her chin.

And we're drooling, too, at the sight, our hearts racing with theirs.

But nothing can prepare us for Redix's turn. After he helps Cade out of the swing and settles her back on the sofa with a kiss, he picks up his first card, scratches it, and nods.

I hope it isn't the FUCK card because I know one is in the stack, but I also know not even Redix's dick can recover that fast. Silas has the shortest refractory period, especially when my pussy's involved. We've trained our swordsmen well, but they need at least fifteen, usually twenty minutes, to rally for another round.

"Mine says,"—Redix stands before our group, his lush lips curving into a cocky grin—"RIM."

Quickly, he turns away.

At first, I don't know where he's going, but when I see him aim for the sex stool, I'm thrilled that my decadent decor is being put to quick use.

Setting the stool made of black metal and leather straps in front of us, it's designed for someone to lie under it and service the person seated above, and clearly, that's what Redix plans to do.

Then, he slowly scratches his gold card next. He grins, silently letting it hang in the air. He's not telling us the name on the card while he considers his favorite flavored lubes waiting on an end table, reading each bottle before he finally selects one to enjoy.

Silas is so hard with me sitting on his lap. He sounds like he can't take the waiting anymore. The anticipation is torture for him.

"Dude," he asks, "who are you rimmin'?"

"Yeah," Cade wonders, "and what flavor did you pick?"

"Whoever it is," Charlie chimes in, "we're all gonna get hot-in-the-ass watching it."

I swear the Erotic Odds are ever in my favor because Redix smiles so lewdly, licking his full lips before casting his stare at the lucky receiver.

"I'll be rimming Naughty Nectarine over... Daniel's lovebud tonight."

Hail to the Shameless Fuck Gods; we all get hot-in-the-ass watching it. How Daniel strips down, kicking his pants away and leaving only his bowtie on while his cock surges hard, his ass sitting in straps hovering over Redix's eager face.

I've never heard a man groan so loud as Redix lavishes him, torturing Daniel with pleasure and telling him not to jerk off until Daniel can't take it anymore. His cock is so hard. He's in pain. He needs to come. His hulking muscles clench with need before our eyes, his full lips parting and begging for release.

Finally, Redix says he can, and with one clasp of his

hand over his desperate cock while Redix licks his ass, Daniel casts his eyes on Charlie, who's fingering herself at the sight, and he comes, growling as ropes of his creamy pleasure coat Redix's abs below him.

"Holy fuck."

It sounds like Silas is desperate, too; he's ready to come at the sight. It was so arousing, but it's Daniel's turn at my Carnal Cards.

Yep, that's what I'm calling them because we are definitely *playing this every New Year's Eve.*

Daniel and Redix stand to recover. Without a word, Redix swipes Daniel's cum off his abs, licking it off his fingers for Daniel to admire before he yanks him into a passionate kiss. It makes Daniel moan at the taste of his arousal in Redix's mouth. Then Redix lets him go. They both catch their breath as Daniel swipes his pants off the floor, putting them back on while we all need another round of drinks.

But nothing can quell the thirst swelling in the room. Like floodwaters slowly rising, even the walls drip with anticipation now.

We're all aware that the only two names left in the stack are CADE and SILAS, and the last to play are Daniel and Charlie.

I press my lips together, holding back any blurts because I also know the last two sex acts.

Oh, my Slut Goddess, I'll blow candles AND dicks to make it happen.

Please, I feel it in my heart. It'll work. It'll be okay. It'll be so right between all of us. We need this. It needs to happen tonight.

Daniel announces, "My cards say LICK and CADE."

He's happy to play his part next, and I squirm in Silas's lap, watching Cade aim for the stool.

"No, no, naughty girl," Daniel corrects her, and he needs to never stop with that accent. "On the bench."

He points to her destination, and Cade smiles, burning to obey while Daniel straps her down. She kneels with her stomach resting on the padded bench, her ankles and wrists bound with her pussy hanging over the edge. All while it's starting to dawn on us who remains.

Charlie is the last to play, and Silas is the last to receive.

And I know what sex act remains while I watch this one, biting my lip as Daniel slides her pearls aside and drizzles coconut lube over Cade's exposed sex.

"Oh fuck," Redix groans from the sofa, watching as Daniel slowly kneels to devour Cade.

The fact that we take turns, that we all share and give and receive, is so erotic. We care for each other. We desire each other. The six of us meld into one sensuous bond that can't be broken now; I can feel it.

We can watch it as Daniel's fingers move to gently fuck Cade's ass while he lavishes her clit, giving her pleasure, sucking and flicking her exposed nub. Cade looks at Redix the whole time, groaning like a wild animal, while Daniel makes her thighs tremble. Then I hear Charlie moaning at their steamy spectacle, too.

Does Charlie realize she's next?

That she'll be with Silas?

Is that getting her off, too?

Because Silas is, I know my husband well. Yes, he's hard as hell with me sitting on his lap. With us watching Cade strapped to a bench while Daniel sucks her clit so hard, she screams, coming with her stare on Redix.

But Silas is sweating, too. His breath is rasping. His

hands hold me so tight. Like he needs me to know, he needs me to be sure, and I am. Emotions tense his muscles, so I turn to whisper in his ear.

"No matter what, I love you. And I know you love me too, more than anyone. You'll never lose me, and you'll never lose her. She loves you too."

He knows who I'm talking about, and I know what my husband fears: that he'll lose everyone he loves just for loving the *way* he loves.

Silas has sworn several times that he'd be happy with only me. He was willing to give up Redix and Cade for me. At one point, he said he wanted to. That he wanted me all to himself, and he wanted the same for me. That he was all mine. But that was before we got married, and I knew better.

I believe that true love, real love, is freedom.

For too long, I wasn't free, and I'll never cage my husband either. He's always had a big heart. Silas grew up alone. He learned to share to have friends, and Charlie was his first. He can't help that he grew up desiring her, too. He was young, and she's gorgeous.

I know Silas desires me above all. And I know better than to force someone to be who they're not. Silas and I were meant to be together. We have the kind of hearts that can share our bodies with others while our souls stay true to each other.

I don't know what he'll do, but I know how I feel about it with every ounce of my being.

This is meant to be as Silas nuzzles my cheek, taking me in the deepest kiss. Cupping my face, I know he'll never let me go. Gently laving his tongue over mine, I know he loves me above anyone else. I cherish him, too, so I'll share him. He's too incredible to cage, too giving to be selfish.

"No matter who I fuck," he whispers over our lips. "You're the one inside me, Eily. My heart won't beat without you. I finally found you and your shoe; you're all mine forever. Promise me."

I dive into his hazel gaze and tell him, "I don't need to promise what's already true. You're the indigo in my rainbow. I can't shine without you, Silas."

The room disappears. The game too. At least for the moment while Silas makes me smile. From the depths of my soul, he does.

"I'll always be the Jack to your Rose," he says. "I'll give you the whole damn board and die for you."

"I don't want you to die for me, but you can give your balls to someone else for the night."

I smile, lifting from his kiss to see Charlie staring at her scratched-off cards.

And I'm usually so good at making people happy. I'm great at reading emotions, too. I'm sensitive to what people feel, but I don't know the look on her face.

She's silent until Cade helps her. Daniel has unstrapped her and helped her off the bench. They both have recovered their breath while we focus on Charlie now.

"We know the name on your card is SILAS," Cade says. "So what's your action with him?"

For the first time in forever, I'm not blurting. More than a filter stifles my mouth. Fear does.

Because I think that's the emotion across Charlie's gorgeous face. Fear and... desire?

Yes, they fight for control of her face. Her soft lips part with lust, but her eyes fill with worry, reading her black card as she reveals its demand.

"FUCK."

Daniel smiles. Redix raises an eyebrow. Cade nods. While it's my game, it's my responsibility.

"You don't have to." I tell Charlie, "It's just a game."

But Charlie looks at the room, considering us. Her pause is long before she stammers.

"Y'all, it's just. It's just that... " She chews her lip. "I feel like... "

Breath heaves from her lungs, her words halting. She glances at me, then Daniel, then finally, she stares at Silas, emotions swirling in her sapphire eyes before she jumps up from the sofa. Shocking us, she runs out of the room.

"Charlie!"

Daniel moves to run after her, but Silas calls out, "Let me. Lemme talk to her. I'm the one she's upset about."

"She's not upset," Cade defends her. "She's confused."

Daniel rakes a hand through his coal waves, his steps wavering, his ocean eyes in a storm.

"None of this is bloody worth it if someone gets hurt, especially my *wife*. I won't stand for it!"

Daniel's getting angry, and it warms my heart. He loves Charlie so much. I think he'd rip limbs from bodies for her, including his own.

"I'll never hurt her," Silas assures him. "You know that. Just lemme go talk to her. I should've done it days ago. We need to get this out there once and for all. Whatever the hell it is."

"Here." I grab a gold condom wrapper from the end table. "Just in case," I tell him as I climb off Silas's lap, urging him to stand, to make this right. "Go get her."

Silas looks at me like I'm half-crazy and half the best wife ever. Both are true.

He asks me one more time, "You sure?"

"Sure as shit," I tell him. "Go fix this because we have

two hours before New Year's, and we'll all six be together and happy and smiling about it, dammit."

He gets up, gently kissing my lips before he rushes to Daniel, snatching him into a hug.

"Just make her happy," Daniel demands, his big hands grabbing Silas's bare back. It looks like he could love him or end him forever. "Whatever she wants, give it to her and make her happy. That's all I ask."

"I promise."

Silas swears it to Daniel before he glances back at me one more time, and I blow him a kiss.

Turning away, he runs after Charlie, and I cross my fingers, making my New Year's wish now.

WHY CHOOSE ENDINGS?

Dear Reader,

I wrote this book in the true spirit of a **WHY CHOOSE ROMANCE.**

It means you get to choose the ending.

I'm giving you a spicy **THEY DO** chapter, where Charlie and Silas finally fulfill their desire. And I'm giving you a touching **THEY DON'T** chapter, revealing why their friendship means so much to them.

I did this because, honestly, I wanted both endings too. I love these characters. They've been in my books and heart for years. I had to give them both endings because, in the end, regardless of their choice, they get their happily ever after.

Xoxo,
Kelly

Charlie

THEY DO

"You blew my mind and was like a dream."

Why am I running?

And where the fuck am I going?

I belong back there, back in that salon, with everyone I love. Loving them in ways I didn't know were possible before this week.

But my bare feet keep pounding like my pulse, chasing this storm of emotions through my veins as I race over gleaming marble floors.

What do I want?

Like two bolts of lightning cracking across the sky simultaneously, it lights up my mind, my darkest desires hidden until now.

FUCK. SILAS.

That's what the cards said. Eily couldn't have divined that. It's fate.

And yes, it's what I want.

And yes, it's what I fear.

But why? With all the shit I've survived, fear is my bitch.

Taking the gleaming stairs two at a time, the exertion feels good; it's familiar and soothing. If I could run a thousand miles, I would, but I'd come right back here.

This is where I belong.

My thundering heart feels it.

I'm safe with Silas. I always have been. We've existed together for so long that I don't even feel myself around him. I just am. I've just lived with Silas beside me.

But right now... I feel everything.

Safety smears into a sensuous ache for him that my body doesn't recognize but welcomes. It's too strong to deny.

Racing down the narrow corridor, I mindlessly seek the familiar destination, our stateroom. *Ours?* Mine and Daniel's.

I don't even think of myself as separate from him. We're one and the same. Daniel's woven into every part of me.

The polished wooden door is heavy as I shove it open. The large bed with its black silk duvet is neatly made, pristine like we were never there, but we were. We made love there, and Daniel wants this for me. I know he does.

"It feels amazing," he told me this morning. Holding me in bed, he said, "Just letting ourselves feel what we want with the people we trust. I'm glad you made us take this holiday. I'm glad you made me talk to Redix. And I hope you'll sort it with Silas too. I want you to be happy like me."

My sweating palm leaves a print on the door's chrome handle as it gently closes behind me, and I grab a breath—several of them.

Staring at the bed, I hear it telling me to do this. To be

happy. It's not that I'm unhappy, but to feel happy *and* free like Daniel is now.

"Charlie!"

Silas calls for me from two decks below. He'll find me soon, and I need to find my answer. I need to face this now.

Alright bitch, are you gonna fuck your best friend?

My pussy jumps to her feet. My clit salutes, standing at attention.

"Ma'am! Yes, ma'am, you are!"

But she's a bad influence. She's ready to fuck the rules and everyone after what just happened. Eily fingered me for Daniel to watch. Silas drank Eily's pussy like a chalice. Cade swung, sucking Redix's cock. Redix rimmed Daniel; *holy fuck, that was hot.* Then Daniel ate Cade's pussy like a buffet, and now it's our turn.

FUCK.

SILAS.

"Charlie!"

His deep voice thunders along with his steps, nearing down the corridor.

Answer me: are you going to fuck your best friend?

I search my logic this time, though it's clouded by lust. Who can think clearly in a room full of sex furniture and hot, half-naked bodies coming everywhere?

Operating half-drunk under X-rated influences, my mind flits her hand, dismissing my concerns with the explicit, hard facts.

Silas has watched you fuck Daniel. And Redix. You've squirted on Silas's face several times, and he's jerked off all over you twice. He talks dirty to you, watching you while you get a DP with his dick in your mouth, and that alone makes you cream.

Come.

285

The.

Fuck.

On.

Bitch, quit cafeteria-lining your friendly fucking ethics. You're picking and choosing which acts cross a line when, clearly, you wanna load your entire plate full of sex with Silas.

Those hard and hot facts, I can't deny.

Hell, they make me laugh.

Who am I kidding? This new feeling for Silas isn't fear. It's just new. It's just lust. And it feels so damn good letting it slide through my veins, like the most luscious drug, relaxing my muscles and erasing my concerns.

If I only feel this. If I stop asking questions and feel this answer, I have no worries, only desire. And I wanted this holiday for six. For sex.

"Charlie Girl?"

Silas huffs on the other side of the door.

And what does he want?

I wait... and wait for his answer too...

Finally, he gently knocks. And will he quit being so goddamn irresistible?

This is his ship. The door is unlocked. He can barge in here if he wants to, but he doesn't. Silas waits for me like he has for almost twenty years.

"Talk to me," he speaks through the door. "We don't have to do anything. Just let me know you're okay."

The vibrations of his deep voice sound worried, but suddenly, I'm not. The thought of him soothes, wrapping around my excited body, drifting right down to my ready, wet sex.

"Just a minute."

I reply, my steps getting bold, aiming for our bathroom.

Goddamnit, if we're gonna do this, we're gonna do it right. Like Silas dreamed for it to happen. I'm gonna make this so damn good for him.

The crew who cleans our stateroom have done their daily job. Not that we leave a mess, but there it is—my red bikini. One of the stews took it from the vanity where I left it and hung it on the fancy, wall-mounted drying rack designed for wet clothes.

My red fringe chemise dress flutters to the floor before I reach and wrap my naked body in the warm bikini.

It's like I'm lying in the sun again. Like I did for so many days with Silas on the beach. I'd read or take naps or just stare at the steely Atlantic while, apparently, I was torturing Silas...

But no more.

Yes, it turns me on knowing how badly he wanted me, and now, I feel the burning desire, too. It controls my mind and steps to the door. Opening it, I stand in a red bikini before Silas and someone get a broom. His jaw hits the floor, breaking our sexual tension into a million sizzling pieces.

He doesn't speak.

I don't breathe.

Desire taps her impatient foot until he finally sighs, "Holy fuck." Grabbing the back of his neck, he can't take his eyes off my body, combing over what he can have. His naked chest heaves at the sight. His semi rouses in his pants, but still, he asks, "Should we talk first?"

Turning around, I aim for the bed and make one helluva show crawling across the silk sheets for him.

"Yeah," I tell him, "we'll *talk* like we're back on the beach, but this time, it ends differently." Reclining on the ivory pillow, hooking my finger, I summon him. "Unless you've changed your mind."

He grins, stepping into the room, letting the door gently close behind him.

"I can change my mind all I want," he says. "But ain't nothing changing my hungry dick that's always wanted to fuck you."

With every step he stalks my way, my pulse climbs, and I love it.

"Goddamn." He shakes his head but won't take his wild eyes off of me. "I can't believe this is finally happening."

I pat the spot beside me.

"You said we should talk first, so let's talk."

Silas prowls across the bed, the sight and smell of him filling me, but it's not familiar anymore. It's new. It's arousing. A half-naked Silas with his hair hanging down tonight is like a new lover with his cocky grin.

Lying down on his side, propping up on his elbow, his gaze roams down my flesh, leaving goosebumps in its wake.

"So whatcha wanna talk about, Charlie Girl?"

I mirror him, not missing that his teasing eyes land on my cleavage, more pronounced by my posture.

"First of all, don't call me that if we fuck. I hear that, and you're thirteen again, not the hot thirty year-old lying hard and half-naked beside me."

"Alright, then. What should I call you?"

"The dirty words you use turn me on. 'You're sweet slut.' 'Your good little whore.' Right, Daddy?"

His eyes slam shut.

"Fuck, I never thought I'd hear you talk to me like that. Or that I'd be lying beside you on a bed, you, wearing a red bikini, and me about to fuck you. You're making me sweat and hard as hell. My fucking heart's pounding so fast, I hope I don't pass out before I do, and—"

"Silas,"—I cut him off—"promise me it won't ruin us."

Because we're always honest like this, we share everything, so we'll say this too.

"It confused me at first," I confess. "All this week, I don't know what happened, but I saw you on the dock, and all of a sudden, my pussy got a mind of her own. And I don't know if it's all the sex I'm having with everyone else or what. But yes, I feel it. I'm sweating, too. I want to fuck you, but not if we lose our friendship."

His eyes soften, his tone, too.

"You'll never lose me, Charlie. We'll always love each other in this way I got no name for, and we know it."

Gently, he reaches, tracing over the scar down my cheek.

Silas knows my story. It floods my heart, but then his fingertip tickles over my lips, and my clit sparks at his touch, firming with that look in his eyes.

"I worried too this week," he confesses. "Like when I realized it could finally happen. That Eily wanted us to and that Daniel wouldn't kill me."

"He'd never hurt you. He loves you, too." I huff, grinning, "Fuck, he's changed this week."

"It was always inside him. Like this was always inside me."

He keeps tracing over my lips, staring at them. We'll never kiss, but he can touch me here, and it ripples down my body, wave after wave of desire. I'm soaking my bikini.

"I'll always love Eily the most," he says. "I'll die for her, and I'll die if I lose her, too. I didn't know love like that until I found her again. But I'll never lie to her, either. I can't deny what happens to my body around you. And she told me to stop feeling guilty about it. That it's natural. She said I imprinted on you. It's some weird shit she read in her vampire-wolf books, but you get the idea. She's wiser than us all, and it makes sense. You were the first person I ever wanted, and I guess my hard dick is a compass, and your pussy is the North Pole."

I laugh. I can't help it. Grabbing his hand, I hold it and flop on my back.

"I love us." I stare at the ceiling. "I love how we can just talk."

"Well, we've been *just* talking for twenty years." He flops on his back beside me. "Please tell me we're finally gonna fuck so I can get this craze out of my body for you. That's what it feels like. Like, let's just do it once, and I'll be fine."

"Shhh." I shake his hand and close my eyes. "Let's just lie here a bit and see if we change our minds."

But we can't.

Desire stirs thick in the air around us. It's hot and steamy. It's driving every part of us to satisfy this urge. Lust itches our skin; we writhe and can't lie still.

Every clock on the planet ticks with impatience, and so does my pussy. She's dripping and pointing at her watch. My excited clit is pacing back and forth, too, like "Bitch! You got two minutes before I take charge."

But I like this new tension between us. I like his familiar heat beside me. I like his hand, sweating in my grasp, and I like letting it build so damn high, so strong, one last time...

Silas tries stifling his groan, but he can't. "Goddamn, Charlie G—" He stops himself, muttering. "It's like we're back on the beach, and I wanna fuck you so bad. I'm going crazy just lying beside you."

"Tell me another fantasy, a dark one you had about me."

Silence fills the air. All I can hear is lust sizzling around us until he confesses.

"That night after I caught you and Daniel in the dunes.

When I saw how he made you squirt, how you came so hard, I went home and imagined us together, too. It drove me crazy. I stood by my kitchen table and imagined you tied to it. Like face down with your ankles tied to the legs in the knots I love, your pussy spread open and wet for me. And I jerked off over my table. I was leaning, braced over it, imagining I was fucking you like that. Like you couldn't fight me. You wanted me to fuck you. You begged me to until I made you come and squirt all over my wooden floors. Fuck, I know it's wrong, but I came so hard imagining us. I even shouted your name when I did."

Oh my god, I can't take it anymore.

"Show me," I huff. Opening my eyes, I turn to find him staring back at me, and I nod toward the tent in his tuxedo pants. "Show me how much you still want me like that."

Without ripping his gaze away, he rips his pants open. But I glance down, biting my lip at his thick, hard cock, flexing and dripping for me.

"This is how I've always wanted you, Charlie," he says. "This is what you do to me. I can't help it."

"You want me that bad?"

"Fuck yes," he growls. "You have no idea what I'm holding back right now. For so goddamn long."

I glance back up at his hazel eyes, and they narrow, hooding with lust. His lips part, his breath getting shallow. Like a dog on a chain, his muscles tense beside me, from his corded forearms to his pecs to his shredded abs, to even his sculpted thighs tensing with passion, with pain.

On instinct, my body reacts to the sight of his desire. It's strong like him, the only force in the room.

"Don't hold back," I tell him. "Do it. Fuck me, Silas, like you wanted to on that beach."

Like the powerful man he is, not the teenager he used to

be, he thinks first, yanking his bowtie off as he plucks a gold condom from his pants pocket before he shucks them away. And thank god, because I almost forgot. Lust robbed me of all my logic, but not him.

He's the man in control now.

Rising naked on his knees, I watch him sheathe his cock before he climbs between my legs, snatching them open.

All the demand knotting the muscles on his body above mine has me craving that he ravish me right now. That he just plunge inside and fuck me so hard, but he doesn't.

His stare is long, like he can't believe it; he doesn't know where to start. So I spread my legs wider, but he growls.

"Don't move. Be still. I'm in charge. I'm getting ready to fuck you so good, and for so long you'll be too weak to walk when I'm done."

Whoever I was years ago? Last week? She's gone, and goodbye. All that remains is a heavy desire; I can't breathe; I don't need to.

Silas leans forward, bracing himself on one arm over me, tenting his perfect body over mine, and this is all I need to satisfy this primal urge.

His mouth lowers, his coconut strands tickling my cheek, his tan skin steaming over mine. Pressing his lips to the shell of my ear, his hungry cock urges against my bikini.

"I'll fuck you like my slut. I'll fuck you like my good little whore. I'll fuck you like I've always imagined, Charlie. Beg me to fuck you now because once I start, I will *not* stop. I won't be able to."

"Please, Silas." I lace my hands through his hair, pressing my lips to his cheek, giving him the beg he wants, the fantasy he's had. "Please fuck me so hard, and don't stop until you make me come, like you've always imagined with your cock coming so deep inside me."

"*Fuuuccckkk*," he growls, his free hand ripping my bikini top aside. His mouth moves down so fast, latching onto my exposed nipple. He sucks so hard my back bows off the bed. The passion in his mouth is sweet pain.

"Oh god," I gasp at its power, at his power.

Ripping the other side away, his mouth seizes my other nipple, sucking and tonguing it as if his thirst will never be satisfied.

"Fuck, these tits," he rasps over them. Going back and forth, he can't decide which of my breasts he wants to devour the most. "Fuck, Charlie. Fuck." While his mouth takes one, his fingertips claim, pinching and twirling the other, and my ribs crack, arching to get more of me in his mouth.

I'm writhing under him, my hips lifting for the erection he's grinding into me.

"Silas, please." I reach down, trying to guide him where the torture is maddening. "Please fuck me."

I know he gets off on my begs. I know it's etched deep in his psyche. Fantasies for this have filled him for years, and they flood me, too, taking my mind that's gone. It's not here. Only our bodies. Only this passion, this desire that's tortured him for so long, and my body, splayed open, crying to satisfy it.

Lifting to kneel between my thighs, his lungs heave, his hair curtains his face as he stares at my pussy, still covered by my drenched bikini. I need him to thrust inside me so hard and so fast, but he doesn't.

Lingering his fingertip under my bikini bottoms, he tickles the inside of my thigh, his gaze wild but his words controlled.

"Are you wet for me?"

"Yes," I huff. I writhe.

"Let's see," he says, gingerly peeling my bottoms aside like he has all the time in the world and hasn't waited forever for this.

His eyes dim, his sparkle clouded by dark need, gazing down at my exposed sex. I swear I'm dripping. I'm glossing my thighs; I'm losing my mind for this.

"Look at you, Charlie," he admires. "So swollen and pink. Look at your clit; it's so hard for me. Clench your cunt for me, too. Let me see how much you want my cock."

I obey, loving the demand and how Silas is so dirty when he fucks. He's not the sweet man I know, and that's fine. I don't want to fuck sweet. I want to fuck wild.

"Yes, that's it," he growls, watching me make my pussy pulse, using the muscles I have across my floor to do it for his gaze. "Yes, look at you. Your pussy's so hungry for my cock to finally fuck you, isn't it?"

Suddenly, he grabs his thick base, slapping the heavy tip of his cock against my raw, exposed clit.

"Shit!" I cry out, a jolt of pleasure shooting down my thighs that jump.

"Say it." He slaps his cock against my clit, again and again, the *smacks* cracking through my thrilled nerves. "Say it. Say my name. Say what you want me to do you."

"Silas." His name moans across my lips, the ones on my face and the ones between my thighs that can't spread anymore open for him. "Please fuck me. I'm begging you."

It's true. It's so damn true as he holds his base and my gaze, barely pressing his tip into my aching entrance.

And the pause he gives, holding us right here, suspended where I'm desperate to feel him finally. Where he's wondered about, fantasized about, craved, and come thinking about.

It's that line we'll cross and never go back. Forward is

the way to go, and it's okay. This is okay. It's what everyone wants, especially us.

Tenting his body back over mine, we're hanging by this luscious thread, about to snap while he demands, "Look at me. Look at me the whole time while I fuck you, Charlie."

And I do. The light in his eyes changes. It shimmers in a golden color I've never seen as I sigh, "Please, Silas," and he gently murmurs, "Charlie," but his first thrust isn't gentle.

It's brutal.

It's amazing.

It punches my core, feral and wild and unrelenting. I cry out, and he does, too. We can't even use words. We can't believe we're doing this, and it feels so damn good, him sinking his cock deep inside me, then over and over again, like instinct reigns supreme. We're not in charge. Lust is. The sweat across our bodies. The clench of my pussy. The maddening pound of his hard cock that won't stop. This fire that's been simmering between us ignites like gasoline on flames, and I'm going fast.

This isn't like when I fuck Daniel. That's a powerful union. The deepest connection. That's where I belong.

This isn't like any sex I've ever had. It's not fucking. It's pure lust. It's starvation satisfied. It's hunger fed. It's thirst about to be quenched, and it's gonna be so damn wet.

"Silas," I can barely speak, reaching for him. Pulling his body down to mine, I'm going to need him like this, his weight securing me while I drop into an ocean and drown.

His grunts get wild. Hooking his arm under the crook of my knee, he takes me, opening me even more. Pinning me down, he stares into my eyes while his massive cock hammers into my body, diving and searching like he knows it's here. It's deep inside me. My orgasm is waiting for him to claim it.

"Fuck, Charlie," he huffs. "Fuck, you feel so good. So goddamn good. I can't believe I'm fucking you." He snarls, "I'm gonna make you come so fucking hard on my dick."

He is.

He's smacking against my clit with the perfect, savage strikes that have pleasure coiling tight in my body. The pussy he's pounding opens for him, taking the pleasure he gives because I'm going. I'm slipping down into that lush, deep place I disappear into before I emerge in a gush I can't control.

And he's watching it all. Our gaze is locked, and his lips shake.

"Charlie, fuck," he sighs, slowing his thrusts, driving each one so deep, shoving out my breath, my sweet cries escaping. "Fuck," he marvels, watching it all, "I'm making you come."

His awe. His desire. His skills and passion and, yes, his love. It's not one we can name or, marry, or need every day. It's not the first in our lives or the one we'll die with, but it's here. We believe in it. We cherish it. We're right here, sharing the last pieces of ourselves.

"Yes, Silas," I stammer. It's all I can do. I'm helpless to it. It's trembling inch by inch up my shaking legs, one over his shoulder, the other wrapped around his ass, feeling his muscles flex, his effort, his weight, his passion. It shakes my head. It's going to be so strong. It's going to hurt with the pleasure I crave.

I grab his hair, my other fist clenching the sheets to hang on. His cock is incredible; my clit is screaming; I can't hold it back. His thrusts are so sweet, so savage, and *oh my god, I'm fucking Silas, and he's so damn good. He's making me come and...*

I anchor my eyes to his and let go.

"Ahhhh!" Bursts from my lungs. Names can't find my mind. Breath can't find my lungs. Pleasure heaves through my body, rippling through my bones; the luscious coil bound so tight releases as I cry out again, showering my body and his.

"*Fuucckk,*" he groans, looking down, watching our bodies join. How my lust splatters his thighs before he pulls out, the ache making me moan and gush again, all over his swollen, dripping cock as he rattles his tip across my wet electric clit, making me spill even more over him and the bed.

"Fuck, Charlie." He's amazed. "Fuck yes, look at you come for me. Look at you squirt all over my cock. Goddamn."

He drives back inside me, punching my core, and my body won't stop shaking; my hips won't stop lifting for more; I'm not in control. I want this too much. I'm whimpering for more as he keeps fucking me. Like he's taking his chance and will never stop, and my body doesn't want him to.

"I'm not done with you," he huffs, releasing my leg over his shoulder. My muscles are liquid with release, but my body can give more. He's doing this to me. Silas is *that* good. He moves like he's about to flip me over, but he surprises me, swearing, "I wanna taste how I made you come on my dick."

Burying his face between my legs, he slings them over his shoulders while he laps at my drenched pussy like a greedy dog in a bowl, and I give his thirsty mouth more.

I can't stop moaning, or crying out, or coming. I don't know what my body is doing, but craving every minute of this. Every minute of Silas making me come on his tongue before he crouches above my body like a wild animal, his chin dripping with my lust while he starts to fuck me again, his thrusts feral.

"You taste so good. You feel so good," he grunts. "A slut, a whore, I'll fuck you so hard, Charlie; I don't care because I'm finally fucking your wet pussy right now."

The piston of his cock is endless like his desire has been for so long, like he doesn't want this to end, and I don't know where we go for minutes until we can't take anymore; I can't take anymore. I want him to feel the sweet satisfaction, too.

Fisting his hair, I pull his ear to my lips.

"It's like I'm tied to your table, Silas. My pussy is so open and wet for you." His sudden groan is deep, his dick pumping hard, the muscles across his back drawing up. "Your big dick is so thick and hard and fucking me so good. Feel how slick and swollen I am for you? Feel how you're making me want you?" His back bows, his breath stuttering, his shaking knees digging deep into the mattress, bracing himself with desperate grunts, his cock not stopping. "You feel so good inside me, Silas. You're making me come. I'm squirting all over your dick and all down your thighs. Feel it. Feel how much I want you."

Grunts of pain and pleasure huff from his lips pressed to my ear. Lips that pant, "Yes, Charlie." Like he's helpless. "Fuck, yes." Like he's letting go. He's finally feeling it, too.

"I want to feel you come, Silas." I scratch the muscles knotted across his back, and his growl fills the room. "That's it. Come so hard and deep inside my pussy."

I clamp down, clenching and using all my might and muscle; I wrap all I have around Silas and take him down with me. I hold him while he cries out, his body shaking until his spine racks and his thrust stills inside me. I feel his thick shaft jump with his deep, quaking groan, straining the veins in his neck as I press my lips to them.

He's coming inside me, and that makes me come again. With a flutter, I tremble around Silas, and he feels it too, panting with a grunt as it takes our bodies one last time, with one last rush of release before we collapse, his body panting over mine.

His weight is comforting. It's new and familiar, and I have to get used to this.

This is us.

I stay wrapped around him, his face buried next to my cheek. Satisfaction soothes through my bones, and his body finally relaxes, exhaling, equally gratified on top of mine. Our breath calms and it's that familiar peace between us, this bond we'll always have.

This is me and Silas. This is who we are now; the world didn't end, nor did our friendship. Sex with him felt so damn amazing, but my heart hasn't changed. Neither has his. I guess this was here all along.

"I feel like a calla lily."

I can't help it. We always joke, and he chuckles. It shakes his body over mine before he gently pulls out and gazes down at me, grinning.

"I only creamed your lilies. You're the one who watered them tonight."

His grin is so cocky, but his eyes sparkle.

"No," I answer, "you can take the credit for that too. You'll be buying a new mattress for this bed."

"Ah, hail no." He wraps around me, twisting our bodies to where I'm resting in the crook of his shoulder. "I wanted that for so long, I'm saving this damn mattress. I'm adding it to my keepsakes for the memory."

It makes me pause. It makes me wonder. But why hold back now?

"Was it everything you thought it'd be?"

"Fuck no," he huffs, squeezing me. "I got a good imagination, but I knew your pussy would be better."

I lift up, challenging him. "All that we just did, our hot-as-hell fuck, and it's just *better*?"

"Alright, it was damn fucking amazing. Thank you very much. You blew my mind and wad like a dream. My dick can finally stand down. But nothing is better than being with my wife. She's the best. I'm just sayin'."

His big smile speaks volumes. He's being sweet. He's telling the truth, and I feel it, too. It was a hot fuck, and we're still best friends. We love each other, and nothing has changed. We just finally scratched that painful itch and now feel the peace of satisfaction.

Poking his sweaty chest, I praise him, "Yes, and that's how it should be—your wife is the best. Because your cock is damn fucking amazing, too, but my husband's is sublime."

"Sublime?" He scrunches his face. "Why you gotta use fancy words? Just say Daniel's dick is the best for you. It ain't gonna hurt my feelings. You got a right to your wrong opinion."

I laugh. "You little shit, you know what I mean."

"So we're back to Charlie Girl and Little Shit now?"

"Yeah, when we're not fucking."

His dark eyebrow shoots up. "So, we're fucking again?"

"One day, maybe." I shrug. "When I'm in the mood for second best."

He throws his chin back, laughing so hard. "Please, tell that to Redix and let me record it. That man ain't ever been in third place for shit."

Bliss bubbles through my veins. I gaze at Silas and see a

new year, a new world for us. All six of us. Together, we'll be fine. Better than fine.

"I love you." I squeeze his ribs. "I love all of us."

Leaning down, he kisses my head, muttering over my tousled strands, "I love you, too, Charlie Girl. You know what you mean to me, and yes, you just blew my mind. I don't feel crazy anymore, but don't make me get all flowery about it; just ask your calla lilies."

He squeezes me tighter, warning, "And we need to go get back to my beautiful wife before we miss our New Year's toast, or I'll never hear the end of it. She'll make me pay by buying her enough glow-in-the-dark monster dildos to circle the globe."

We jump up, and I strip off my drenched bikini while Silas quickly disappears into the bathroom, discarding the condom. When he returns, he stands naked and relaxed before me, watching me with a grin, and I shrug. He agrees, shrugging back with a satisfied look. Grabbing my hand, like when we were young and are even better now, he leads me back to the salon.

Back to the ones we love.

Silas

THEY DON'T

"You can try for one ending or another, but fate decides your happily ever after."

I'm not a dick.

"Charlie!" I shout from the bottom of the stairs.

I'm a man chasing after my hot best friend with my beautiful wife's encouragement. I'm a man racing up a winding staircase with cherry wood banisters inlaid with sparkling chrome. The mirrors on the curved wall of the round stairwell are thin and stacked, designed to look like the Empire State Building.

This fancy ship may not be my style, but it's mine. My ship. My life. My marriage and my friendship.

I'm a man damn lucky to have it all.

Because I know where my best friend's going, it's where she always goes when she needs to think. Charlie likes to lie down and hug a pillow while she decides her next move. And for so many years, I'd lie right beside her.

Yes, dammit, I'd get hard doing it.

I've given up trying to keep my dick down around Charlie. Damn thing's got a head of its own.

Eily thinks it's funny. Of course, she notices. She's a meteorologist for my cock. She can always predict which way it's gonna blow.

This morning, Eily told me that I "imprinted" on Charlie.

For a second, I thought it was new slang for coming on someone, but then my wife high-schooled me.

I held her in my arms. I always wake to my sunrise, to my Eily in my grasp, and usually, my morning wood poking between her cute ass cheeks.

I wanted to make love to her this morning. Like I was full of feelings, watching how amazing Eily's been with everyone this week. For so long, she had no friends. Well, she had one shitty friend, but now she has five of us who adore her, and I get overwhelmed by how giving she is, how she's truly the best thing in my life.

"You're hard for me this morning,"—she giggled, shaking her ass against me—"but I think you should save it for Charlie tonight."

I nuzzled into her neck, kissing her sweet spot. "But I want *you*."

"You want *me*, but you've imprinted on Charlie, and you need to see it through."

"I did *what*?"

My wife is so cute and creative and confident. Half the time, I don't know what brilliant shit she's talking about.

Twisting in my grasp, she stared up at me like I was crazy. Like I'd never heard of air or water.

But no, she was talking about her vampire-werewolf books.

"Like, when you were growing up," she said, "you

imprinted on Charlie, like Jacob, the werewolf, imprinted on Renesmee, Bella and Edward's daughter. It's not love. It's more. You're whatever she needs. A protector. A friend. A lover." Her grin grew while her hand blindly reached for what belongs to her. "And you get hard for her, I see it. And with the way you get hard for me, too, I don't know how you don't pass out with all that blood leaving your brain and rushing to this cock."

I couldn't lie to my wife; I love and respect her too much. Besides, my body can't hide what my brain can't make sense of.

"So," I asked her, "did Jacob cry in a chair for months and scream in his sleep waiting for the girl he printed?"

"*Imprinted*,"—she rolled her eyes—"and no."

"Then how did their story end?"

I couldn't believe I was asking about her teenage vampire books because you can be damn sure I ain't watching all five movies to know the ending. Unless... Eily asks me to. Then I'll hold her so tight and heckle the screen the whole damn time.

"Jacob fulfilled his destiny, and they all lived happily ever after."

"So me fucking Charlie is your happily ever after?"

"No." She climbed on top of me. "You and me together is our happily ever after." She smiled, nuzzling her nose against mine. "You fucking Charlie is fulfilling your desire. Your hard cock deserves a happy ending too."

She made me laugh, showering me with kisses before she finally made love to me with all the feels I have for her.

But now, I ain't laughing. I feel worried.

"Charlie!" I call out for the second time, half expecting to find her halted in the hallway, waiting for me.

But I don't.

I make it to the wooden door of the stateroom where she and Daniel have been staying this week, lifting my fist to bang on it.

But...

I stop...

All the times I've waited outside Charlie's door come rushing back in a flood of memories. Most are sweet, the boy waiting on his crush. But some are so heartbreaking. Sometimes, I knew Charlie was crying and alone on the other side of the door. Sometimes, I was all she had, so I'd rush in. I wouldn't knock. I was too worried about her. Like Eily said, I always protected her, just like she protected me.

Eily's right. "Love" can't describe what Charlie means to me.

I didn't have siblings, and neither did she. I didn't have true friends. I was too different, and Charlie was the same, but we had each other. She lost her family like me. Though she could never get hers back, I did. Then I found Eily, while she found Daniel, and together, they made a new family.

All the while, yes, I wanted her. But even more, I wanted her to be happy. And that's all she wanted for me.

"Charlie Girl," I huff, talking to her closed door again. I know she can hear me.

My heart, my fist, my mind: they pause. They wait.

And finally... I hear myself.

Sometimes, when you don't know the answer, fate provides it. Sometimes, you want a lover, but every day, you need a friend more.

I swing the door open. This is my ship, my best friend, and I'll always take care of her. "Talk to me."

I find her standing in the middle of the room, turning to stare back at me, caught in the same dilemma.

Yeah, she's wearing sexy lingerie. Yes, her face is breathtaking. Her blonde mane is seductive, and I can see her amazing tits. The tempting pearl thong Eily bought the women to wear traps my glance, the string of pearls disappearing between Charlie's sweet pussy lips.

Fuck, there goes my dick again.

It can't forget this week—this night.

But I remember my heart.

"We don't have to do anything." My steps seek her. I wrap my arms around her, pulling her head to rest against my shoulder. I've done it a thousand times. "Just let me know you're okay."

"Just a minute," she mutters against my bare skin.

Seconds feel like forever when you hold someone, waiting for their answer.

"I'm just confused," she finally sighs. "And you're half naked and hot as hell and smell like coconut and sex, which makes it worse."

I chuckle. "Well, I ain't confused. I'll always be your friend, and if you're confused about fucking me, too, then we ain't doing it."

Her lungs exhale in my grasp. She melts in my arms like my deciding for us lifted a weight off her shoulders. She nuzzles into me tighter, wrapping her arms around my waist. I kiss her vanilla strands as she huffs against my naked flesh.

"But what about your fantasies and my red bikini and me being really horny right now?"

I laugh harder.

I can't help it.

"I'm horny too. Hell, can't you feel it? I'm holding my best friend, and I ain't gonna fuck her, but damn, you're half-naked and hot as hell, too, and my hard dick is well aware. It always has been. Then you tell me you're horny for me too, and that ain't right. You're gonna be torture until my dying day."

"But I don't want to torture you." She lifts away, confronting my gaze. "It tortures me, too. Silas, I'm not used to wanting you, but clearly, I do. My body wants to fuck you but—"

I shake my head.

"There's no 'but' in fucking," I tell her. "Well, unless you're butt fucking—asses, I prefer—but you know what I mean. If you gotta question us, then there's your answer. We know who we are. We don't fuck. We're best friends. You're my Charlie Girl, and I'm your Little Shit,"—I smile— "unless you eat an entire bag of corn chips."

Laughter takes her eyes; it lifts her lips and matches mine.

Fuck, this is what I mean.

We can't lose this.

"Now… " I keep going. I gotta make her happy; I promised Daniel I would. "If you wanna butt fuck, that hole's fair game."

Softly, she punches my chest.

"So, you'll eat my pussy and love it when I suck your cock, and you wanna fuck my ass, but you draw the line at my pussy?"

"There ain't no line at your pussy. There's a giant, bright pink pointing neon arrow that reads, 'FUCK ME, SILAS.' You were my wet dream girl for over a decade. That ain't changing. But neither are we. Let's leave your pretty pussy to my fantasy."

"But that's where I get so confused." She gently bangs her forehead on my chest, like I'm a wall and I will be for her. "My pussy really wants to fuck you, but my heart tells me we shouldn't."

"You remember when we almost did? We weren't kids anymore. I was twenty-four."

"Yeah," she sighs, tracing over my nipple. It tickles. I'm in a constant state of arousal around this woman, but this is more. It's pensive. It's taking us back.

"I was leaving for Spain," she says, "for my job on Daniel's show. Of course, I didn't know I'd fall in love with him and all that would happen next, but that night before I left, I was so filled with premonition it scared me."

"So you called me to come over." I reminisce. "Of course, I did, with strawberries in hand, and we hung out, drank our fair share of rum. We weren't drunk, but I could tell you didn't wanna be alone. That something was changing for you."

Her fingertip rings clockwise over my erect nipple like she's tracing over all the time we've spent together.

"You stayed with me so many nights; my pillows smelled like you."

"But we never fucked," I remind her. "We never did anything but me holding you until you fell asleep. Of course, I lost oxygen to my brain—that explains a lot—because all my blood was in my dick rubbing against your ass, but hey, that's what friends are for."

"But that night," she remembers, "I fell asleep in your arms and had the most erotic dream. It was blue water everywhere, and I was with you and someone I didn't know, and I woke up and—"

"And you kissed me."

Suddenly, her head lifts, her glance grabbing mine.

"I don't remember that part. I just remember waking up

and being this close to wanting to fuck you, and it scared me. I thought all the rest was a dream."

"Trust me, it was very real, but I could tell you were half asleep."

"So we've kissed?"

"Yeah." I trace my fingertip over her bottom lip. "You kissed me for so long and gave me tongue, too, and reached for my cock. You started stroking it and moaning my name."

"I did?" If I used a cattle prod, I'd shock her less. "Are you bullshitting me? I thought I just dreamt that part."

"Hell yeah, I'm every woman's dream." I love giving her shit. "But that night, it was real, and I was so damn hard. My heart was beating so fast my ears were ringing. I wanted to fuck you so bad. Like it would've been us making love because I was in pain. I was so in love with you, Charlie. You moaned my name and rubbed your body against mine, stroking my hard cock, and kissing my lips. I'm man enough to admit that I wanted you so bad right then; I wanted to cry because I wouldn't do it. You were half-asleep. You were confused. You were my best friend, and I could've been your lover, too, but not like that."

"Silas, I never wanted to hurt you, especially that night. I remember sorta waking up in your arms and feeling so safe with you. I was suddenly attracted to you. I wanted you so bad, too, but then I felt guilty about it and started crying. I remember that."

I pull her back into my embrace, knowing why she felt guilty for so many years, knowing all that Charlie's survived.

"All those times," she sighs against my chest. I feel her lips on my skin, but it's not a kiss. She's speaking to my heart. "All the times you were there for me, Silas. When my parents were killed, you slept on the beach with me because

I couldn't go in our house, not for a week, and you held my hand when I finally did. You even burnt a sage stick and said it was magical, that it'd make their spirits happy, and I believed you, though I knew you bought it at the damn head shop." She squeezes me tighter. "Thank you."

"All the times you were there for me." I squeeze her back. "You even took family leave and flew home from Afghanistan when my parents kicked me out. I felt like the world abandoned me, but not you. You told me to be proud I'm bi, and I was because you were proud of me first. That week, you helped me buy bed sheets for my grandma's old house. And you taught me how to make my bed like a fucking Marine. But apparently, you found all the childhood stuff I'd thrown away, too."

"It wasn't hard. You left it in a trash can you never wheeled out for pickup. It was begging to be saved."

"No, *I* was begging to be saved. And you did. You saved me, Charlie. I had no one else but you."

I rub her arm, and I gotta tell her this.

I need to give us this peace.

"After that night," I tell her, "I thought we would be something more. Like when you came home from working in Spain, we'd finally be together. That I'd marry you. Then I saw that viral picture of you passed out in Daniel's arms and all the love in his eyes for you, and it hurt like hell. I felt like my dream died."

She pulls back, letting me see the tears spilling down her cheeks.

"I never want to hurt you, Silas. I love you."

"I know you do, but that's just it, Charlie Girl. My dream didn't die. I finally woke up to my destiny, and it's Eily. Like fate was waiting for me to find her again. We all dream of what we think our life should be, but if we let it, if we wake up, the real thing can be so much better. I finally found Eily, and you went and married a motherfuckin' British superhero, so here we are."

She rears back, gently pinching my nose.

"And you married a talented, smart, and sweet babe-a-licscious. *And* you have Redix. *And* you have Cade. *And* you have billions."

"I get no pity from you?"

She grins. "No pussy either."

"That's fine." I shrug. "I married the best pussy ever."

"Yep," she says, "just like I married the best cock ever."

I narrow my eyes. I guess I'll always question, so I gotta ask.

"So, had we fucked, like me hypothetically fucking your pussy, because me fucking your ass is happening, just sayin'. But that night before you left for Spain, if we had fucked and I had rocked your world, do you think you still would've fallen in love with Daniel?"

She pats my chest, her smile crinkling that scar.

"You mean, if I had rocked *your* world, would you still have fallen in love with Eily?"

The answer hits me. I don't have to search for it. "Yes."

"Exactly," she says. "We'd still be right here. You can try for one ending or another, but fate decides your happily ever after."

"Speaking of... " All this talk makes me remember. "We better get back downstairs for our New Year's toast, or I'll never hear the end of it from my beautiful wife."

"What are we gonna tell them?" She steps back, grabbing my hand. "Eily and Daniel really wanted us to... "

She pauses, like it embarrasses her, and really? After all we've done? It's kinda sweet.

"They wanted us to finally *fuck*." I state the obvious.

"Yeah... that."

"Oh, they'll be fine. I have a feeling whatever kinky stuff the six of us do tonight to ring in the new year will leave them well-satisfied."

I tug her hand as I lead her back to the salon, back to the people we love. But at the top of the stairs, before we make our final descent, she yanks me back into a hug.

"I love you, you little shit."

She wraps around me so tight, and I close my eyes, kissing her forehead. I kiss everything we could've been but love who we are now even more.

I wouldn't change a thing. Except coming on her calla lilies. That shit was embarrassing.

"I love you, too, Charlie Girl."

Eily

EPILOGUE

"I GOTTA TAKE CARE OF THE CLIT CLUB."

One year later

"They can share the wood."

I snort, "Like *we* just did."

Silas chuckles at my reply, but the debate continues.

"Alls I'm sayin'," he keeps talking, aiming the remote at the flatscreen like it's a red laser pointer and he's giving a PowerPoint presentation, "is that wood is big enough for both of them to fit."

"Sorry, mate." Daniel stuffs his mouth full of popcorn, but that doesn't stop him from arguing back. "It's not possible. The director said it himself—the wood wasn't big enough for Jack and Rose to share. Look, rewind it. He tries to get on, and it starts to sink."

"He didn't try hard enough to get on the wood. If they had tried a different position, he could've fit."

Silas debates, clicking the remote, going back a few frames while I glance at Charlie beside me, reclining against

Daniel's chest. We exchange silent, satisfied grins, but we're also team *V* and can't let that pun hang in the air without taking the point.

"That's what *we* just *proved*," Charlie snickers and Daniel goes for her waist, tickling her while his naked legs wrap around her tighter.

The bed in our stateroom is warm from our four bodies and the three hours we've spent cuddling, eating popcorn, and watching *Titanic*. Which I find a particularly twisted tradition to start, given that we're about to set sail for the Cayman Islands.

But I won't be having nightmares about icebergs. My mind is flooded with hot memories of what the four of us just did when we arrived.

It's been months since we've been together—any four or six of us. Life's been busy and full of surprises this year.

Yes, we hang out for birthdays and some weekends. Yes, we've had a few more hot nights, especially in Luca's Charleston hotel. But mostly, it's us hanging out like friends, trying to squeeze in time together between work and life.

But all our pent-up desire and the tease of this New Year's holiday on our ship again put us in a frenzy. As if we could wait until tonight? Until our naughty gift game tradition?

Not possible.

Daniel started it.

Silas poured him his first rum and coke of the holiday, but that's not what Daniel wanted to drink. He grabbed Silas and pulled him in for a thirsty kiss and, all aboard! Our voyage had begun. Clothes were off, and so were we.

In typical Silas fashion, he spoiled me, too. He insisted that Daniel fuck me while Silas stood over us, letting Daniel devour what he craved while Charlie was very content to watch our threesome in the main deck salon. Touching herself, she came right after I did, and that took Silas with a growl, filling Daniel's groaning mouth; Daniel was the last to finish. We didn't even make it to our stateroom.

But for the second round, we did. That was Charlie's turn. We gave the men enough time to rally, and they sure did. Especially when I recorded Charlie's gushing DP on our bed.

I swear, she's still the Queen of the Cumshot. Though I'm getting better. I'm now the Duchess of the Dicksplash, so I gave everyone a cum blanket for their birthday, but my girl, Charlie, got three for her twat water.

I gotta take care of the clit club.

I love how the four of us share, but yeah, we miss our other couple.

"Oh my gosh, you two." Charlie sits up, leans over, and grabs her phone off our nightstand. "I'm not listening to this *Titanic* debate all week."

"What are you doing, babe?"

"I'm gonna look it up." Charlie reclines back between Daniel's legs, answering him as her fingertip taps across her phone. "And once we settle this, can we move on?"

"Nah," Silas replies. "We're gonna experiment. We're gonna test my theory this week."

"What are you gonna do?" I ask Silas, reclining between his legs. "Rip a door off the hinges and throw in the Caribbean? It won't be an accurate test. The water's not freezing."

"Freezing or not," Silas leans down, murmuring over my ear, "I'm giving you *all* my wood, Eily. Till the day I die."

I laugh. I can't help it. Especially when Silas nuzzles into my neck, knowing that's my spot.

"Stop it." I giggle because he won't. "You're gonna make me pee."

"Go for it." His chuckle is deep in my ear, deep in my soul. "We've already drenched the bed."

"Okay, y'all." Charlie sits up, naked and cross-legged between Daniel's massive thighs. "Riddle solved. This recent show here," she turns, nodding toward Daniel to make her point, "featuring the director of *Titanic*, twenty-five years after the film was made, conducted an experiment in a freezing pool with props and actors just like in the original scene and they found that—"

A ringtone hits the air. Silas's phone sings out with "The Devil Went Down To Georgia" as he reaches for it on the opposite nightstand.

"Speaking of," Silas says, answering the FaceTime call we've been waiting for. Holding his phone up high, he taps the button. "Hey, dude."

He was expecting Redix, but Cade appears, lying on a bed, too.

"Hey," she says. "Miss us?"

"Of course," Charlie answers. "How are you feeling?"

"If I were an inch taller, I'd be round," Cade answers, flashing the screen down. She's wearing a white sports bra with black sweatpants pushed below her very pregnant belly.

A big hand wearing a golden wedding band appears across it, caressing her body. The voice it belongs to, deeply rumbling, "You look beautiful."

Cade turns the phone to share the screen with Redix. "Yeah, but I feel like a tick," she replies with a grin while he kisses her cheek.

"We miss y'all already," I tell them, "and we haven't even left the dock."

"Doctor's orders," Redix answers. "She's due any day, and I'm hoping for a New Year's baby."

"The hell you say," Cade fusses back. "We're going at it again in another hour. I need this baby out of me now. I'm not waiting six more days."

"Is that true?" I ask because lately, I'm suddenly curious. "That sex can start labor?"

"It sure is fun trying," Daniel chimes in, and Redix laughs, agreeing.

Cade casts a suspicious grin at the sight that must fill her screen. Me, Silas, Charlie, and Daniel, nude in our bed, clearly reclining after a post-foursome fuck. The sheets are as mussed as me and Charlie's hair.

"It looks like y'all have started some sexy things of your own," she says.

"We gotta keep the horny tradition going," Silas answers her. "Because y'all are coming back next year, just sayin'."

The five of them chuckle, agreeing, while I can't stop this burst in my heart. It's too full of love and hope and excitement. Our life is beyond perfect. We're so blessed, and we've waited long enough.

I've watched Charlie and Daniel with their cute kids this year and Redix and Cade with Glory. It kinda gave me this weird, sweet ache. And now, Cade's so beautiful and pregnant and ready for another girl, it blurts from my mouth.

"But what if I'm pregnant next year?"

The deep gasp of Silas's chest is audible. His lungs sink beneath my weight lying back on him, and he drops the phone, shocked.

"Eily... " His tone drops, too, his arms reaching to turn me around in his lap so he can ask me. Like he doesn't believe what I just said. "Are you serious? You're ready?"

Charlie picks up his phone, holding it while she, Daniel, Cade, and Redix fall silent, giving us this moment.

Resting my hand over the heart that belongs to me. The one pounding in Silas's chest, I can feel it under my palm, all our hopes and dreams. All of his questions have been answered. All of my fears are gone. And we're right here, exactly where we belong. We're surrounded by love, by friends, by lovers, by family—we don't follow the rules. We follow our hearts.

"Yes," I tell Silas, tears welling in my happy eyes because they're forming in his. "I'm ready. After this trip. After the New Year. Let's start trying."

Every kiss from Silas grabs me, body and soul, and this one is no exception. Clasping my cheeks in his hands, he pulls me in, wetting our kiss with whose tears I don't know.

"Looks like they're gonna start trying right now."

Redix's voice lulls through the air, making us chuckle, our lips still seeking the other's.

"Do you want some privacy?"

Daniel's English accent makes his request sound so formal, though we're buck-ass naked, four people in bed and two more on the phone watching us.

"No," I huff over Silas's lips. Glancing their way, I see tears in Charlie's eyes, too. She's happy for us.

And dammit, this is supposed to be another XXX-rated holiday escape, not a sweet Hallmark movie.

"Y'all,"—I sit up, straddling Silas—"we're not starting yet. I want one more week of dirty fun and naughty gifts. I'm gonna fly my little slut flag all week. You should see what I bought at Stacey's store."

"Oh, it'll be a damn dirty and naughty week, alright," Redix adds. "Is Luca there yet?"

"They'll be here in an hour," Silas answers.

"Damn, I'm jealous," Cade sighs.

"Damn, are we ready for Luca?" Charlie wonders.

"I am."

NOT THE END

Want a free bonus epilogue?
Join my newsletter at KellyFinley.com
THIS HOT AND HUMOROUS BONUS EPILOGUE FEATURES OUR SPICY SIXSOME IN LUCA'S HOTEL.

WANT MORE OF THE SIX?
GET READY FOR ANOTHER HOLIDAY ESCAPE IN
HALLOWEEN FOR SIX
THIS TALE OF SPICY TRICKS & TREATS FEATURES THE SIX AND OTHER CHARACTERS FROM TEMPT HER, MAKE HIM & SHAMELESS GAME.

MEET REDIX'S BEST FRIEND, LUCA MERCIER.
A SINGLE DAD & BILLIONAIRE DOM IN A WHY CHOOSE ROMANCE
READ MAKE HIM FOR FREE IN KINDLE UNLIMITED

ALSO BY KELLY FINLEY

"THE QUEEN OF SPICE"

-All Interconnected Books Available in Kindle Unlimited-

CHARLIE & DANIEL

PROTECT HER, Prequel

PIERCE HER

HUNT HER

CHASE HER

A SPICY, ROMANTIC SUSPENSE, ALPHA HERO & BADASS HEROINE TRILOGY

REDIX & CADE with SILAS

AFTER HIM

WITH HIM

AN ANGSTY SECOND CHANCE TO A MMF WHY CHOOSE DUET

SILAS & EILY with Redix and Cade

ALL FOR HIM

A SWEET & FORBIDDEN CINDERELLA RETELLING POLY ROMANCE

STACEY & HER TRIO OF MEN

TEMPT HER

A MMMF ALPHA HEROES & SASSY HEROINE'S REVENGE ROMANCE & AUDIOBOOK

THE SIX with

Silas & Eily; Redix & Cade; Charlie & Daniel

HOLIDAY FOR SIX

A Spicy, Lots of Friends to Lovers Poly RomCom & Audiobook

LUCA & SCARLETT

MAKE HIM

A Single Dad/Billionaire Dom, Why Choose Romance & Audiobook

BEAU, BLAIR & COLTON

***SHAMELESS PLAY*, Prequel**

SHAMELESS GAME

A Frenemies to Lovers, Why Choose, Football romance

THE SIX & all of these MCs in a spicy week

HALLOWEEN FOR SIX

A Spicy, Lots of Friends to Lovers RomCom & Audiobook)

Join my newsletter for what's next in this spicy world. I also share sneak peeks, giveaways & more.

Kelly Finley.com

"The Queen Of Spice"

@KELLY FINLEY BOOKS

ACKNOWLEDGMENTS

My husband and best friend: I wake up to coffee and your sweet notes. Your love and support keep me writing. I'm lucky I found you, Silver Fox.

My family: I love you all, and for the ones who read my spicy stuff, well, I warned you.

My friends: More like partners-in-crime because y'all are the best bad influences. I just wish I could see you more, but when I do, damn, I'm blessed.

My Book Team: Deborah, you are a Proofreading Goddess and always so encouraging. Thank you, Lori, for this gorgeous cover. Bree, you're the best PA ever!

My Beta Team: Bree, Dani, Deborah, Jay, and Marsha. I love y'all! Thanks for your comments, edits, and texts. They either crack me up or crack the whip.

My ARC & Hype Teams: I love the spicy family we're building. I cherish your posts, reviews, and support. I love your DMs, too. Keep 'em coming! I truly can't do it without you all.

#Bookstagram & #BookTok Followers: It's true. There *is* a community and a world of friends online. I'm overwhelmed by the amazing people I've met. Every day you make me smile. Thanks for your comments and support. They keep me writing.

Author Friends & Mentors: You inspire me. You school me. You help me. Thanks for the Zooms, emails, and chats. You keep me strong.

Best for last - READERS: Thank you for giving your time to share this spicy story with me. When I get your messages, posts, and emails, they are the greatest gifts. And I promise to keep giving you more spice. Big hugs.

ABOUT THE AUTHOR

Kelly Finley hates writing bios but appreciates that you made it this far. So here you go...

She lives in the Carolinas with her sexy husband and cherished family. A rebel with many causes, she fancies black leather, dirty jokes, big hearts, and smart mouths.

Her books are so spicy that her readers started calling her "**The Queen of Spice,**"...and she wears her crown with pride.

Dedicated to writing books with proud love and shameless heat, she's most likely at her keyboard putting the next spicy story on the page for you.

Want to connect with Kelly and her readers? Get her newsletter at KellyFinley.com, join her Spicy Book Babes on Facebook, and share the fun on her socials.

tiktok.com/@kellyfinleybooks

instagram.com/kellyfinleybooks

facebook.com/KellyFinleyBooks

goodreads.com/goodreads_kelly_finley

bookbub.com/authors/kelly-finley

amazon.com/author/kellyfinley

Holiday for Six

Kelly Finley

© 2023 Kelly Finley Publishing, LLC

Visit the author's website at www.kellyfinley.com

ISBN: 979-8-9866222-8-6 (eBook)

ISBN: 979-8-9866222-9-3 (paperback)

Proofread by Deborah Richmond

Cover design by Lori Jackson

Made in the USA
Middletown, DE
21 November 2024

65131773R00201